"YOU WANT TO KNOW MY SECRETS?" AMELIA ASKED.

"All of them. I wish to know everything about you," the highwayman replied.

"Like where I keep my fortune, or why I never carry any valuables around?"

"No, nothing like that. I can get money from the others."

Her nerves tightened when he mentioned others. Other women. She knew he must have robbed others. But somehow she'd taken to thinking that she was the only one. Did he kiss the others? Kidnap them? Hold them close enough to feel his desire?

"From you, Amelia, I want more. I want to know your heart." When he placed his hand over her heart, flat against her breast, she gasped, her every nerve whipping to attention.

"I want to know your soul. To know every inch of you." He drew closer still, his mouth lowering until his lips almost touched hers. "Inside and out."

Also by Sherri Browning
THE SCOUNDREL'S VOW

Once

Wicked

SHERRI BROWNING

A DELL BOOK

Published by
Dell Publishing
a division of
Random House, Inc.
1540 Broadway
New York, New York 10036

Dell® is a registered trademark of Random House, Inc., and the colophon is a trademark of Random House, Inc.

ISBN: 0-440-23528-6

Printed in the United States of America
Published simultaneously in Canada

July 2000

10   9   8   7   6   5   4   3   2   1

OPM

For my mother, Donna Topping Cote,
who taught me that I could do anything.

And for my father,
Harold Wesley Browning,
who inspired me to do what I like
and to like what I do.

With thanks to Lisa Stone for her wonderful instincts; to my grandparents, Donald and Mildred Topping, for the endless support; to Barbara and Jack Erwin, for making me feel at home; and to Laura Sieben Jerry, for sharing my wild past and for encouraging my once wicked ways.

And a very special thank you to Sean, my husband, who put up with so much while my broken wrist healed. *I couldn't have done it without you, hon.*

Chapter
1

The boys were wild tonight.

Amelia knew her uncle must have had a devil of a time trying to settle them down after she'd gone. Normally, she left Holcomb House well before bedtime. But when the boys had pleaded with her to tell them one more story, she hadn't been able to resist their entreaties. Amelia had a soft spot in her heart for the orphans under her uncle Patrick's care. She could hardly refuse them such an easy indulgence— but the boys needed their rest, so she'd spun a tale that hadn't made them beg for another. Usually, she told of pirates and soldiers, giants and heroes, fodder for the young lads' dreams. Tonight, for her second tale, she'd spun a yarn of a princess being saved from a curse of eternal boredom by a knight on a charging white steed. Princesses? Romance? Her tale was greeted with a universal groan from the lads. She couldn't end it fast enough to suit them, and at last she'd been dismissed to go on her way.

But the story she'd told was with her even still. *Eternal boredom.* As she rattled along in the coach bound for home, she watched the scenery drift by her window—the same scenery she saw every week on her return from the orphanage. She had settled into a regular, predictable routine, but she would not wait for a dashing knight to come and save *her.* She was well used to taking care of herself. And knights on white horses . . . well, honestly. They made for nice fairy stories, but these days knights simply did not exist in real life as they did in books. If she wanted excitement she would have to go out and find it. It certainly wasn't going to come looking for her.

"Oh!" The coach gave a sudden lurch and Amelia tumbled forward, catching herself just in time before she pitched straight across the seat. "Do take care, Foster!" she shouted. Skilled driver though he was, Foster never slowed the horses enough before leaving the smooth, well-traveled road just outside of London for the rougher, less-frequented country lane that led to Briarwood, her beloved estate.

The coach pitched again and she went flying into the air, only to land hard on her seat. One would think she was riding on wood planks for all the good her pretty crimson cushions did when Foster traveled at such speed! What had got into the man tonight?

"Foster!" she cried at the top of her lungs, but not loud enough to break the din of the rumbling wheels and thundering hooves. "Foster, do slow down!"

But Foster only drove faster. Resigned to being tossed about uncomfortably, Amelia stopped fighting to hold her place and allowed her body to be jolted, jarred, and swung to and fro as they rollicked along into the forest.

She looked out into the growing darkness but could make no sense of anything except the branches and twigs that whizzed by, occasionally scraping at the window, and a mysterious, shadowy blur that easily kept pace with the carriage. What was that? *Who* was that, rather? A horseman rode at their side. She could make him out now, though he was difficult to see as he was all in black and the horse was black as well.

Suddenly, the coach jolted to a halt. Amelia pitched forward, straight off the cushions and onto the cold, hard floor between the seats.

The carriage had stopped. And the rider? She heard a *clip-clop* of hooves, then nothing. She began to rise but froze when she heard the scratch of boot heels on gravel outside the carriage.

"Good evening, sir." A strange voice.

"And a—a—a good one to you." Foster was

apparently uneasy, but he said nothing to soothe her or inform her of what had happened. And she was suddenly too apprehensive to ask.

"Tell me, would you happen to have five shillings for a crown?"

"It's money you want?" Foster asked. "Take it. Take it all, just leave me be, ruffian!"

Take it? Was he a robber, then? Amelia started to rise, struggling to pull herself back up onto the seat.

"Ruffian? But, sir, I assure you, all I want is change." A loud *thunk* was followed by a brief gurgling noise. "And that's the sort of change that will do nicely."

Amelia dropped back to the coach floor and froze in position. What had happened? Had he murdered Foster? A highwayman *and* a murderer? Dear Lord! A knock sounded on the door. Her mouth went dry as ash.

He was coming for her next.

She looked around, left to right. A weapon! She needed to protect herself. Whatever could she do that might possibly frighten him off or convince him not to hurt her? A knock on the door echoed in the coach.

"I don't like to storm in uninvited," the voice hailed her. It was unnaturally deep in tone. And a bit scratchy. She imagined the rogue to be seven feet tall and five feet wide. A regular bear of a man. And she would be helpless against him. The voice called out again. "Won't you open the door?"

Amelia stayed stock-still. She simply could not move.

"Very well, then. But if you persist in being impolite, you can't expect me to be on my best behavior. . . ."

Chills bumped up all over her flesh at his menacing tone. If he'd been on his best behavior when he murdered Foster, what would he do to her at his worst?

Amelia was too fearful to sit up, but she stretched out her leg, kicked the latch with her toe, and pushed the door open ever so slightly.

"That's better. Let's have a look at you."

And *she* wanted a look at *him*. Amelia squinted into the darkness, trying to make him out. All she could see at first was black. Black clothes. Black mask. Black scarf wrapped around his head. And then she could see the whites of his eyes as his gaze traveled from the door to her foot, following the outline of her leg as his gaze swept up her skirt.

Amelia pulled her leg back sharply and curled it under her bottom to allow her to sit more upright. "Wh-what do you want?"

His piercing stare left her feeling vulnerable. Exposed. She shook her head, demanding that some little bit of sense return to the thoughts spinning uninvited in her mind. Of course he couldn't see up her skirts. It was dark. Too dark to make out much of anything. The highwayman stepped forward, his body almost blocking the entire doorway.

The soft glow of the moon, almost completely

hidden by the clouds, framed him, and she could at last see the outline of the body that stood before her. He was a large man, but not nearly so large as she'd imagined. To fit in the door he would have to duck his head a bit, but then, so did she. His shoulders were wide and straight. She couldn't tell what his hair would be like under that scarf, and the scarf itself was unlike anything Amelia had ever seen a man wear. The rogue didn't even wear a hat! Instead, he'd wrapped his head up like some sort of gypsy or storybook pirate, exotic to an extreme. With the light framing him from behind, she could hardly make out the features of his face, until he suddenly parted his lips and indulged in a slow, sensuous smile.

His straight white teeth shone even in the dark. His grin was mocking, almost as if he teased her to increase her fear. It worked. Her heart was beating so fast she thought it would rise up into her throat and choke her. She couldn't move—she wasn't even sure that she could speak.

"Money," she said softly, her voice barely a whisper though she could have sworn she'd shouted. "There. Take it. Please, take it and go."

She motioned to her reticule on the floor at her feet. It had fallen with her and slid toward the door when the coach had stopped. He looked down at it and back up at her. He still wore the same wicked smile that so unnerved her.

"No. I want you to give it to me." A hint of

mischief broke through the gravelly depths when he spoke this time. "Come out here and place it in my hands yourself."

His words sent a cold bolt of fear right through her. Did he mean to—to have his way with her? She tried to swallow and could not. Her heart *had* risen into her throat for certain. "P-please. Don't hurt me." She was surprised to find she had gotten the words out.

"Hurt you?" He threw back his head and laughed. The cavalier scoundrel!

"Please." She was aware there was a pitiful imploring in her tone, and, yes, she would beg him for her life if she had to. There was so much she hadn't done. So much she wanted to do.

"I won't hurt you, princess. Inflicting pain is far from my desire."

"But Foster?" She sat up a little more, growing braver as she grew curious. "What have you done to him?"

"I've only knocked him on the head to make my work a little easier. In a few moments he'll come to and be fine, save a little headache. Now, come out and give me my spoils. Don't make this so tedious. You're ruining all my fun."

"What?"

"I said come on, then. I'm at this for the entertainment as much as for the treasure."

"The entertainment?" She could scarce believe her ears.

What did he expect, for her to serve tea and crumpets and make his robbery less of a bore? Entertainment, he wanted? If she had a weapon she would show him some entertainment, all right.

"Adventure, danger, daring deeds. I'm in for the thrills, angel, and truth be told, this has all been a mite too easy so far. Your driver practically played dead as soon as he saw me. I'd hoped at least for a little more fight from you."

"Well, I'm sorry to disappoint you." Amelia's mind raced. He wanted her to put up a fight. Flight was more on her mind than fight. She was fast on her feet from chasing after wayward orphaned boys, and she was certain she could outrun him if she bolted between the fringe of trees ahead. But Foster—she couldn't leave him. She had to know that her driver would survive. She started to get up.

"Not to worry. I'm sure I'll find some way for you to make this all a bit more amusing," he said.

Closer to him now, she could see his mask rise a little on the left side as he spoke, as if he'd raised his eyebrow underneath. *More amusing?* She shifted back a bit. What could he possibly mean?

Before she could decide whether to move forward or retreat farther into the carriage, the highwayman reached in and grabbed her around the waist.

Amelia screamed and struggled. "Unhand me! Let me go, blackguard!"

"Hush now. Enough. No one can hear you.

There's no one else fool enough to take this route at night. There are brigands in the area, or haven't you heard?"

He put an end to her fight with a simple clasp of his arms tight around her middle. She couldn't move, couldn't breathe. It was as if he held her with thick iron bands. The bones of her own elbows became weapons against her as they pressed sharply into her sides with the pressure of his arms around her. But she wouldn't give up so easily. She bent her wrist at an awkward angle and gripped the edge of the coach door with her fingers. She didn't want to come out, and he couldn't make her.

"Ow!" As her fingernail bent back and scraped the side of the coach, she howled in pain and let go. Unfortunately, he *could* make her. As soon as she found her footing she tried to shrug him off, but by then he'd released her.

As the moon slipped out from behind the clouds, Amelia was torn between trying to get a good look at the robber and stealing a glance at her injured finger. It hurt like the devil, and pain won for the moment. She glanced at her hands, which shook even as her finger throbbed in pain.

"Did I—did I hurt you?" The highwayman stepped forward and took her hand in his own. Forcefully. Couldn't he even allow her the dignity of examining her own wound? "Yes, it is a small scrape. Your fingernail managed to stay in the coach, I'm afraid. At least, the upper portion. But no blood. See? You'll be fine."

He held her finger up for her to survey the damage and quickly tossed it down again, dismissing her so easily. She shook her hand to prove her reestablished ownership. It still hurt, but the pain was beginning to subside. He was right—she would be fine.

"Now, where's my money?"

"*My* money is still in the coach. Take it if you must, and leave me . . . please." Her tone betrayed her growing impatience. If he hadn't killed her yet, she assumed he wasn't going to, and she simply wanted to get the whole humiliating experience behind her and move on. She'd been frightened, humbled, and now hurt. She only wanted to get home!

She must have stood still pondering for a moment too long. He grabbed her by the shoulders and shook her lightly. Her nerves snapped like the cord of a whip. How did she know he wouldn't hurt her? He'd knocked out Foster in the wink of an eye, and despite his protestations he could have much worse in store for her. Her breath caught as his gaze, silver and eerie in the moonlight, bore into her. "I said I wouldn't hurt you, but I'm not one to fool around. Go fetch your reticule and bring it here. Now!"

"No," she answered, surprising herself. "I will not! You want it, get it yourself. I've had enough!" And she had. The brute—would he force her to further humiliation? She wouldn't have it. If he wanted her money, there it was. If robbing her was truly his goal, he would get on with it and waste no further time with violence.

She was right. He grunted slightly at her refusal but turned away from her to stalk back to the carriage. Bag in hand, he returned quickly. She stood still, watching, as he tore through the delicate lace trim and ribbon binding to drop a few pound notes and some odd crowns into his palm. It was all she had. The corners of his mouth dropped down in apparent disappointment.

"Is this all you carry?" His head whipped round to the coach and back at her.

"You expected more?" She half laughed. "Because I ride in a fine carriage? Yes, I have money. But I don't need to carry it all around with me, you know."

Smug, she crossed her arms over her chest. But as he started for her she dropped her arms and haughty attitude in a heartbeat.

"Lord," he groaned. "I told you not to fear me. Here."

He held out her reticule to return it. Her hand shook as she took it from him. He slid his palm over her fingers and squeezed, but not with the firm grip she'd expected. He slid his hand down hers and held her wrist as tenderly as he might hold a wilting flower.

"There. Was that so terrible?" His voice was a raspy whisper. He stepped closer, bringing her hand to his lips. "A kiss to soothe your wound."

Ever so gently, he touched her finger to his mouth. His lips were fine and soft. Her gaze, she realized, had become trained to his face. She could make out the stubble of a few days' growth of beard, and his straight white teeth parted in a roguish grin.

"See? You needn't fear. I'd rather give pleasure than pain to a lovely thing like you." Fearful again, her skin pricked. "A shame we haven't time. What's this?" He stepped closer and reached for her chest, grasping at her necklace. "It's a pretty little bauble. Give it over."

Without a fight she reached up, unclasped the necklace, and handed him the jewel.

"What else have you got?" He didn't step back but put his finger under her chin and directed her face up to meet his inspection.

"Nothing," she answered. "Isn't the necklace enough?"

He held it up to study it in the moonlight. "Hm. Perhaps. It looks dear." He lowered it again and continued his study of her face. "Your driver should be waking soon. I will let you go."

She couldn't contain her sigh of relief.

"Ah, but not without a price," he added. "You haven't yielded nearly as much as I expected. Just so the night's not a total disappointment . . ."

She opened her mouth, prepared to argue. Who was he to hold her to any expectations, to be disappointed in her goods? He was a lowly robber, for God's sake. If he was disappointed, he deserved it!

But she never got to speak. He wrapped his arms around her waist and pulled her body hard against his. His mouth covered hers and he swal-

lowed all her words before she could say anything.
For a moment she thought he would swallow her
whole as well. She gasped inaudibly as he slid his
tongue between her lips. His kiss was deep, probing.
She had never experienced such a kiss. Any kiss.

And she enjoyed it. He intrigued her. She nearly
forgot herself and went along with him. Perhaps he
was a master of seduction as well as robbery? But she
couldn't allow herself the indulgence of finding out.
She had a reputation to protect. And he—he had
some nerve to think he could rob her and make love
to her all at once! She struggled in his arms, flattening
her palms against his steely chest and pushing with all
her might to force some distance between them.

He stopped abruptly and pulled back. "That's
it, princess. Now I consider the evening a complete
success."

She was enraged. "How dare you!"

He smiled a crooked, cocky smile and turned
around to leave. He did not reply until he reached
his horse.

"That's the privilege granted by the mask. I do
as I dare."

"Coward!" she shouted after him, taking a few
short steps forward. "I'll bet you aren't so bold without a mask to hide behind!"

He laughed but didn't glance back until he had
fully mounted. "Perhaps. Perhaps not. Would you
really like to know?"

Just then Foster let out a low moan. Amelia ran
to his side to tend him, but she couldn't resist one

last gibe as the robber prepared to ride off into the night with her money, her necklace, and her pride in his pocket. She would have the last laugh.

"The stone is paste. Ha!"

He turned around on his horse. "What's that?"

"It's paste. Worthless. Now, go away and let me help my driver."

Foster moaned again as if on cue. She reached up and patted his cheek. "It's all right now, Foster. We've been robbed. He hit you. Hard. On the head. Can you hear me, Foster?"

Foster groaned. "Aye?"

She began to climb up to sit next to him, but a pair of hands firmly grasped her shoulders from behind and wrenched her around.

"Worthless?" The highwayman stood before her again. "Did you think you could tease me with that bit of information and I would just leave? What else have you got?" He pressed her against the side of the coach. The carriage rails rammed into her back, but she preferred the wooden edging to the feel of his long, lean body against hers. One minute he'd been on his horse, and the next . . . Oh, she'd been such a fool to bait him! What had she been thinking?

"I—I haven't anything else."

"We'll see about that." His eyes raked over her slowly, from head to toe.

"What are you going to do?" Her breathing became rapid, more rapid than her heartbeat. She couldn't catch her breath. At least she had the presence of mind to tuck her left hand behind her, concealing her ring with her skirts. He hadn't taken her ring and she meant to keep it that way.

"That's it." He grabbed her hand, wrenching her arm up. He no longer seemed to care if he hurt her. "What have you here? Aha! A ring. I glimpsed it earlier, but I meant to leave you with something. Clearly, you don't deserve such kindness. I'm taking it."

"What? You can't!" She gasped and pulled her hand back, hiding it again behind her skirt. "It—it's an old thing. Paste as well."

"Then you shan't be too upset to part with it. Give it here."

"Please! It's all I have."

He looked at her, his gaze narrowed so that she could hardly see his expression, and he did not answer her. He gripped her firmly by the wrist, pried her fingers apart, and slipped the ring off.

He held it up to the moon's glow. "Paste, indeed! *Now* I've had a satisfactory evening." He turned and started toward his horse.

"You'll get the noose for this! I'll alert the constable—"

"He'll have to catch me, won't he? And I'm afraid that won't be possible." He mounted and looked back at her, gestured as if to doff the hat he was too ungentlemanly to wear, and urged his horse to a gallop.

"You'll pay for this!" she screamed after him as he rode. "I'll see to it!"

"See to—see to—I'll slow down, miss." Foster was awake but clearly lost in a haze. He leaned over the seat and grabbed repeatedly for the team's reins that lay in front of him, missing every time.

As the highwayman's dark silhouette disappeared down the road, the sound of hooves fading from earshot, Amelia elbowed aside her driver and climbed up onto the box. "Never mind, Foster. Take your ease." She took a firm grip of the reins. "I will get us home."

Chapter 2

Another glass, Trudy. Hell, bring the bottle! I'm feeling wild tonight!"

His nerves still on edge, he downed the shot as soon as it was delivered, placed the glass back on Trudy's tray, and sent her to the bar with a pat on her behind.

"Watch it, love." Trudy turned around before heading back for his bottle. "Me Davey's at the bar tonight. He'll charge you extra for the slap and tickle."

"Ha!" Dylan Marlow laughed, a long low chortle. "I've got plenty to spare."

"Well, that *is* a surprise." Trudy winked. "In that case I'll hurry on back to you."

Wild. He still felt wild, his nerves skittering in

time with the popping of the sausage Davey was fry-
ing up for a late supper of bubble and squeak. He'd
done it. He hadn't actually got all that much to show
for it, but the important thing was that he'd really
done it. And now that he'd done it once, he knew he
could do it again. And next time he'd choose his
victim more carefully. He'd target a dowager duch-
ess or a bird-witted spinster sort. Someone fool
enough to carry a large sum of money and jewels.
Someone without a body so lovely as to distract him
from his purpose.

Before long he'd have enough to fix his ship.
And then he'd have money to spare. More than he
could ever possibly need.

"To the *ton!*" he shouted, grabbing the bottle
off Trudy's tray as she returned.

"The *ton?*" Trudy shook her faded red curls.
"Why's you want to toast them? Never did anything
fer the likes of me or you, lot of filthy hypocrites."

"Ah, but they have done something for me,
Trudy. And they will continue to serve. I repeat—to
the *ton!*"

The *ton.* They didn't appreciate half of what
they had, so it may as well be his for the taking. If he
had the kind of money that kept fashionable London
in . . . well, in fashion, he'd know what to do with
it and it wouldn't be wasted in showing off. He
wouldn't merely spend his money or throw it away
on endless displays of blummery. He would put his
money to work for him so that neither he nor his

heirs, whenever he got round to creating some, would ever be wanting again.

He poured out another shot of whisky and held the glass up to the candle. It was dark at Boltwood's Tavern, more so in his secluded corner than in the rest of the place, but when he studied the whisky by the light of the flame, he fancied the color was about the same tint as her eyes.

Her eyes? Why was he still thinking about them?

He'd tried to remain indifferent to her throughout the robbery. When he first saw her, after she'd opened the door so hesitantly, he'd been tempted to crawl in and comfort her. She'd seemed so vulnerable and small that he had to steel himself to get the job done. And when he'd pulled her out . . . well, she wasn't nearly as small as he'd expected, nor as vulnerable as he'd first supposed. She was fearful, yes, and she should have been, but she hadn't exactly cowered. And the dressing-down she'd given him—aye, she was a bold one. He appreciated her giving him just a little bit of a challenge.

At first, when she'd kissed him back instead of falling limp in his arms, she had won enough of his regard that he'd thought to leave her the ring. But after she teased him with the fact that the necklace was paste, how could he resist going back? He had to answer her challenge—and bring the haughty miss down a notch or two. Going back may have been his mistake, though, for it was then that he'd noticed her eyes.

They glared at him in the moonlight with the ferocity of a cornered beast, yet the amber warmth, the smoky intensity . . . they were there too. Yes, her eyes were the same hue as the whisky and as alive as the dancing flame that illuminated his glass from behind. He'd kissed her to quell the wild impulses inside him. If circumstances had been different he would have kissed her again, for no other reason than the pleasure she could provide. He'd been too busy to think of women for a while. But now, with the prospect of wealth in his not-far-off future, he might be able to take his ease and let loose, to engage a mistress.

The door creaked open and a gust of wind followed, extinguishing the lamps closest to the entrance. Marlow's candle flickered but didn't go out. Someone had come in. The constable? The hairs at the back of his neck stood on end for the merest second. Then he took a breath to calm himself. No one would look for him here, so far from the scene. He had summoned his old friend Thomas, and that was probably who it was.

Dylan had been meaning to contact Thomas since his own return to London last year, but he had been putting it off, hoping to get his affairs in order first. Solvency was a long way off, though, and Dylan was lonely. He needed a friend. Thomas was the one man who'd always understood him, the only person he could trust.

Was that him? He peered through the smoky haze. When Dylan had sent the note he'd thought he would know Thomas anywhere. Dear old Thomas Selkirk. The Honorable Thomas Selkirk. They'd grown up together, after all. Now he wasn't so sure. It had been years. . . .

"Thomas!" Dylan rose and gestured, hazarding a guess though he couldn't see quite clearly. "Over here."

"Marlow? Is that you?" Thomas laughed at sight of him. "I thought it might be, when I got the note. Who else would send such a cryptic missive, and unsigned, to meet at a dockside establishment?"

"And for whom else would you venture out at this hour, and to this part of town? You knew it was me all along, else you would not have come."

"So it is Dylan Marlow indeed." Thomas approached, reached for Dylan's hand, and pumped heartily. "How long has it been?"

"Who keeps count? Any number of years."

"Quite." Thomas put his hand to his chin, a reflective gesture that Dylan remembered well. Reflective. Staid. Dependable. Same old Thomas. Dylan was glad to see him. The two had been inseparable in youth. Thomas had followed Dylan on all his pranks and capers. Ever the voice of reason, Thomas would try to talk Dylan out of all sorts of schemes, only to end up helping him in the end or living vicariously through his friend's exploits. "I haven't seen you since you were—" Thomas paused uncomfortably.

Dylan was more than willing to fill in the blanks.

"Thrown out of Oxford for stirring up a debate to question the existence of God?"

Thomas couldn't hold back the smile now. "Yes, that would be correct. Are you—are you still an atheist?" Thomas whispered the last word as if he couldn't bring himself to say it aloud.

"Still? Ha-ha! I'll fill you in on a little secret." He beckoned Thomas closer as if he were going to whisper, then shouted, "I never was! But it was fun to have them all on. Come and have a seat. Another glass for my friend, Trudy!"

"So you risked all that, got expelled and sent away from home, for a lark?"

Dylan grew serious now. He hadn't counted on getting thrown out of Oxford, truly. He'd really meant to rile only one particular priest. But the prank had gone awry and so he'd had to face the consequences. Dylan's father had been rather understanding, but his uncle had been gravely disappointed in him.

His uncle, the Earl of Stoke, was a man of some means and much property. Sire to no children of his own, he'd taken Dylan under his wing at an early age and had financed his education, with the intention that Dylan would be heir to his uncle's title and estates when he came of age. The atheism prank had cost him his uncle's regard, and he had been disinherited. But Dylan could spend only so much time in regretting his actions. Years had passed. Now laughter was his only recourse.

"I don't need the Earl of Stoke's money, Thomas."

"No?" Thomas screwed up his nose in the way that he had always done as a boy to express his skepticism.

"No. Soon I'm going to have plenty of my own."

Trudy brought the glass at last and set it down in front of Thomas. Dylan watched, amused, as Thomas followed her departing derriere with his eyes.

"A comely lass," Thomas voiced his approval at last.

"Trudy? She's a decent sort," Dylan agreed. "But she's nothing compared to the one I met tonight."

Thomas's eyes widened. Dylan just stared back. He didn't know what had got into him, why he felt the need to say it—why he was still thinking of her at all.

"Oh?" Thomas sat back, waiting to hear.

Dylan filled his friend's glass with whisky. "Here, a drink first. And then I'll tell you all about my latest adventures."

Thomas sipped his whisky slowly. Dylan downed his in one gulp and savored the heat as it spread through his body.

"That dockyard straight over there . . ." Dylan put his finger to the cool pane of the window. It was too dark to see out into the night, but he knew where he was pointing and Thomas just nodded along. "It's mine. All mine."

"Your father's business?" Thomas asked. "You've taken it over at last?"

"My father passed away. He left the fleet and warehouse to me."

"I'm sorry," Thomas said quietly, and took another sip of his drink.

"Oh, yes. I am too. I miss him. But you'd be especially sorry for me if you could see the condition of the ship. The one that's left." Dylan refilled his glass even as he cautioned himself to slow down. If he kept up he'd be well into his cups before the night was half over. Time to ease off. "She's in a startling state of disrepair. Not seaworthy, certainly."

"Dear. I really am sorry," Thomas added.

"No, no. You needn't be sorry for me, my friend, for as always, I have—"

"A plan." Thomas's eyes lit up. He sat forward. "And what is it this time?"

Dylan hesitated. He hadn't seen Thomas in a long time. He wasn't sure that his friend was prepared to hear about his latest exploits. Dylan leaned across the table toward Thomas so that he could keep his voice down. "The ship needs repair. The warehouse could use a bit of work. Equipment, labor, parts . . . it will cost."

"Indeed. A pretty penny," Thomas agreed, and looked down, his cheeks growing red.

"And that's where my plan comes in."

Thomas began to fidget. He interrupted Dylan

before he could speak again. "Look, I may as well tell you now. Please, stop. You need an investor, and I wish I could help. But I can't—I still haven't come into my inheritance. I'm running out of money myself. A man can take out only so many obits, and—"

"Thomas, hush." Dylan waved him off. "No, I don't need your money. Is that what you thought?"

Thomas said nothing, but his eyes expressed his relief.

"I know your father is still alive, and stingy as ever, I would wager."

"Ever so." Thomas laughed.

"You'll come into your inheritance soon enough, not that I would wish ill on your father."

"Oh, no. I understand."

Thomas's father was an abominable man. Judgmental, cold, and harsh. Thomas could never live up to his father's standards. No one could. But Thomas did put in an admirable effort. Of course, living up to his father's idea of what a gentleman should be did cost, and Thomas himself had no money save the paltry annuity his father allowed him. To make ends meet and maintain his image, Thomas was forever borrowing against his future inheritance. It made Dylan burn inside with anger. Lord Selkirk had all the money in the world. Why should Thomas have to be forever in fear of running up debts? All his father had to do was raise Thomas's annuity. But he wouldn't.

The same was true of Dylan Marlow's own uncle. His uncle, the eldest son, had inherited the earldom and all the family's wealth and estates, while Dylan's father, a second son, was left to shift on his own, expected to take orders or enter into service. He made do as he could in running the shipping business that he had sold his military commission to purchase. Dylan's uncle disapproved of his younger brother's dalliance in trade, and so he'd cut him off from any further assistance.

Then, after Dylan's birth, the earl had reestablished communication with his brother and had tried to shape Dylan into the son he'd always wanted. But Dylan was very much his father's lad. He abhorred hypocrisy and scorned the selfish tendencies of his rich uncle. The Earl of Stoke couldn't abide anyone flouting his authority, which he perceived Dylan had done by carrying out his prank at Oxford, and so Dylan, like his father before him, had been disinherited.

And Dylan Marlow was left with a lingering distaste of the upper class. The *ton* lived their flagrantly wasteful lives while the lower classes—sometimes their own relatives—went starving to their deaths.

That was why he saw nothing wrong with robbing them blind. Why shouldn't he play the highwayman and claim a little of the wealth that the *ton* routinely took for granted?

While he tried to think of a way to explain his actions of the evening to his friend, he took the ring out of his pocket and absently began to fiddle with it. Her ring. Yes, it was a pretty bauble. Gold band, with tiny diamonds surrounding a rather large opal. Opals didn't command a high price normally, but this one was unusual. Fiery. Brilliant. Like her. He shook his head, returning to his appraisal of the ring. He could sell it for a fair enough sum. But no. He would hold on to it. It would be a token to celebrate his first robbery.

She had been quite upset to part with the ring, he remembered suddenly, his conscience nagging at him. But she probably had a dozen more, at least. Hell, she probably had fifty rings that were more valuable than this paltry one. And this one alone was likely more than a year's wages for her butler or her maid. Why should he feel bad? No, he shouldn't. He wouldn't.

He did. But it was only because he kept thinking of her eyes, and her pretty face, and her perfect womanly figure. She was just the right size. Not too big, not too small. A slender waist. A fair-size bosom.

"Nice piece." Thomas interrupted Dylan's thoughts as he emptied his glass and leaned across the table. "Are you going to tell me where you got it?"

Thomas must have had an inkling that Dylan hadn't actually acquired it through legitimate means. His friend always sensed when he was up to something, and Dylan had hinted that he'd been involved in unseemly deeds from the start.

"It's hers."

"Hers?"

"The girl I mentioned, the one I met this evening." He picked up the half-empty bottle and refilled his friend's glass and his own.

"The girl, yes. You mentioned you'd met a female. Now, who is she? And *how* did you meet?"

"I robbed her." Dylan picked up his glass and sat back, a slow smile spreading over his face.

"You what?"

He enjoyed his friend's flustered reaction. "I had a glorious evening, Thomas."

"Tell me about it," Thomas insisted.

Dylan hoped that the bond between them was strong enough that what he was revealing to Thomas wouldn't send the man running to alert the constable. Growing up, they'd both run in the same circles. Thomas, the son of a baron, was of the same relative importance as the favored nephew of a powerful earl. Now they inhabited different worlds. Thomas, heir to a barony remained accepted in society, while Dylan, fallen from his uncle's favor and with no title of his own, had slipped from society's notice almost altogether.

"Yes, as I was saying, I had a glorious evening. Tonight I wasn't Dylan Marlow, inconsequential nephew of a nobleman."

"No? Then who were you?"

"I was a highwayman," Dylan said matter-of-factly.

"A highwayman," Thomas repeated, his mouth gaping and his eyes widening with awe.

Seeing his friend's delight at living vicariously through him again, Dylan related the entire tale of how he'd waited in the woods for a carriage to pass, had almost given up when the road remained untraveled, and then had perked up and charged out when a coach at last happened into the area. He told Thomas how he'd knocked the driver out with a light, quick blow to his head with the butt of his pistol. How, despite the quiet, he'd known there was a lone occupant huddled within the coach. How he'd convinced her to open the door and hand over her money herself.

How he'd kissed her in the moonlight, her lips as soft as rose petals and so yielding . . . up until she'd decided to fight him off.

"And then you took her ring?" Thomas was on the edge of his seat, waiting to hear every detail.

"Well, her necklace. I had to go back and torment her to get the ring."

"Torment her?" Thomas's Adam's apple rose in his throat and then fell.

"Mm. It made her fairly angry." He leaned forward and whispered, "But I think if I'd kissed her again, she would have forgiven me."

"You—you didn't kiss her again?" Thomas was almost disappointed.

"No. But perhaps next time . . ."

"Oh, Marlow, no. You can't mean to do this again. It's a fool's game. If you get caught—"

"I won't."

"But surely she would have reported the incident. The constable will be watching the roads now. They'll set up patrols."

"Bah." Dylan waved him off. "I know my way around the roads and through the paths and clearings in the woods. And Fergus can outrun any horse—"

"Fergus?" Thomas bolted up in his seat, alarmed. "You're *still* riding Fergus?"

Fergus was the horse Dylan's uncle had given him when he was just a boy at Harrow. The horse he had named after his uncle—Fergus Marlow, Earl of Stoke—just to be obnoxious.

"He's fast," Dylan said, defending his beloved horse.

"But he's so . . . old. You're bound to get caught. Now, listen to me."

"Here comes the lecture." Dylan rolled his eyes.

"I'm serious, old chap, please listen."

"Very well."

"I know you are strapped. And it feels awful. I do understand, believe me. I hate not having money while everyone around me is swimming in it. But robbing? And treating a woman like that—just grabbing her? I can't condone it. You can't just go around taking what you want from those who have more and scaring innocent people. We have to make do with our lots. You'll find a way to fix your ship. Perhaps you could marry."

"Marry? Well, of course—why didn't I think of

that? I have so much to offer." Dylan snorted. "Who would have me?"

"There are certain young ladies who have plenty of money and can be easily charmed by a good-looking man who knows how to flirt. And if that fails, there are certain wealthy dowagers who appreciate a man for other . . . um, skills."

Dylan threw back his head and laughed. He knew what his friend was getting at, but leave it to Thomas to put it so delicately. He could either try to sweep an innocent heiress off her feet or he could become a kept man, living to service his mistress for the benefit of the extra coin she might toss in his direction. Neither lot appealed to Dylan Marlow.

"You can't be serious. I'll not endure being tied for life to a coquettish ninny simply to reap the benefits of her fine fortune. Nor could I manage to perform stud service to a beastly widow."

"Oh, I'm sure *you* could manage it."

"Even I have limits, my friend." In his school days Dylan had been a notorious rake. He still managed to indulge in the pleasures of the flesh when he had the time. But to be forced to do it, night after night, with the same unappealing woman? No. It wasn't his game. He preferred highway robbery.

"So you will go on stealing?"

"Only from those who have plenty to give."

"It's wrong, I say. You're risking your life. I can't allow it."

"You can't stop me. I mean, you wouldn't.

Would you?" Dylan raised a brow. He'd felt certain he could trust his friend not to turn him in, but now he did have a moment of doubt. "I'll never hurt anyone. These people have more money than they know what to do with, Thomas. Why shouldn't I have a little? And the girl—I daresay she enjoyed the whole adventure."

"Leave it to you to rob a poor girl of her fortune, only to steal her heart along with it. The ladies always adored you, Marlow. What was your haul?"

"The ring. A necklace. Some coin . . ." Dylan was careful not to reveal a specific value. If he'd taken too much, Thomas would lose respect for him. Too little, and Thomas would say it wasn't worth it.

"Well, that ring can't be valued too highly. And if the necklace wasn't dear . . . I'm sure she'll weather the loss. Society girls have far too many jewels. Perhaps she learned a little lesson about riding at night unchaperoned. At any rate, you didn't hurt anyone." Thomas sighed. "You're sure this isn't a permanent vocation for you, this robbery business?"

"I want only enough money to be able to fix the ship. Then I'll stop. I swear. I'll never steal from those who don't have more than enough to give."

"We're talking about my friends, here, Marlow. People like me. How can you tell who has enough to give and who doesn't? I myself—"

"I know." Dylan put his hand over Thomas's and stared into his eyes. "I'll choose my victims carefully. Who knows? Maybe one day I'll even pay a few of them back."

"It's a noble thought to return the money, but I fail to see how you'll keep track. Still, I won't turn you in." There was resignation in Thomas's voice. His hazel eyes reflected the soft light of the candle and held concern for Dylan. "But promise me one thing."

"Anything. What is it?"

"Allow me to introduce you back into society, bring you around to some parties and entertainments. If you meet some of my illustrious friends you may decide to stop robbing them and start—"

"Start sleeping with one of them? For money?" Dylan laughed.

"You never know. You may find a woman who catches your fancy, either a marriageable girl or a willing widow. All I ask is that you give it a try."

"I rather like being a highwayman. I get to wear these natty clothes. Don't I look dangerous in black?"

"Hm." Thomas wasn't laughing along. "And how will you look in a hangman's noose?"

"Good point." Dylan stroked his chin, mulling it over.

"So you'll try it my way?"

"One party. I'll attend one little soiree, and if I don't find a woman who will both satisfy my high tastes and serve my monetary requirements, I'll go back to robbery."

"Very well." Thomas looked pleased. He always did enjoy his role of trying to keep Dylan on the straight and narrow. Even if he rarely succeeded.

"Lady Melbourne is having a garden fete a week from today. It will be brimming with eligible young heiresses—and some tolerable old dowagers too. I just know I can find you the right woman."

"Confident as always, Thomas."

"You'll be a big success. The ladies never could resist your charm."

"Then, to success." Dylan wasn't so sure of this new plan of Thomas's, but he lifted his glass out of good humor.

"To success!"

Chapter
3

Amelia stormed into her bedchamber.

Her maid, used to seeing her mistress in only the best of moods after a visit with her uncle Patrick and the boys, bristled at the sound of the door flinging open and flying straight into the wall, but she still hastened to close it quietly after Amelia had entered. It wasn't often that Amelia was angry, but when she was, no one wanted to stay close to her for long.

"The bed's ready. Hot water's all poured out. I'll leave you. . . ."

The maid was obviously in a hurry to go, likely wishing to spare herself a tirade. Amelia knew her servants hated to be around her when she was in a temper, but she wanted to be heard. She needed a friendly ear. And if she couldn't know any peace this night, well, no one in the house would either.

"Lettie, I've been robbed!" she shouted at the maid. She knew she shouldn't shout, but, honestly, what else was there to do? "Robbed!" She stamped her foot as if to add emphasis, and then she began to pace at the side of the bed.

Dear Lettie stayed still and listened while she railed.

"He could have taken my money, and he did, but was it enough?"

Lettie began to answer.

Amelia cut her off, shaking her finger at the air in front of her. "No! It wasn't. He had to have my necklace too."

As Amelia stormed by her, Lettie flattened herself against the door, as if she wished she could shrink away. Amelia abruptly stopped pacing. There was no point in frightening her servants. No point especially in upsetting her maid. Lettie was more than a maid. She was a good friend. "Oh, Lettie. What am I to do?"

Amelia went back to the bed and threw herself down on the nicely smoothed bedsheets.

"Miss. I'm—I'm so sorry to hear of your ordeal. You weren't hurt in the robbery, I hope?" Lettie came and sat by her.

Amelia sat up to face her, still angry but keeping herself calm. "No, Lettie. He didn't hurt me. Not that he didn't want to, I'm sure. The ruffian!"

"Ruffian? So it was a lone man?"

"A highwayman." She spoke the word with every bit of malice she could muster, and still it came out in a breathy sigh of a whisper. Surely too good for *him*, the blackguard. Why couldn't she manage to insert the proper scorn into her tones? "It was awful!"

Lettie stroked her back while Amelia buried her face in her hands. "There, there."

"Truly." She lifted her gaze to the maid. "You should have seen him. He was—he was like something from a nightmare. Almost seven feet tall, perhaps. And all bulk. He could have killed me."

Perhaps she exaggerated just a bit. Surely, he wasn't near seven feet. But he was tall. And he did use his strength to push her around. She could still feel the grip of his hands around her arms. Beyond a doubt he'd left bruises on her skin.

"My! You poor dear! Terrorized on the road." Lettie hugged Amelia, who let herself relax in the comforting embrace.

"He got my ring." Amelia, secure with the knowledge of being in her own home, in her own room, finally felt safe enough to cry. "It was my mama's ring." She bit her lip and studied the space on her finger where the ring had been. There was an indent around it, as if she still wore the ring. But it was gone. Gone forever.

Her ring. Her one tangible reminder of her mother and her mother's stories, told to her each night in this very bed. Her father, the hero of all her mother's fairy stories, had given her mother the ring when he first realized she was his one true love. Amelia knew all about it, because her mother had told her. The story of the ring was her very favorite bedtime tale. And now the ring was gone. It was as likely she would ever see it again as she would find her one true love. Her parents' marriage was rare, she knew. The chances of her ever finding the happiness they'd shared . . . well, she'd all but given up on the possibility. She sobbed aloud once more.

"I know, dear. I know. Let it out."

"But he—he—" She was about to tell Lettie of the robber's further insolence, but she swallowed the words. No, she wouldn't tell. Why give him that much power, the power to let word get out and soil her reputation? She would keep to herself the fact that he had kissed her.

But she was dying to ask Lettie what a kiss should feel like. Was it natural that her pulse raced just to think of it? That her nerves tingled all throughout her body? No. It couldn't possibly be natural to feel so intrigued by a man who had so rudely accosted her. Threatened her. By God, he'd taken her ring!

She hated him!

Amelia rose and went to the washbasin, taking a towel in her hands and twisting it with a vengeance. "If I ever see him again, I swear I'll—I'll kiss him!"

She pulled at the towel so tightly that she nearly ripped it in two. Ah, it felt good to let herself release the rage she'd been holding back. . . .

But her maid simply stared at her, her eyes wide

with incredulity. "It's a figure of speech, Lettie. I wouldn't really kill him, though I am plenty angry."

"Oh, but—" Lettie broke off, laughing slightly. "But, darlin', just now you didn't say you were going to kill him."

"I—I didn't?" Amelia looked at her maid. Had she gone daft? Of course she had said it! She'd stood right here, wrenched the towel between her hands, and swore that she would kill him.

"No. Perhaps you meant to, but that isn't what you actually said."

"Then, what did I say?"

"You said, and I quote, *If I ever see him again, I swear I'll—I'll* kiss *him!*"

"Kiss him?" Amelia dropped the towel in shock. "Don't be ridiculous."

She coughed and bent to pick up the towel. She had to get hold of herself, pretend not to be as flustered as she suddenly felt. "You must have misheard me, Lettie. I'm certain I said I would kill him. Kiss? Ha! The man robs me and all you can think of is kissing? Oh, Lettie, you are an original. I'm so glad I have you around."

"Me, original?" Lettie's little black eyes narrowed. "You're the one who said it."

"Oh, do go on!" Amelia went over and hugged her maid to her. "Yes, I feel much better now. Thank you, Lettie. You always know just the thing to say to restore my good humor."

"But—"

"No need to help me with the buttons. It has

been a long night. I'm sure you'd rather be off to bed. I'll manage. You may go now."

"Go?" Lettie was clearly surprised.

From the state Amelia was in when she'd entered, the maid had probably thought she was in for a long night.

"Mm-hm. Go on. Good night, Lettie. We'll talk more in the morning." She put up a good front of humming cheerfully while she began to remove her own dress, so Lettie would take heed and go. The maid didn't waste any time with leaving, lest Amelia change her mind.

And once she was alone Amelia stared into her mirror, looking long and hard at the woman who had been well and truly kissed. She did look a bit different perhaps. Somehow older and more refined. She stroked her cheek with her hand. Then she saw it again—her bare finger. No, she wouldn't be taken in.

"I'm going to get you, highwayman," she sneered at herself in the mirror, where she pictured his shrewd silver stare. "I'm going to get you and get my ring back. You'd best be on your guard."

Lady Melbourne's garden tea.

Amelia had almost forgotten it entirely until Lettie reminded her at breakfast. She had managed to avoid society all week, since the robbery. It wasn't that she was intent on staying in, but she did have so much to do to plan her own ball, set to take place later in the month. Her ball, of course, was for the purpose of raising money to replace the leaky roof at Holcomb House. Lady Melbourne's tea was just another event, a chance for the lady to show off her new jewels or to advance her family's social agenda. But, much as she wanted to decline the invitation, Amelia needed to attend in order to ensure the presence of Lady Melbourne and her wealthy, influential friends at her own ball. It was all part of the game.

Amelia hated playing games, and she hated the idea of spending another afternoon avoiding the advances of the foppish dolts who courted her. Except for Chadworth. Lord Chadworth, at least, managed to hold her interest. Every time they were together he took the time to ask her questions and to really listen when she answered. It impressed her. While others had asked her opinion on a range of topics, none of them took time to really look in her eyes or to even pretend to take an interest in her response.

Perhaps Chadworth would be at Lady Melbourne's. He managed to appear at most, if not all, of the Melbourne events. Surely he would liven up her afternoon.

"Lettie, I'll wear the new lavender ensemble."

"The lavender? I've already laid out your green dress."

"The green is nice. I had planned to wear it, but, then, I will be in a garden."

"I thought that was the point. Green in a garden. You'll blend right in to the surroundings."

"Hm." Amelia thought aloud. "Suddenly, I

don't wish to blend in. It would be nice to stand out today."

Lettie stood still, blinking rapidly. It was what she always did when she was confused by Amelia's behavior but didn't dare to question her. Poor Lettie had been doing a lot of blinking in the past week. Amelia decided perhaps she would offer her an explanation at last.

"Lettie, I've been thinking. Life around here is getting too predictable. It's time I made a few changes, livened things up. Perhaps it's time I considered marriage."

"Marriage?" Lettie blinked more rapidly still, but her mouth turned up at the corners. Clearly, she liked the idea.

"I'm not getting any younger. Some would already call me an old maid. I am past twenty, after all."

"Posh, by but a few years—" Lettie interrupted herself when she realized she was arguing against her case instead of for it. "But, indeed, time does pass quickly. You have always wanted children." Lettie smiled unabashedly now.

"Yes, Lettie. Children. A half dozen at least. Can you imagine them running around? Oh, what a lovely thought! Hm, but we are getting ahead of ourselves. Marriage is the first step I must consider. I think I'm ready to fall in love."

Lettie laughed, trying desperately—and ineffectively—to smother her giggles with the back of her hand.

"What? Is something wrong with the notion of my being in love?"

"Miss—" Lettie laughed harder, then took a breath to control herself. "That's just like you. *I think I'm ready to fall in love.* It doesn't come that way, if you'll pardon. Love simply happens. You don't plan for it or put it on your schedule of things to do. It just happens."

"Most inconvenient." Amelia smiled and pretended to wave off her maid's protests. She knew she couldn't make love happen. But there was nothing wrong with trying to help it along. She would never find the kind of love her parents had shared—a full-blown inferno—but surely she might find a little spark out there somewhere. Thinking of Chadworth did make her feel warm inside. Was it the beginnings of love? "I don't like to wait around and hope something simply happens. Why can't I make it happen? Add it to my calendar: falling in love, right between Lady Melbourne's tea and my ball."

She was half teasing, of course, but Lettie wouldn't argue. She merely shook her head and went off to assemble Amelia's wardrobe.

An hour had passed and he hadn't seen anyone suitable.

"Well, you haven't given it half a chance," Thomas chided him. "Most of the ladies are just beginning to arrive. You've barely met anyone save our hostess. And what did you think of her?"

"Of Lady Melbourne?" Dylan nearly choked on his coffee.

"Yes. She seems to have taken a fancy to you. It wouldn't hurt you to stay on her good side."

"But—she's an old woman. And she's married, for God's sake." Even if her age did not deter him, Dylan would not dally with a married woman. Christ, he had *some* scruples.

"Married, yes. But not above the occasional affair. Half her children aren't even her husband's, or so the rumor goes. She's powerful, Marlow. And rich beyond your imagination. Don't write her off so easily."

"No one is rich beyond *my* imagination, Thomas," Dylan quipped, and took another sip of coffee. "Besides, I'm bored. Highway robbery has it all over this social drivel as far as excitement."

"Give it a chance, my friend. Just another two hours."

Dylan didn't answer but waved Thomas out of the way so he could observe the new arrivals. Four new ladies had just come in, all of them young and a few of them tolerably pretty.

Thomas followed Dylan's gaze to the gate and began naming them down the line. "Lady Sarah Billings."

"Rather horse-faced, don't you think?" Dylan was ready to dismiss her.

"But she has a nice figure. Look at the way her dress hugs her bosom. And she has quite a fortune.

Plus, with a title of her own, she won't much care if you are of rank."

"Hm, all right. I'll think about her. Next?"

"The Sloane sisters. Kitty and Margaret. Pretty, but they haven't got much to offer. And, then, you'd have to put up with them fighting over you. They bicker constantly."

"Now, that does sound interesting. And perhaps I can yield a higher income if I take two for one."

"Marlow, you're a cad." Thomas laughed.

"That's why you like me." He was about to make another gibe when his breath caught in his throat. A fourth lady had made her entrance.

The newcomer was unquestionably lovely. Her hair had all the shine and color of spun gold, and she had the face of an angel. *His* angel. There was no doubt about it. She was the one.

"Amelia Benedict? Oh, yes." Thomas noted Dylan's reaction right away. "She is a prize. But you may as well forget about her."

"Why?" He was instantly curious. Forget her? How he'd tried!

"She has no interest in marriage. Or so the rumor goes. She has turned down a half-dozen offers, and she has a ready entourage of suitors to whom she never offers the slightest bit of encouragement."

"Not the slightest?"

"Well, there is one man. Lord Chadworth. He seems to have intrigued her. If she does marry, he will be the one."

"Who says?"

"Everyone."

"The hang with *everyone*, Thomas. *Everyone* hasn't counted on my arrival. I plan to shake things up for this Lord Chadworth fellow, and her other suitors while I'm at it."

"I'm telling you, it won't work. She is a Benedict, Marlow. Of *the* Benedicts. Proud family. Rich. Ancient lineage. They lost their titles years ago over some trifling scandal—if she marries, people speculate it will simply be to restore a title to her name. She certainly won't need to marry for fortune."

Dylan paused, the acute feeling of disappointment tugging in his gut. So she was one of *them*. He should have been pleased; her money made her a suitable marriage candidate. But she was of the *ton*—not just among them, but one of their celebrated few. He'd hoped she would be more like himself. On the fringe. The news that she was from a renowned, fortunate family put a dulling coat on an otherwise brilliant package. Still, he would have her.

"She's an heiress, and she's exquisite. Plus she has just the sort of temperament that I find challenging. No question about it, Thomas. She is the one." Marlow set his cup down on a nearby wrought-iron table and brushed his hands together decidedly.

"How do you know? You haven't even met her yet."

"Oh, indeed I have. Do you recall my robbery?"

"Yes?"

"She was my victim."

"By Jove, Marlow, we must get you out of here!"

"Not at all. She'll never recognize me. I wore a mask. And I spoke in gravelly tones quite unlike my own."

"You expect a mask and a deepened voice to protect you from recognition?"

"Well, that and the fact that we are in Lady Melbourne's gardens. She'd never expect the scoundrel who robbed her to turn up in polite society."

"Hm. You may have a point there. But take heed, Marlow. Do be on your guard."

"She'll never know me, I assure you. Now, be a good lad and make the introductions."

"Introduce you? To Amelia Benedict? Oh, no. I don't know her well enough. She's quite out of my circle."

"Very well. I'll handle it myself."

"But—you can't just walk on up and—Marlow!"

Ignoring his friend's protestations, Dylan left Thomas and crossed the room to where Amelia was just now allowing Lady Melbourne's niece to pour her out a cup of tea.

Dylan leaned back into a row of hedges, paying no attention to the low branches that scraped his ankles and the mud that enveloped his shoes. He needed to observe her without drawing attention to himself.

By night she had been alluring—by daylight she was stunning.

Moonlight lends a certain loveliness to almost all young ladies, but to see her now, under the shade of Lady Melbourne's garden canopy, her beauty shone like the sun reflecting off a garden pond. No wonder she'd had offers; the men would be lining up in droves even if she were penniless. But that she had a fortune to boot—oh, the luck!

Her whisky-tinted eyes he well recalled, but he certainly hadn't expected her hair to be so fair. Of course, that night she'd had it tucked up in a bonnet, with only a few stray tendrils framing her delicate face. A brown-eyed blonde. Not so typical. For Amelia, he guessed, what was typical would never do.

She went to stand alone on the other side of the hedge, not too far from him. Her eyes seemed to search the crowd. Was she looking for someone or trying to escape? He couldn't tell which. One thing was certain: She didn't have an interest in being a part of the party. And that served his own purpose well. He drew closer, unnoticed, as her gaze swept across the faces of those gathering in the garden.

He needed an in with her, something that would allow him to speak without having first been properly introduced.

Reaching deep into his pocket, he found a delicate silver filigree bracelet, a little trinket he kept with him that was useful on just such occasions. It was pretty but not worth much of anything.

When she turned her head to the other side of

the garden, he tossed it to the grass at her feet and waited a moment. She finished her search and returned her attention to her tea. Dylan waited another moment and made his approach.

"Excuse me, miss . . . um, begging your pardon." He stooped down and picked up the bracelet. "Did you drop this?"

Her whisky-tinted eyes, which had shone with such a soft glow in the moonlight, turned on him suddenly. She peered at him so sharply, with such a fiery gaze, that he thought her mere stare would burn him through.

"No," she answered curtly. Then, as if realizing she'd been rude, she added, "It is not mine. Thank you."

And as soon as she spoke the words, before he could address her again, she turned on her heel and walked away.

Dylan looked after her, stunned. He'd never been cut so thoroughly by a lady. Women liked him. They always had a strong reaction to him. A strong, *positive* reaction. At least they did at first glance. After they got to know him better, some of them found they began to like him less. He didn't have much patience for fawning lovers, after all. But on first acquaintance he was a pleasing fellow. Charming, in fact. He could catch and hold the interest of any woman he chose.

Except this one, apparently.

Across the room she held her hand out to a

brute who had just come through the gate. To *him*, she bowed slightly and smiled widely. A large, sweet grin that displayed her perfect white teeth.

Dylan stood watching, still in shock, and muttered under his breath, "Haughty female!"

"Hm, some do think so." Lady Melbourne approached him directly.

"Forgive me, my lady." Dylan bowed quickly, embarrassed by his faux pas. He hadn't realized anyone was nearby, let alone his hostess.

"Bah, think not of it. Some *do* think it. Especially the younger ladies. The jealous ones, upset with her for stealing all their beaux—and not caring a whit for them herself. But others would say she is the picture of generosity, simply an angel."

An angel. He hadn't been far from thinking so himself at first. With her soft, pretty face and fair, golden features, her appearance was certainly angelic. But her behavior?

"And you, Lady Melbourne? What do you think of her?" With his hostess he realized he could be a bit more direct.

"She is somewhere in between perhaps." Lady Melbourne seemed undecided on the case of Amelia Benedict, and as reputation had it, this lady was rarely undecided about anything.

"A holy demon?" Dylan smiled his cocky grin, and Lady Melbourne threw back her head and laughed. Ah, so he hadn't lost his charm after all. After Miss Benedict's cold reaction to him, he'd begun to wonder.

"Oh, Mr. Marlow. I will enjoy having you around." Lady Melbourne took his arm, though he hadn't offered it, and began to lead him to the nearby stone path.

"Will you?" Dylan was trying to decide which course to take with this new little flirtation.

Lady Melbourne didn't interest him. She had a pleasing enough figure and abundant dark hair. Fine eyes. The only thing to indicate her age was her skin, which wasn't as tight as it might have been twenty years ago. Her face was smooth, but her neck showed a host of wrinkles and discolorations. Still, her maturity enhanced her appearance. Likely, she was a more handsome woman now than she had been in her youth. Marlow had been with a few older women, but this one was married. No matter how rich or how powerful she was, he felt no desire to court her affections.

Fortunately, the lady did not seem to have any intentions of making love to him. If anything it appeared she was trying to aid him in his cause.

"Mr. Marlow," she spoke in a low whisper, "you're going to escort me on a brief turn about the gardens. Your lady is with Chadworth now. He is sure to suggest a walk in order to separate Amelia from the crowd."

"Why will he try to get her alone?" Marlow's skin bristled. If Chadworth was ready to propose to her, and she accepted, it would be all over for him.

"Simply to bring their acquaintance that much further along." Lady Melbourne continued to hold his arm and speak in a whisper, though she smiled gaily to guests as they passed by. "He won't propose yet, not to worry. She has shot down too many suitors for him to press his luck so soon."

"Yet? Then he does mean to marry her?"

"Who can tell with Chadworth? Chad likes to keep himself a mystery. It's why he appeals to so many of the women. Not that I need to tell *you* what a woman likes."

Marlow was startled by her boldness. He'd heard of Lady Melbourne's manner, but he never expected her to be so blunt with a man she'd barely met. Of course, she had enough money and power in her circle that she needn't worry much about her reputation, and she never had. For all her days, Lady Melbourne had enjoyed a high place in society and social acceptance on a grand scale. She could be a valuable ally.

"Have I a chance, or is she already in love with this Chadworth?" Dylan decided if he wanted to know his chances, he may as well be as direct as Lady Melbourne.

"With my help you'll have more than a chance. I hope to see you succeed on a grand scale."

Marlow didn't question the lady's motives now. As they strolled leisurely through the garden, he simply thanked his good fortune that he had someone so influential on his side.

Chapter
4

Thank goodness, Chadworth had arrived!

When Amelia entered the garden and didn't see him, she'd feared he wouldn't come. And then, when she became the target of yet another fortune-hunting rogue, she'd cursed herself for not wearing her green dress after all. Perhaps if she'd blended into the scenery she could have avoided the attentions of yet another would-be suitor. Of course, this fortune hunter had been quite handsome, really, hadn't he? She had been startled when she looked up into his eyes, blue as the cornflowers along the adjacent fence. Rather striking, but she could not be taken in. A bracelet in the grass, indeed. Did he expect her to be fooled so easily?

Fortunately, she'd seen Chadworth enter almost as soon as the fellow accosted her, giving her an excuse to hasten off. Now she was pleased she'd worn the lavender. Chad had already given her a half-dozen compliments on her appearance.

And almost immediately he had taken her arm and asked her to walk about the gardens. He led her down a fairly secluded path, but she was not nervous. Chad was the perfect gentleman. But, she wondered, was he the perfect gentleman for her?

Amelia stole a glance at him as they walked along in silence. Chad's hair was almost the same shade as his warm brown eyes. His strong jaw and slightly pointed chin added just the right regal effect. Chadworth was the picture of nobility, a proper gentleman. His manners reflected his upbringing. He was well-spoken, indicating his education and interest in intellectual pursuits. Plus, Chadworth had already inherited his family property, a nice estate in Farnham where he held his baronial seat. And he had recently purchased the seemingly requisite London town house. All in all he was a catch, and yet her heart did not beat faster to have him by her side. Why was that? Surely she could fall in love with him. He held all the right credentials.

"Oh, do look there." Amelia pointed up the path, eager to start a conversation. "Forget-me-nots. Aren't they lovely?"

"You fancy them?" Chadworth asked, escorting

her to the patch for a closer look. "I would have thought most women prefer roses. But, then, you are not most women."

He bowed slightly and she blushed at his compliment.

"Oh, I like roses too. But they aren't my favorite flower. I don't think I have a favorite, actually. Too many beautiful flowers. So hard to choose . . ."

"I don't find it difficult at all." He drew closer. "I can name the loveliest flower in the garden in a heartbeat."

He touched her chin and tilted her face up to meet his. Now her pulse *did* race. She thought perhaps he might kiss her, though, of course, it wouldn't be proper. The highwayman had taken the liberty, but he was a rake, a cad. Still, she would truly like to be kissed again. For the life of her she had not been able to forget what his mouth had felt like on hers. . . .

"She's standing right in front of me."

"Who?" Amelia snapped back to attention and looked around, left to right.

"The loveliest flower, Miss Amelia Benedict. I was talking about you." Chadworth looked into her eyes. The corners of his lips turned up in a slight, bemused smile.

Chad's lips were thin. The highwayman's had been full and soft. But why on earth was she comparing them? Why was she thinking of the highwayman at all when she had Lord Chadworth right in front of her, taking an obvious interest, saying such sweet things. . . .

"You flatter me." She smiled and turned back to the path, aware that her actions may have made her appear coquettish to Chad. "Perhaps we should get back."

He followed her, restoring her hand to the crook of his arm as soon as he caught up.

"We have company," he observed, motioning ahead.

"Lady Melbourne, I see," Amelia acknowledged. And the man who'd tried to form an acquaintance with her earlier by asking if she'd lost a bracelet. It seemed there was no escaping her potential suitors. Now she would have to suffer an introduction, and there was no telling what liberties the man would try to take once properly introduced to her. Well, for now she was safe with Chad.

"Come, Lord Chadworth," she suggested boldly. "I don't wish for our time together to be interrupted. Let's hasten back the other way."

His eyes narrowed at her suggestion, and then he smiled. She expected him to take her up without pause on her offer to advance their intimacy.

Instead, he surprised her. "They've already seen us, Miss Benedict. To run off now would be rude. Come, we'll make a foursome."

And before she could protest, he called out a greeting to Lady Melbourne and bid her to come join them. Bother! She would be introduced to yet another suitor after all.

"We've caught them." Lady Melbourne tugged at Dylan's arm. "They know we have them in sight, and they can't pretend they have missed us."

At last he would get a proper introduction. She couldn't cut him now. "Indeed. You are a clever woman, Lady Melbourne. I'm most grateful."

"Hm. The time for gratitude will come later. Now is the time to capture her interest. Where is that bauble you tried to snare her with?"

"Excuse me?"

"The bracelet. I saw the whole thing, Marlow, don't play ignorant. A rather amateurish trick but not completely without its possibilities. We're almost upon them. No time for delay. Give it to me."

Without hesitation he slipped the trinket from his pocket and slid it onto the lady's wrist. He saw her plan, and it was a good one. Why hadn't he thought of it? Lady Melbourne would pretend that Dylan had successfully returned the bracelet to her—its owner—removing any chance for Amelia to suspect that he had ever meant to fool her into making his acquaintance. It wouldn't do for her to think ill of him before she even got to know him. Now he could start over with her more properly.

"Why, if it isn't Lord Chadworth and the lovely Miss Benedict." Lady Melbourne's tone changed from a conspiratorial whisper to a high-pitched social chirp in the wink of an eye. "Enjoying my garden paths?"

Chadworth muttered something about the

forget-me-nots, observing Dylan with a narrowed gaze. Miss Benedict cooed politely about the lovely day and smiled wide, her eyes shifting to reveal her insincerity. Dylan knew the *ton* and their silly affectations. He could read them all by now, even if he refused to adopt their so-called manners. Again, he felt disappointed in her for sharing in the sort of false joviality so common among her set. If she didn't give a hang to meet him, why didn't she just say so?

Ah, but in her own way she had earlier, hadn't she? And that hadn't suited him either.

Lady Melbourne made the introductions.

"Mr. Dylan Marlow . . ."

He could see Amelia's lips repeating after Lady Melbourne, though no sound came out. She seemed to know the name. How? Unless she was extremely well studied, she wouldn't know him from a beggar.

Or a highwayman. His lips curled up in his own secret smile.

"Mr. Marlow has been kind enough to restore my bracelet. I'm ever so grateful." Lady Melbourne waved her wrist around dramatically and held her hand to her bosom most affectedly.

Marlow would have applauded the performance, but he was too busy waiting to see Miss Benedict's reaction. And she did not disappoint. Her whisky-colored eyes widened in shock.

"*Your* bracelet? Dear, I'd—" She blinked back her surprise and recovered herself, casting a congratulatory—and apparently genuine—smile in Dylan's direction. "Well, Mr. Marlow. I must give you credit for your determination. How very kind of you to find the bracelet's owner. I confess I would have thought it a lost cause."

She'd thought it more than that, clearly. Amelia Benedict had suspected his bracelet discovery to be a poor attempt to win her regard, and now Lady Melbourne had proven her quite wrong. Indeed, if Lady Melbourne weren't married, he may have considered entertaining Thomas Selkirk's suggestion to make her his mistress. She was delightfully playful and blessed with a wicked sense of justice. Just the sort to appeal to him, normally. But he had set his sights on Amelia now. His fond gratitude, delivered to Lady Melbourne in privacy before he could leave the fete, would have to do.

And for her part Lady Melbourne seemed to have lost interest in him altogether. She latched on to Chadworth's arm and began to lead him up the path, demanding to see the very forget-me-nots that had commanded Miss Benedict's attention. It suited Dylan fine, for now he had Amelia Benedict's complete attention.

"Shall we?" He motioned for them to follow their hostess and Chadworth.

"Indeed." Miss Benedict did not take his arm but started to walk quietly forward.

"A lovely day for a garden party," Dylan commented, closing the distance between them and beginning the light conversation he despised but that the situation required.

"Yes. I thought it might rain. But it hasn't." Amelia was quiet for another minute, and then her curiosity must have gotten the better of her. "I haven't seen you before, Mr. Marlow. Are you new in town?"

"No," he replied. How much of his background it was safe to reveal he still wasn't certain. He'd been out of society for some time. And his uncle was gone off to Scotland. Besides, when the scandal had broken, Miss Benedict would have been just a girl, maybe off to school herself. And, at any rate, none of his undoing—his expulsion, his uncle's disinheriting him—had happened in proximity to London. He was probably quite safe. "I'm sure we must have seen each other at one event or the next. These things do all run together."

"Perhaps." She studied him and pursed her lips, unconvinced.

"And I have been out of town recently, visiting my uncle."

"Your uncle?"

"You may know him. The Earl of Stoke?"

"The Earl of Stoke?" she repeated, clearly impressed. Yes, he would say his relation to an earl did raise her interest markedly, and again he felt a pang of disappointment that it should matter to her at all. "No, I don't know him directly. I know of him, of course."

"Of course." Dylan turned his attention to the primroses lining the path and suppressed a wily smile. Now, perhaps, would she consider him suitable to court her acquaintance?

She grew quiet again, and he let her be. He walked on slowly, stopping now and again to study a stray flower. It wouldn't do to act too interested in her.

Up ahead, Lady Melbourne and Chadworth stopped and looked over the forget-me-nots. From the corner of his eye Dylan noticed that Miss Benedict had stopped as well. He followed her gaze—she watched Chadworth move in rather close to Lady Melbourne as they talked animatedly and gestured over the flowers.

"The forget-me-nots seem to have inspired their share of interest today," Dylan said, determined to engage Amelia in conversation while Chadworth and their hostess were otherwise occupied. "I hadn't realized ladies were so fond of them."

"Of forget-me-nots?" Amelia asked, startled. "Lady Melbourne has an abundant patch of them, I suppose."

Her gaze drifted back to Chadworth. A telling sign. She was in danger of becoming too intrigued by this Chadworth fellow. Dylan did have his work cut out for him.

"Tell me, Miss Benedict." He took her hand and led her forward, though she had stopped as if to maintain a deliberate distance from Chadworth and their hostess. "What flower do you fancy the most?"

She didn't look at him, apparently distracted by Chadworth's leaning closer still to Lady Melbourne, but she answered him anyway. "I don't like any, truth be told. If I get too close to flowers, they make me sneeze."

How delightfully unromantic of her. It took him by surprise. The lady was different, indeed. He'd known it when he'd first met her, and her confession confirmed it again in his mind. A woman who didn't like flowers—certainly she was different from any woman he'd ever known.

"Well, let's get you out of this garden, then, shall we?" He put his arm around her waist and led her directly to Lady Melbourne and Chadworth, not giving her a chance to form an argument. "I say, it's looking like rain, Lady Melbourne. And you've been absent from your duties long enough."

All eyes turned to him, startled. His tone was intimate and demanding at once, as if he knew Lady Melbourne far better than one day's acquaintance would allow. In fact, he was being rather rude. But he didn't care. He sensed that his only shot at winning Amelia's interest away from Chadworth in a timely fashion depended on him showing the utmost regard for Amelia's welfare and opinions, and he was ready to oblige.

Unfortunately, she was not ready to be obliged. Amelia stepped forward in protest. "Rain? Oh, no, Mr. Marlow. We were just speaking of the delightful weather, were we not? It isn't going to rain."

"But—" He was about to intervene again, for

her sake. Did she not see that he was trying to save her? "The flowers?"

She turned to him, mouthing a hasty "shh," before turning back to the others.

Chadworth and Lady Melbourne looked on, their stares of surprise turning to expressions of bemused curiosity.

After a moment Lady Melbourne spoke. "How kind of you to remind me of my duties, my dear Mr. Marlow. I have arranged this garden party for a purpose, after all, and we'd best get to the unveiling before the rain falls."

She came away from Chadworth and took Marlow's arm, stepping in front of the others to lead them back to the party.

He hadn't expected Lady Melbourne to reclaim his attentions. Now Amelia was annoyed with him and back to clinging to Chadworth's arm. He felt as if he was again at the starting line, with no progress made at all. His only consolation was that Lady Melbourne was smiling wider than ever and congratulating him, in a low voice, for his genius at having made Chadworth jealous.

Chadworth? Jealous? Now, why would the man be jealous of *him* when Chadworth was the one with the treasure of Miss Amelia Benedict walking at his side? Dylan hoped his patroness knew her business better than it seemed at the moment, because he couldn't afford any mistakes.

———

The nerve of the man! Amelia grew increasingly vexed as she studied him from the rear. He cut a fine figure, it was true. His clothes were not expertly fitted to his form, but she could still make out his fine musculature, his solid build. His tight, firm—

Oh, honestly, why was she even looking at Mr. Dylan Marlow, the blackguard? Was it *his* place to betray her sensitivity to pollen? Why had she said anything at all to the man? He was just like all the others, thinking she was a useless little ninny who wanted saving. The only man who didn't fawn all over her was Chadworth. And Marlow would spoil Chad's good opinion of her by making him think she was so infirm and frail that she couldn't even bear to be around flowers.

Flowers, of all things.

What woman couldn't stand to be around flowers? It was unnatural. Strange. She didn't want to be strange. And how else was a man to show his blossoming regard for a woman but to bring her a bouquet of flowers? No, it wouldn't do for anyone to think she couldn't stand them.

"Or petunias?" Chad queried.

"I'm sorry. . . ." Chadworth had been speaking to her as they walked along and she just now realized it. What had he been saying? "I was studying the pansies over yon and I lost track of the conversation."

"That settles it, then. You have answered my question. I asked if you preferred the petunias or the pansies." He strode away from her, stooped, plucked a pansy from the row, and returned, offering it to her.

She could smell it faintly as he held it out, and she knew from the tickling in her nose that if she took it from him it would finish her. She pushed it away quickly. "No. I mean . . . well, I prefer almost anything to pansies."

"Oh." Chad looked down at the flower and back up at her, confused. "I see. Forgive me." He dropped the pansy and crushed it with his boot heel. "An end to pansies, then. Death to all pansies!" he shouted triumphantly, his lips curling up in a smile.

Then, with his hostess directly in front of them, he dashed over to the patch of pansies and did a frantic, funny little dance for Amelia's benefit, gaily stamping the life out of them all.

"Oh, Lord Chadworth, do stop!" Amelia called, but she couldn't stop laughing to save herself. He was just too delightful, too whimsical, too spontaneous.

Perhaps her plan of falling in love wasn't so farfetched after all.

She could be in love with such a man. A man with not a care in the world, not a whit of regard for propriety. For decency. It was most improper for Chadworth to laugh like a fool and to ruin Lady Melbourne's garden. Yet he did it. He risked Lady Melbourne's wrath and social ruin—why? For the sake of pleasing her?

If so, it was a compliment of the highest order. And even after Chad stopped his outrageous stomping and Lady Melbourne turned on her heel to glare at them, her anger well apparent, Amelia was giddy. The mere look on the lady's face made her giggle so hard she had to cover her mouth with her hand.

"You have a quarrel with my pansies, Lord Chadworth?" Lady Melbourne's eyebrow was raised to a dagger-sharp point, and it did cause Amelia some concern now.

Her laughter died and, with short huffs, she got control of her breathing. They were drawing a crowd. First one, then two, now three and four heads poked over the hedgerows, eyes round with curiosity. A few even came into the aisle to see what caused such a commotion.

And there was Chad, stepping out of the pansies, his fine shoes caked with soil and stains from the leaves. He resumed his position at her side, and though she hadn't offered him her hand, he took it gently and placed it in the crook of his arm.

"Indeed I do, Lady Melbourne. They were causing Miss Benedict some distress, and so they had to be destroyed."

"I see," the lady mused. She seemed to be mulling it over. The crowd continued to grow, and no one dared even gasp in the event they might miss something. Mr. Marlow, the rogue who started it all, stood politely at Lady Melbourne's side, not saying a word.

"I suppose it's a good thing Miss Benedict didn't take offense to Paul here." She motioned to the gardener, who stood off to the side trimming a rosebush and looking none too pleased to be suddenly at the center of attention. "I'm loath to think what you may have done to *him* for Miss Benedict's sake."

Titters raced through the crowd of onlookers. A number of girls blushed for Amelia's sake at claiming such attention. A few of the matrons. smiled knowingly in her direction.

Amelia felt it her responsibility to add to the game, but with Marlow's eyes upon her she found herself quite unable to come up with anything at all amusing to say.

Why did he study her so, and why did she care? Oh, that man! She cursed the moment she even bothered to acknowledge his acquaintance. How did he have such power to vex her? She barely knew him. He bothered her only because she allowed him to do so. In a moment's inattention she had betrayed a weakness to him, and now she simply had to speak with him again, in private, to assure his silence, then she would think of him no more.

The hour was early, and she had all day to enjoy Chad's company. Already the crowd was moving off toward the fountain, and Chad took her arm tighter to escort her along.

"It's time to see why Lady Melbourne has assembled us all, I suppose." Lord Chadworth walked very close to her. With every step she took, she could feel his thigh brushing hers through her skirts. "I believe she means to make a presentation."

"Oh? We shall see." Amelia smiled, but her thoughts kept turning in her mind. Where was that Marlow? She wouldn't have any peace until she could clear up her misunderstanding with him. She had lost sight of him in the crowd. He was with Lady Melbourne, she assumed, but so many people had gathered around that it was impossible to tell.

Chadworth stayed by her as the crowd drew closer to the patio. Lady Melbourne's voice rang out loud, but Amelia barely listened as the lady droned on. Something about a statue. They'd all been gathered to Lady Melbourne's garden for the sole purpose of glimpsing her new statue. Amelia sighed. Any excuse for a party.

Amelia stopped trying to see over the sea of heads and turned her attention to the man at her side. She'd rather study Chadworth's profile than a boring statue any day. Except when she turned she was disappointed to see that he was no longer there. He must have gone off to get a look at the statue himself, she thought. But how much interest could one possibly have in a block of carved stone?

As the crowd let out a collective sigh of pleasure at the unveiling of the statue—which Amelia gathered was a depiction of Psyche to make a pair with Lady Melbourne's favored figure of Cupid—she strolled back toward the pavilion. It was too early to leave. And perhaps, if she stayed, she could rejoin

Chad to partake of the buffet. Still, she was just as happy to find a seat on a bench by herself for a few moments to observe the crowd instead of being a part of it.

"I'm afraid I won't be stomping in any flower patches to win your approval, but perhaps you will allow me a seat." The voice, deep and familiar, came from behind her. She jumped. Her solitude was not to last, apparently.

Without turning around she gave him leave. "You may share my bench, Mr. Marlow." She did wish to speak with him, after all.

He sat, not on the other side of the bench as she supposed he would, but so close that his leg was pressed up against hers. "Not interested in the unveiling, Miss Benedict? I thought you might be right up front to take a look."

"Why should you think that?" she snapped, immediately on the defensive.

"Cupid and Psyche. Rather a romantic pairing. Ladies like romance, or so I thought."

"Most ladies like flowers too, I suppose."

"And you don't. Indeed, you aren't like the others."

"It isn't that I don't *like* flowers. And hush."

She was acting shrewish, and there was no need. Yet with Mr. Marlow sitting so close, studying her so intently, she felt nervous. She wouldn't meet his eyes, and his breath was hot on her cheek. But, she warned herself, she had best be a little less vinegar and a little more honey if she intended to get her way of things. "Please. I do sneeze, sometimes, when I'm too close to flowers . . . but I do like them, truly."

"Forgive me." He backed away slightly. "I didn't mean to presume—"

"Of course, Mr. Marlow. I'm sure. I would ask you a favor, though?"

He leaned closer. "Yes?"

She looked deep into his eyes. With his ink-black hair she wouldn't have expected him to have blue eyes. And such a startling blue at that—very light and clear, like crystal. He had beautiful eyes. And they looked back at her, as if trying to figure her out. She didn't want to be assessed. "I want you to forget what I told you about the flowers. I—please. Just don't tell anyone."

He smiled. Her gaze hadn't moved from his eyes, but she knew he was smiling just from the way the faint lines at the corners of his eyes crinkled. He was too young to have such lines around his eyes, she would have thought. But he did.

"Don't tell? Hm. Intriguing. So your intolerance to flowers is a well-guarded secret, is it?"

Her stomach tightened. Had she just given the man more ammunition to use against her instead of encouraging him to forget the whole issue?

"No. Yes." He confused her. She didn't like the feeling. "I mean—I'd simply rather people didn't know."

"People? Like Chadworth, for instance."

"It has nothing to do with Lord Chadworth,"

she protested. Heat rose to her cheeks. Of all times to blush!

"Really?" He toyed with her.

"Yes. I'd just . . . well, it isn't anyone's business. And you wouldn't be a gentleman if you went around blabbing my secrets."

"Who told you I was a gentleman?" His smile turned to laughter.

She asked him a simple favor and he *laughed*? Now he'd done it. She was angry. "Oh! I should have known I would get nowhere talking to a man like you."

"A man like me? We've only just met and you think you know me so well?"

"I know you tried to play the hero earlier, in rescuing me from the flowers. Do you think I need rescuing, Mr. Marlow? Did you think that would impress me?"

"I don't know. It seemed to have worked for Lord Chadworth."

"Whatever do you mean? I abhor rescues. I don't need saving, from anything or anyone. Do you understand? I am perfectly capable of taking care of myself."

He took her hand in his and studied it, tracing slow circles over the base of her gloved fingers. It was a moment before he looked up again. "Perhaps you are. But every woman likes to be saved now and then, I think. It is my position that you, in particular, Miss Benedict, need a hero in your life."

She snatched her hand back quickly and shifted away from him as far as the bench would allow. "Ridiculous."

"Is it? Perhaps it was offensive when *I* tried to rescue you, Miss Benedict, but you seemed to rather enjoy Lord Chadworth's dance in the pansies all for the sake of winning your approval. Everyone's talking about how Lord Chadworth risked offending Lady Melbourne all for the sake of Miss Benedict. The ladies are practically swooning with envy." He paused and stood up, making ready to take his leave. "And I think you rather enjoy it. I do believe that it isn't so much having a hero that you protest, but that you want to have your choice of heroes."

She did not answer but glowered at him. How dare he think he could sum her up so easily!

And yet, perhaps he was right. She balked when he'd tried to rescue her, but in the end it was exactly what Chad had done to her delight. And hadn't she deigned to judge Mr. Marlow before he had even made an attempt to criticize her?

He stood there, smiling down at her, watching as she evaluated his accusations. She'd been a hypocrite. And she had nothing to say for herself.

He doffed his hat and walked quietly away.

And even as Chad returned to her side, asking to accompany her to the buffet, Amelia found herself looking for Mr. Marlow in the crowd.

Chapter
5

Dylan Marlow needed a London address.

No longer did it suit his purposes to sleep in the dockyard office or to nod off in a dusty corner of Boltwood's Tavern. If he meant to pursue Miss Amelia Benedict—to really pursue her—he needed a fashionable abode. There was no way around it. And the only place that was suitable—that he could afford—was Oakley Place, his uncle's Mayfair town house.

The day after the Melbourne garden affair, Dylan prepared to move into his new home. The Earl of Stoke was off to Scotland, he knew, and only a few of the servants would be left behind. Mrs. Fredericks, the housekeeper, had adored him in his youth. Like his uncle, she'd thought of Dylan as nearly her own son. Only she wouldn't have disowned him so easily over one foolish mistake. Would she?

He hadn't ever spoken with her after the incident. The big blowup had occurred at Hensridge, his uncle's country manor, and Dylan had never returned to the town house again. How much would the housekeeper know of his undoing? She could know everything and send him packing. Or she could know very little and have enough sympathy for his current position to let him stay. He had to take his chances.

Once he was moved in to a proper household, he could have cards printed up and make his visit to Miss Benedict's estate, Briarwood.

It wasn't likely he would be invited to any future social events. Selkirk had called in enough favors to get Dylan an invitation to Lady Melbourne's garden fete, and while Lady Melbourne seemed to take a liking to him, there certainly wasn't a strong enough regard between them to encourage her to use her power to help him climb the social ladder. Dylan wasn't part of Amelia's crowd yet. It would make courting her difficult for the time being. But once he managed to get closer . . .

He would simply have to find ways to run into her. At Melbourne House he'd heard of Miss Benedict's approaching ball and charity auction. He hoped to get to know her well enough to earn an invitation. One invitation from her could lead to others, and before he knew it he would have her where he wanted her—her lovely body at his beck and call and her fortune at his disposal.

The thought occurred to him just as he strode up the walk to his uncle's front gate. His lips curled in the most mischievous of grins just as Mrs. Fredericks herself emerged from the house to sweep the stoop at the entrance. She took one look at him and threw up her arms, sending the broom flying to the lawn.

"Dylan, lad, is it really you?"

Lord, he hadn't seen her in years, and yet she knew him straightaway. Dear old Freddie. He had called her Freddie because *Mrs. Fredericks* was too much of a mouthful for him to manage in his youth. Most of his childhood he'd forgotten, or he'd taken pains to put it to the far recesses of his mind. But Freddie . . . well, he was glad to see her again. He hadn't realized how much he'd missed her.

"It's me, Freddie. I've come back." There was no sense in going through the formality of calling her Mrs. Fredericks. She'd always been a sentimental sort, and he was willing to indulge her.

"What with that smile on your face, I knew you right away. Don't just stand there, man. Come give your old nanny a hug!"

He did as instructed, bounding forward to Mrs. Fredericks's waiting arms. She was as stout as ever, a good solid woman, and it was comforting to be held in her warm embrace again. Before he was released he blinked back a tear from the corner of his eye. Never would he have imagined that he would be so affected. He'd shut out his past, hardened his heart, or so he'd thought. But he couldn't deny that he still harbored some tenderness inside him.

He'd been loved in the past. He remembered the feeling and treasured it. His mother had died giving birth to him, but Mrs. Fredericks had become like a mother to him upon his moving in with his uncle. The years he had spent at Oakley Place had been golden ones. He'd had his uncle, Mrs. Fredericks, and wealth at his disposal. On occasion he would be allowed to visit his father at the docks. He'd planned to return to Oakley Place after Oxford, and then—one mistake, and in a heartbeat it had all been stripped away from him. He returned to his father, but by then the man was old and tired. His father didn't live much longer, and Dylan was left with the dockyard and a heap of debts.

"All right, you can let go now. You've done squeezed the life out of me."

"Sorry, Freddie." He released her and stepped back. "It is good to see you again."

"Hmph. I'd like to believe that. How many years have you been gone now without so much as a word? You could have at least stopped in to say good-bye." She stepped away from him and crossed her arms over her ample chest.

"Freddie." He gave her the look he'd used in childhood to win her over when he'd misbehaved. It still came naturally to him, after all these years, to make his eyes wide and his lower lip droop to a slight pout. She never could resist him. "I *have* missed you. Honest. But I couldn't come round. I've had business. And—"

"And what? You were afraid of what your uncle might say to see you show your face here? That I can understand." She relaxed her posture and drew near him again. "But he's gone now, the old goat. Off on holiday. Been on holiday the past two years, at least. It's safe for you to come inside and take a cup of tea."

He hesitated. So she *did* know about his falling out of favor—and she didn't seem to care. But what about the others? Could he risk word getting out to his uncle that he'd come back to the house? He'd told himself he was ready to risk it, but now he wasn't so sure. His pride was stronger than he imagined. "I don't want to be a bother."

"A bother? Well, heavens! You've never worried about being a bother in all your days before, I wager. Dylan Marlow does what he likes, and . . ."

"And likes what he does." He smiled, finishing the old motto he used to shout around the house to all who would listen. He hadn't thought of it in years, perhaps because it had lost its flavor. He didn't like what he was doing, did he? Stealing, conniving. If all went according to plan he would swindle a young lady out of her fortune and not bat an eye. He wasn't supposed to care.

In the end he would get what he wanted. And he

would see to it that Miss Amelia Benedict got something out of the bargain as well. She had plenty to give, and he was a damn sight better for her than Lord Chadworth. What was the harm?

The pang of guilt returned. He knew the potential harm, but he fought like the devil to quash his fears. In her set, they all used people. Self-advancement was the sole concern of the members of the *ton*, so why should he balk at making it his as well?

"It's only Nan and me, besides." Mrs. Fredericks's voice broke into his thoughts as she took his arm and started to tug him toward the entrance.

"I'm sorry?"

"Inside. Nan and I were left to look after things. And old John, but he's out on some errands. Lord Stoke took most the staff to Scotland with him. Except for a few rooms, the house is closed up. Only takes the three of us to keep it in order till the master decides to come back."

Dylan's spirits lightened immediately. Only three servants? And all of them had been fond of him. The situation could not be more to his advantage. Freddie, Nan, and John would let him stay. With a Mayfair residence to call his own, he was well on his way to respectability—and into Amelia Benedict's good graces.

For four days he had searched for her to no avail. Did she not take part in the usual forms of entertainment for the *ton*? She'd missed a luncheon of Lady

Jersey's that he was sure she would attend, and she had not put in any appearances at Almack's. He couldn't gain admittance to such events, but he had done his best to be aware of them and to keep watch outside for any sign of her. He'd been to the areas where she would likely shop, dine, or stop to be seen, and he hadn't caught a glimpse of her. His hope rose. Perhaps she wasn't as enmeshed in the high society he loathed as he'd first suspected. No. It had been only a few days. More likely she was ill. He would give it time.

After five days he finally decided he would not see her unless he sought her out at home. It would be awfully bold of him to simply drop in on her, of course, but he was beginning to consider it. His finances were severely strained. He had to make progress, and soon, but for now he had other matters to attend to.

He had been leaving Fergus at home and taking one of his uncle's horses during his excursions to search for Amelia. She hadn't recognized Dylan as her robber, and it was equally unlikely she could identify his horse; however, it seemed an unnecessary risk to allow her to see them both together. A week without exercise would be too much for Fergus to bear, though. Too many days in the stables would take the spring out of the horse's step.

Fergus had whickered wildly as Dylan saddled him up, and now that they were riding about Hyde Park near the river, he was so lively that he might have been mistaken for a younger horse by those who didn't know better. Dylan himself was having such a grand time of it that he nearly didn't see Amelia Benedict in time.

There she was, walking along by herself as if she hadn't a care in the world. She was rich, Dylan reminded himself. She probably *hadn't* a care in the world. At least, she wasn't bogged down with the same kind of worries that ate at him day in and out.

Before he could be seen, he steered Fergus back to a more secluded lane and tethered him to some trees. Despite his horse's earlier burst of energy, Fergus now seemed content to rest in the shade.

"There's a good fellow." Dylan gave his horse one last stroke and started off.

Amelia had been meandering along, not in a hurry to be anywhere, from the looks of it. Dylan knew he could catch her if he kept up a brisk pace. With her plain bonnet his lady was easy to find in the crowd. Amelia had no need for the frippery or feathers that so many women seemed to prefer. She was a woman of elegance and simplicity, and Dylan admired her taste.

"I say, Miss Benedict!" He called out to get her attention, trying to still his beating heart and catch his breath enough to sound as if he were approaching casually.

She turned, squinting back at him. Her eyes widened upon recognition. "Good day, Mr. Marlow."

He took quick steps to close the distance between them and walk at her side. "It is a good day now that I've met up with you." Dylan spoke carefully, still trying to regulate his breathing.

She stopped and stared, her eyes narrowed with suspicion. "What do you mean by that?"

Breathing easily now, he took time to answer in a way that he thought would win her over—with honesty. "I'm sorry. It was a rather poor attempt at flirtation. I only meant that the day is always better when I have a lovely lady by my side."

Amelia seemed to consider it as she walked on. He kept pace. A second later she stole a glance at him, her lips turning up in a fetching smile. "Do you have many good days, Mr. Marlow?"

Why, was she flirting with *him* now? With her question Amelia seemed to inquire if he spent time with other lovely ladies in the same fashion. How was he to answer? "As many as I can."

She nodded, still smiling, and strolled across the bridge, stopping to admire the river below. He stopped next to her, allowing his hand to stray close to the elbow she rested on the rail. Some gentlemen rode by on the opposite shore, drawing her attention. Amelia looked back at him. "And why aren't you riding? It seems a fine day for it."

What could he say? He couldn't let on that he had abandoned his horse for her. "I'd love to, but my back . . ." He arched as if to lend credence to the sudden lie. "I have an old injury that acts up. I'm prone to backaches now. It doesn't allow me to spend much time on horses."

"Oh." She seemed surprised. "I'm sorry."

Dylan was grateful for the opportunity to toss in the lie, actually. It would serve to further separate him from the dashing horseman who'd robbed her. "As am I."

As if embarrassed about forcing him to admit his weakness, Amelia turned her attention back to the river. Dylan did likewise, trying to come up with a new topic of conversation.

"What—what's that?"

Dylan looked up, following her gaze to a patch of fabric drifting swiftly down the river. As the current brought it closer, the patch grew larger until it looked to be an entire woman's skirt and then . . .

"It looks like—" He couldn't say it, once he figured it out. It was a woman. Dead.

The color began to drain from her face as realization took hold. He held his hands out to steady her. The group of men on horseback had apparently seen the corpse upstream and had drawn the same conclusions. They came racing back toward the bridge and around the other side, shouting about trying to get her out. One of them raced to fetch the constable.

Amelia looked on, apparently shaken but eager to help. "The poor thing! What can we do? She'll need towels. Brandy, perhaps? That should restore some warmth to—"

"Miss Benedict," Dylan pleaded, gripping her shoulders tightly as she tried to dash off to where the men were trying to haul the body out. "Amelia." He shook her lightly. She looked stricken, her face a mask of pain.

"No. Please, we can help."

"There's no help for her now. You know that, don't you?"

"I do. I know she's—she's dead." Her lashes fluttered, as if to contain her tears. "A suicide, do you think?" She put on a brave face, trying to mask her horror with a show of morbid curiosity. He admired her attempt.

He'd been finding much to admire about Amelia Benedict, and it made him shift uncomfortably even as he drew her into his arms. "It's not for us to worry. She's gone, whether on purpose or by accident. Let us look away and say a quiet prayer for her."

Gently, lightly, Dylan embraced her. Amelia buried her face in his shoulder, surprising him. He'd expected her to pull away. He breathed in her lavender scent, allowed his fingers to stroke the stray curls at the base of her bonnet, and wondered what she would look like with her hair unbound and free. What it would be like to come home at the end of a long day at the docks to find her waiting in his bed. He felt himself harden at the mere thought, and he pushed away from her before his desire overcame him and frightened her.

She blushed a little, as if embarrassed to have taken advantage of his attention. "I simply need to sit down a moment."

He escorted her to the bench at the base of the bridge and held her hand until she was seated.

"Shall I sit with you?"

"That's not necessary." She looked at him dismissively. "I'm really quite well now."

"If you're all right, perhaps I should see if they need any assistance."

Amelia's gaze was trained on his face. "No. Those men will manage without you. There were enough of them. And . . . And . . . your back."

"My back?" He'd almost forgotten his earlier excuse.

"Your infirmity. You could be hurt."

"Yes. Quite right." He sunk his hands deep in his pockets, ashamed though there was no true weakness to be ashamed of. The way she'd said it—*your infirmity*. There was some clear disappointment in her tone, a hint that it made him less of a man in her eyes. Now he cursed himself for having made it up at all. He meant to win her over, not put her off. Was he his own worst enemy? "Shall I escort you home, then?"

"No." A moment ago she had allowed herself to relax in his arms. Now she would hardly look at him. "My driver will be meeting me shortly. I've no need for assistance. Thank you, Mr. Marlow. You may go."

You may go? Clearly he'd been dismissed. Normally he wouldn't stand for it. He would argue. He would rail. He wouldn't let an arrogant heiress think she could get the better of *him*. Alas, he had little choice if he meant to stay in her good graces. Her wishes would be his command—until he could gain the advantage after their marriage. Then she would see who was master in their house. If he chose, at the right time, he could have her on her knees, begging for the privilege of serving him. Ah, yes. He smiled wickedly.

"Some other time, Miss Benedict." He leaned a little and tipped his hat in parting. "Some other time."

Dylan Marlow left her feeling most unsettled.

It was the suicide, Amelia had told herself until she almost believed it. Death didn't frighten her, but to be confronted with it in the middle of a weekday morning . . . well, she hadn't expected to find a body floating in the river, of course. Such a sight would unnerve the calmest of souls, even her uncle Patrick.

Amelia wouldn't tell her uncle. Oh, no. He would be worried for her. For the same reason she hadn't informed him of the robbery. But she would see him today. She was on her way to Holcomb House now. How would she keep it from him? Surely he would notice that she was upset and that she wasn't wearing her ring.

The first order of business was to calm her nerves. She could hide her hands and distract him from the absence of her ring, perhaps, but a frazzled state of mind would alert him right away that something had happened. If he started asking about her walk in the park, he would get her talking, and if she started talking about her distress, one thing would lead to another and she wouldn't stop until she'd told him the whole story of both her grim discovery of today and the robbery of weeks ago.

Again she thought of Dylan Marlow's blue eyes. The sight of them, wide with concern for her, popped into her mind unbidden. A tremble went through her. Her stomach tightened. It was only nerves. She'd seen a dead woman—thankfully, not up close. Amelia could tell that it was a corpse floating there—and a feminine one by the fact that it wore skirts—but she hadn't really gotten a look, thank goodness. When she thought of the poor woman, her heart flooded with pity; however, her skin didn't prickle. Her nerves didn't dance. It was only when she thought of being in Dylan Marlow's arms that her heartbeat raced frantically.

It couldn't be Dylan Marlow who gave her a case of the quivers, certainly. She didn't like the man. He turned up in odd places, at unfortunate times. He was a bother, if anything. Not only did he know that she was sensitive to flowers, he was there when she happened upon a body in the river. She'd allowed herself to be comforted by his embrace, for goodness sake. How embarrassing! She hardly knew the man. What would he think of her? What would he say about her? What if he told the story about town?

Amelia Benedict nearly fainted in my arms. . . .

She could imagine the way word would get round. Once again she found her reputation at the mercy of Dylan Marlow, and she didn't like it at all. This time, though, there was no point in going to him and asking him to keep quiet. It would only make it worse. She didn't even want to see him again. But his blue eyes were proving ever so difficult to forget.

Amelia felt a little feverish as her pulse began to pound again. The apothecary? She could stop and ask for a salve or something on her way to Holcomb House. No. Shopping. The purchase of a new bonnet would soothe her for a time, and then on to Holcomb House to see Patrick and the lads.

Chapter
6

"Amelia, muffin, where is your ring?" Uncle Patrick took hold of her hand and studied it as she reached for the sugar scoop. "I've never known you to be without it. Even when you're baking."

She was wondering when he would notice. By now she'd thought she was almost safe from discovery. But suddenly, in the tight quarters of the pantry, Uncle Patrick had become observant.

"Oh, I've lost it." She tried to answer quickly and get on with her business, but she knew he would not let the subject drop. She could only hope to distract him. The sugar barrel was almost empty; perhaps replenishing it would divert his attention. "Where is the sugar, Uncle?"

She spotted it in the customary location, the top

shelf of the cupboard. "Ah, there it is." She stood on tiptoe and pulled at the corner of the heavy sack. Refined sugar was dear, and her uncle would never let her risk dropping it, even to satisfy his curiosity about her missing ring.

"Let me get it." With one nudge Patrick pushed her aside and reached for the heavy sack, which was easily within his grasp. Patrick was about the tallest man she had ever seen, and one of the most intimidating to look on. The collar he wore as a priest did little to soften his imposing appearance, but when Amelia looked in the dancing blue eyes that hinted at his mischievous personality, she forgot about his size and wondered why the boys in his care at Holcomb House got so silent and obedient in his presence.

She loved her uncle dearly—his vivacity, his strength, his kind heart. There seemed to be no other men quite like him. Because she had such respect for her uncle—the man who had left a prestigious position at Oxford to serve as her guardian when she lost her parents—she couldn't lie to him should he press for more details.

And he did.

"There." He grunted as he dropped the sack to the floor and tore it open. "Your sugar. Though I think you've used enough of the blasted stuff already. Do you want my lads to be bouncing around all night? And now, what about the ring?"

"The boys will be fine. I'm making only enough for them to have one maid of honor apiece. And besides, I won't be here at bedtime tonight, so what care I if they are a rowdy crew?" She laughed, once again hoping to draw his attention away from her ringless hand. Her uncle cleared his throat, his blue eyes darkening in concern. The time had come to confess. Patrick had a keen sense of humor, but he knew when to get down to business.

"The ring. Yes, I know." She held up her fingers and blew on them to clear them of flour dust. Already, the mark on her hand that indicated where the ring had been was beginning to fade.

"What happened?"

"I was robbed."

Patrick opened his mouth, immediately concerned.

"I was not hurt. No one was hurt—well, Foster did have quite the headache, but he's fine now. And I handled myself quite—"

"Inappropriately?" Patrick raised a silver eyebrow. "You were traipsing out alone again, were you not? Haven't I told you about the necessity of keeping a manservant?"

"Foster's a man."

"Lot of good he is when he is busy trying to keep an eye on the road. I thought I made it clear that you weren't to be out at night without a protector. Where did it happen? And when?"

"On the road from here to Briarwood, outside the city limits—two weeks ago Tuesday."

"Tuesday." Patrick sighed and buried his face behind an enormous hand. "You were leaving here. I kept you late, with the boys. It's all my fault. I should have seen that you were safely escorted before letting you go. I didn't even ask you about finding your way home."

"You were busy with the boys, trying to get them settled. I'm a grown woman, Uncle. I don't need you to ask after me or find me an escort. I'm quite capable of—"

"Getting yourself robbed on the open road, apparently." Patrick shook his head. "Was the brigand caught? Did you alert the constable?"

No, she hadn't bothered to alert the constable, and she hadn't exactly been on the open road either . . . but why worry her uncle further by telling him she had instructed Foster to cut to the narrow back road through the woods? "No need to alert the constable. He hardly got away with a thing—save the ring." She looked at her hand again. She truly missed her ring.

"Can you identify the man?" Her uncle leaned forward, his blue eyes boring into her. "If you can, I'll send for the constable now and we'll give the word to have him apprehended."

"No. I don't recall much about his appearance, but I can't forget those evil little silver eyes of his." She shivered with the memory, but the feeling that went through her was more one of curiosity than disgust. She had been thinking about him constantly. Much as she tried, she couldn't forget the way he had kissed her.

Patrick must have noticed her blush. "Tell me,

Mellie-muffin, this wasn't some romantic intrigue, was it? Your highwayman wasn't merely some young nobleman in disguise, taking your ring as a little love treasure to present back to you later?"

"Uncle Patrick, my word! You're such a romantic! Do you think I would go along with such a scheme? This man was—" She stopped and thought of him, remembering his silhouette framed by the light of the elusive moon. Her heartbeat picked up speed. "He was dangerous, Uncle Patrick. A consummate villain."

"A villain, you say? Even more reason to alert the constable."

"No." She stepped forward and put her hand on his arm to add impact to her words. "Please. I'll be more careful. I'll take a manservant on my outings if I am to be out past dark. I'll even have Foster stick to all the main roads. But let's not tell anyone, hm?"

"If you prefer to let it pass, I won't try to stop you—but only since you were unharmed. I know the ring was precious to you, but your safety is far more important. And even without your mother's ring in your possession, at least you still have your memories."

"I know, Uncle. The memories are what count. I'll always have those, yes. And I shall be careful. I promise."

"Hm." Patrick studied her for all of a second before his nose wrinkled up in disgust. "What's that smell?"

She sniffed. The air was full of a bitter, heavy

stench. Smoke. "My maids of honor! Oh, my first batch was due out and I forgot all about it!"

"You go on and get them, then. I'll bring you your sugar."

Without even thanking him she rushed off to tend to her baking.

When she got to the kitchen she was encouraged to see that smoke was not yet streaming in abundance from the oven. She grabbed a towel and dashed over, opening the door in such a rush that she nearly burned the edge of her hand. But as she looked in, she knew her efforts were wasted. Her tarts were well and truly ruined. Black as coal. She would never complete a second batch before she had to leave. Just as she removed her charred tarts from the oven, her uncle entered the kitchen with the bag of sugar, a smile playing about his lips.

"Oh, Uncle. It's no use. The sugar was for the lemon curd to fill the tarts and—" She sighed. "They're not worth filling. The boys will have to do without my maids of honor today. And I had so wanted to make them a treat."

"Your presence is always more of a treat than your baking, Mel." Uncle Patrick tried to hide his smile, but Amelia caught the twinkle in his bright blue eyes.

It was late, anyway. She had to get ready to attend Kitty Sloane's tea. "Dear, I must be going. I'll wash up and say good-bye to the boys. They should be finishing with their lessons soon."

"Not soon enough, I'm afraid. Sister Hortense

will have them occupied for the next hour at least. They ended their lessons early yesterday when rain started leaking into the classroom. They've moved to the east parlor today and will be working to make up their missed assignments. But I'll tell them you've sent on your kind thoughts."

"Very well." Amelia dried her hands on a towel and removed her apron, dusting some stray flour off her skirt. "I'll just go."

Her uncle said not a word but raised his brow. Amelia sighed. "Of course I will be escorted, Uncle; Eliza Fairmont is accompanying me. She always travels with her aunt Bitsy—who, as you know, is anything but. Traveling with Bitsy is as good as traveling with any man. I'll be alone for only the short time it takes me to get to her house. And, besides, it's daylight."

"The Fairmonts live clear across town. And it looks like rain. Why don't you stay here?"

"Uncle Patrick, I've made a commitment. You're the one who has always told me the importance of keeping my commitments. And what's a little rain? I won't melt."

"Indeed. You're right. Have a good time. And take care!"

"I will, Uncle," she promised. "I will."

The rain didn't start until he had positioned himself in the alley across from the Boar's Blood Tavern.

He didn't much like getting soaked, but his hat

and cloak kept him somewhat protected. Beneath the cloak, he wore a shirt of black silk and black tight-fitting trousers to allow easy movement. Dark colors would help him to avoid being spotted and the rain, falling harder by the minute, would provide an additional shield from identifying eyes. Thomas would think he'd gone insane, attempting a robbery in midday barely on the outskirts of London. And truly, Dylan knew it was a tad ill-conceived to think he could pull it off, but he was growing desperate.

He had to have some money if he meant to call on Amelia Benedict properly. He would need to rent a carriage, since he couldn't just ride up on a horse after telling her he had back problems. Besides, arriving in a carriage would lend him an air of respectability. And of course he should have some new clothes to make him look the proper gentleman. It was too late to call in a good tailor for today's visit— he would have to borrow what he could from his uncle's closet and try to make it work. But he was determined to see Miss Benedict at home today.

He had to keep up a relentless presence in her life. He could wear her down. There had been colder women in his past, and none of them had been able to resist him for long. Amelia would prove no different in the end.

But even as he thought it, a pang in his gut told him otherwise. She *was* different, and that was precisely why he hadn't been able to stop thinking about her for days on end. It was damn odd, this single-mindedness. All of a sudden it was as if he slept, ate, and breathed Amelia Benedict. He shook his head, sending drops of rain flying from his hat, and tried to keep his mind on his plan. He needed her money to get the fleet back in business, he reminded himself. That was all.

Dylan breathed deeply, the stench of London's muddy streets bringing him back to reality, restoring his mind to its purpose. Any minute now, a target would approach. The Boar's Blood was growing infamous for its high-society clientele; Dylan had heard it from Thomas Selkirk. Betting on racehorses had become an increasingly popular activity among aristocratic ladies. They had to sneak off to place their wagers, of course, as it was completely unacceptable for women to gamble. Many risked the good opinion of even their husbands to place wagers in secret. According to Thomas, Lady Linden was caught at it just last week.

Typically, the ladies would set off for a ball or tea, then divert their drivers to the Boar's Blood and send a manservant in to place a wager or two before going off to the event they'd planned to attend. Midafternoon had become the Boar's Blood's most crowded time of day, when the ladies could take advantage of their husbands' visits to White's and place wagers undetected. Selkirk had heard of the practice from a former mistress. Of course, when Thomas had passed on the anecdote of Lady Linden's discovery to Dylan last night, he had no idea that his friend would use the knowledge to his advantage—but how could Dylan resist?

Women sitting in unattended carriages whilst they waited for the servants to place wagers and return? Ladies always wore their good jewels to tea, to show off. It would be an easy take. A carriage would come, the driver would go in, and Dylan would make his move. He would leave Fergus tied to a post across the road, cross over and let himself into a carriage, hold a blade to a lady's fair cheek, and strip her of all she held dear before her driver could even return to his post.

He would have to be quick, though, and complete his business. Fergus was fast but not agile enough to avoid a direct and immediate pursuit on London's crowded streets. It wasn't worth the extra risk. The roiling down low in his gut questioned if any of it was worth the risk.

Then he remembered Amelia Benedict and the enchanting effects of her whisky-brown eyes. Her figure. Her soft lips. And of course, he reminded himself, her enormous fortune. That's what he was really after.

Carriages came and went and Dylan continued to watch them, his eyes focused in rapt attention as he waited for the perfect one.

At his side, Fergus was a patient animal, barely moving much less whickering during the hour they'd stood together waiting. Dylan was wet, and it grew colder. Just as he nestled closer to the horse to soak in the beast's body warmth, he saw a new carriage arrive. The Fairmont carriage. Bitsy Fairmont was a foolish old woman who had a legendary collection of jewels and lacked enough sense to leave them all at home. Perfect, indeed. Dylan watched as the driver left his box to go inside. His hand clenched and unclenched the hilt of his dagger, restoring feeling to his wet, frozen hands.

It was time.

Chapter
7

The Fairmont carriage had creaked along slowly through the muck. Occasionally, it had paused and Amelia cringed in fear that they'd become stuck. She should have insisted on her own carriage. Foster never had problems driving in the rain. But Eliza Fairmont's aunt, Bitsy, was to have accompanied them. Bitsy, a creature of habit, preferred to have her own staff around her. Of course, Bitsy had taken ill at the last minute, leaving Amelia and Eliza alone and stuck with no choice but to take the Fairmont's carriage after all. To keep herself distracted from the impossible slowness of Eliza's driver, Amelia had kept up an endless stream of conversation.

And though she hadn't meant to say a word of it to anyone, Amelia realized she had recounted the whole story of the robbery to her friend, including the bit about the kiss. Eliza sat before her now, eyes wide with shock.

"Well, what do you think?" Amelia had already made the mistake of telling the tale. She may as well hear her friend's reaction to it.

"I think your uncle is right. You shouldn't be traipsing about so late, unescorted. Anything could happen."

"Anything could, yes. And I don't know that having an escort would have helped, truly." She blushed at Eliza's admonition. She'd hoped her friend would agree with her that she wasn't in the wrong to be out alone.

"Of course it would have. You may have still been robbed—a shame, that. I'm so sorry for you, dear." Eliza's eyes held a look of genuine concern. "But . . . well, you can wager he wouldn't have been so bold as to kiss you if you'd had someone else along." Her lips pursed in shrewish accusation.

"Perhaps." Amelia agreed, and yet deep inside she acknowledged that she was glad she *had* been alone. She couldn't tell Eliza, of course, that the kissing was the most exciting part of the experience, the one thing she would repeat if only she could have the chance. It was madness, she knew. But after days of thinking about her midnight bandit and his sultry kisses, she had to own—to herself anyway—that she had enjoyed his tender assault and that she longed for more.

Just thinking of him made her heart race.

She hated the man, of course. The highwayman was an accursed villain, and she wanted with all of her heart to see him again in order to have her chance at revenge. She wanted her ring back so desperately. But she couldn't forget his body. The way he held her. His smell, a mingling of smoke and sea air. His lips, commanding hers. His eyes . . .

"It is romantic, I must admit." Eliza sighed breathily. "A rogue having his way with you under the moonlight—"

"Nothing romantic about it." Amelia dusted off her hands, as if to free herself of the memory of him. It was romantic, but she needed to keep up an apathetic approach. It wouldn't do to have Eliza thinking she'd liked this ruffian's treatment of her. Lord, she'd already revealed enough! "And he didn't 'have his way' with me. He robbed me, yes, and took liberties he shouldn't have, but you are right. My uncle was right. Let that be a lesson to us not to travel a—"

The carriage jerked to a halt and Amelia jumped.

"We're stuck! I knew it! We should have taken my—"

"No, we aren't stuck," Eliza replied, coming out of her dreamy torpor. "We must be at the Boar's Blood. Dobbs, the driver, has business here."

"Business? At a tavern? What could he be—"

"Shh. Very secretive. Aunt Bitsy tells me we must allow it. My aunt says Dobbs is having an affair with the tavernkeep's daughter, and the news would simply kill his wife, Winifred, if she were to find out. Winifred also happens to be Aunt Bitsy's favorite maid, you see. We must keep her happy to keep her in our service. Auntie's plan is to let Dobbs stop now and again at the Boar's Blood to see his lover when Winnie is least likely to find out about it."

"Why doesn't she just put a stop to it and tell Dobbs he must end it immediately?" Amelia knew Eliza's aunt was daft, but she never ceased to be amazed by the stories Eliza told of Bitsy Fairmont, which proved the woman's complete lack of sense beyond a doubt.

"She can't. She likes Dobbs, and she tells me she is afraid that if she forces the issue, he will leave. Then where would she be?"

"Able to hire less-bothersome servants, I imagine." Amelia tried not to roll her eyes. "How long will he be?"

"Just a few minutes."

Amelia laughed. "A few minutes? Indeed? It must not be a very satisfying love affair."

"Hush now, he'll hear you. . . ." Eliza looked out the window. "Oh, I can't see. The window's all steamed up. And listen to that rain!"

"Yes, it sounds dreadful. As much as I admire Kitty Sloane, I doubt even one of her most successful teas is worth coming out in this squall."

"We won't be sorry once we arrive, I'm sure. Kitty is a perfect hostess, and she'll have so many different types of sandwiches that we'll—"

The door swung open, interrupting Eliza

midsentence. A man had opened it and, as casually as if he belonged there, stepped into the carriage and seated himself beside Amelia, next to the door. From head to toe he wore black. The ladies stared, speechless. At first Amelia had consoled herself with the thought that the poor man had climbed into the wrong coach. What with the heavy rain it was an easy mistake.

And then his dagger snaked out from beneath his cloak and seemed to crawl beneath Eliza's nose with a life of its own. He held it there, poised as if to slice Eliza's nose clean off should she dare to so much as wink. Amelia's mouth went dry. Eliza, she could see, had taken a deep breath as if to scream, but now she stared at the blade held steadily against her face. Amelia barely paid heed to the big black phantom beside her; she just silently willed her friend to breathe. Eliza exhaled and began to sob.

Amelia had taken to thinking of her own robbery as some sort of foolish game. But now, with the sudden appearance of this new rogue, his dagger at the ready, she was reminded that robbery was deadly serious business. Her blood pounding in her veins, Amelia braved a look at the stranger.

"Now, now, ladies. Don't scream. Don't make a sound. What I want from you is very simple and—"

"You!" Amelia's fear was instantly replaced with anger. He hadn't yet looked in her eyes, but she knew his unnaturally deep voice at once. "How dare you rob me twice, you rogue!"

She sat forward in her seat, pink with indignation. No longer was she afraid of the dagger. Yes, it was sharp—a moment's assessment had proved it to be a serious weapon—but now her full attention was on him. Her highwayman. It was too much to bear, too much to believe, that he would have the audacity to rob her again!

He stared back at her, his full lips falling open as if he were equally shocked to see her.

"You." He shook his head, beads of water rolling off his black hat and onto poor Eliza, who was still frozen with fear. At least he wore a hat this time to cover that infernal scarf. . . . Amelia shook her head. This was no time to be concerned with the fashion sense of thieves.

"Are you following me? How dare you!"

"Following you? Oh, that's rich!" He bantered back, but didn't miss a beat as far as keeping her at bay. He whipped the blade away from Eliza's face to press the tip ever so gently to the base of Amelia's neck.

She lifted her head to avoid the weapon's sharp point, but she dared not flinch before him. His cocky grin was sharper than the dagger.

"Oh, yes. You had so much to offer last time that I set my cap to finding you again."

His wit, too, was sharp as the blade he held. It cut into her, prodding her wrath to dangerous levels. Not again!

"Out with it. What do you want?" she snapped.

"Ha. Not much from you, if memory serves . . ." He relaxed his dagger arm and began to turn back to Eliza.

Amelia sat forward, ignoring the weapon, ready to defend herself against his insults if nothing else. She had plenty of wealth to offer; she was simply too wise to cart it around with her. But she quickly realized that to argue her worth with a robber was scarcely the best way to prove her wisdom, so she grunted and held her tongue.

He jerked the knife back to her throat. "You, stay!" The commanding tone she recalled returned to his steely voice, and a shiver ran down her spine— from fear or excitement, she couldn't tell. "Stay put, and don't move a hair. And you," he looked back to Eliza, "your money and your jewels. In the sack. Now!"

Eliza's head flitted back and forth. Her eyes blinked rapidly. Clearly, she had no idea what to do or say. But why should she, Amelia thought; Eliza had never been robbed before.

"Just do as he says, Eliza. Do as he says and he won't hurt you."

"Quickly," he added, his eyes turning back to Amelia as soon as he could see her friend begin to move. A grin flashed across his face. "We must stop meeting like this."

"Hm. And still we've not been properly introduced." She tried to sound huffy, but secretly she was pleased when he returned his attention to her.

Was she jealous of the attention he was paying Eliza? Ridiculous.

The blade's edge was dangerously close to her throat. She could feel the tip graze her delicate skin, and she felt a flutter deep in the pit of her stomach as her pulse accelerated at the contact. Though she was careful not to reveal her excitement, she found her gaze drawn to the dagger and let it trail down to his hand, which was enclosed in a black leather gauntlet. Aware of her interest, he let up a bit on the pressure of the point and trailed the blade down her dress to the valley between her breasts. She sucked in a breath, stayed perfectly still, and dared to meet his gaze again.

"Introductions may come." His lips curled up. He was decidedly amused at her discomfort. "But not today."

"You are no gentleman, Mr. Highwayman."

"I thought we'd determined that last time we met."

"No gentleman, alas . . . perhaps I could convince you to return my ring?" Even behind his mask, she could see his eyes had widened. Those cool eyes somehow looked a tad warmer than she'd remembered. With her tongue she traced the outline of her lips. Perhaps with a bit of flirting she could have her way? "Sentimental value."

"Sentiment commands quite a price on the open market these days." His lips tightened to a thin line, as if he struggled to restrain himself. There was the cruelty again. She'd almost forgotten his nasty edge.

"You've sold it! I can't believe—" Amelia leaned forward in anger.

"Perhaps." He sat back but kept the knife in place. "I told you not to move."

"Here." Eliza, finished with her task, handed the bag back to the robber. He didn't even bother to look at her, just took the bag and tucked it under his cloak. His eyes remained trained on Amelia.

"Everything. It's everything I have." Eliza's voice quavered.

"Very well." His smile returned as he addressed Amelia. "And you? What have you for me this time? You know I have my price."

"A price on your head, when I'm through with you." She stayed still but allowed herself the indulgence of returning his arrogant grin.

He leaned forward in the seat and trailed the tip of his dagger across the fabric of her bodice, so gently he didn't leave a scratch on the crepe. But she could feel the blade, and she imagined his fingers in its place. Her nipples hardened and strained against the fabric. She didn't even want to breathe for fear of breaking contact, though she prayed he couldn't tell how much she wanted him.

He traced a circle with his knife around the tip of her breast and leaned in closer still. When he was nearly upon her, he withdrew his weapon. But he didn't reach for her with his hands. Instead, only his lips met hers, and with an ardor she didn't expect from herself, she kissed him. She was ready for him, and when his tongue shot between her lips she took it between her teeth and drew it farther in. For a moment she didn't know anything but him—his mouth, his tongue . . .

The carriage rocked and began to move forward.

It took them both a second to lift their heads and to realize that the driver had returned. Eliza was faster with a response. She ignored the dagger now pointed with little seriousness at Amelia and turned to pound on the glass and scream her head off.

"Shush, Eliza, do you want to make a scene?" Amelia hissed, still caught up in the dizzying pleasure of the highwayman's kiss.

The carriage jerked to a halt.

He'd be caught, then, so easily? He'd get the gallows for certain unless . . . he could make an escape.

He sat calmly next to Amelia. He looked at her, looked at Eliza, looked at the door just as it jerked open.

Dobbs poked his head in. "What the bloody—"

The highwayman interrupted Dobbs, shoving the heel of his boot under Dobbs's throat. "A robbery, if you please."

Dobbs held his hands aloft and stepped back.

"Good man. Let us through, then, hm?" The highwayman lowered his leg and replaced the knife at the base of Amelia's throat simultaneously.

What did he mean, *us*? And why was he pointing the knife at her?

Sharply, he reached in and jerked her across the seat. She let out a little shriek in surprise.

What on earth was going on?

"I'm taking this one as my hostage. If you don't want her dead, you'd best not send the constable after me."

A thrill ran up her spine. She was to be his hostage? Entirely at his mercy? Alone with him? She was scared to death and filled with anticipation at the same time. What was wrong with her?

His hand bit into the flesh of her arm, and fear began to win out. She stared at Dobbs, her eyes wide, as the highwayman pulled her in front of him. She couldn't move an inch, not even to look back at Eliza as her friend began to sob.

"No! Please . . . leave her be."

"He won't hurt me, Eliza. I know he won't."

"Not unless I hear another scream," the highwayman sneered between clenched teeth, and wrapped his arm tight around her waist. With the other hand he sheathed his dagger. She breathed a sigh of relief. Now she had to worry about his arms, and his sheer strength, but not about sharpened steel.

"Not one sound. And you, driver, get back. I'm taking the lady to my horse, yonder," he gestured through the rain, "and we're riding away to safety. I'll return her unharmed when I deem it safe. But send anyone after me, and I swear—" He lifted his finger to her cheek and stroked it gently before he slipped his hand under her chin and made a cracking noise low in his throat, as if he meant to break her neck.

"Go, then." Dobbs, the coward, kept his hands in the air and stepped back to allow them free passage. Eliza muffled chokes and sobs against the back of her hand.

The rain slapped against Amelia's face as the highwayman pushed her toward the edge of the road and followed directly behind, his arms tight around her the entire time. She struggled to turn, in order to reassure Eliza of her well-being.

"Don't fret," she shouted. "Go ahead to tea and pretend nothing has happened!"

She squinted to see if Eliza had heard her through the howling wind. Rain seemed to come from all directions, but she thought she saw Eliza respond before strong hands jerked her away from the scene.

"Come on. They'll be after us in seconds flat."

She heard *him* well enough—his mouth was practically right up against her ear, his breath so hot she thought it would burn her.

"And they might catch you—more's the pity," she muttered.

"Through here!" he shouted, tugging her into some brambles and practically dragging her out the other side. She was soaked to the skin and so numb with cold she barely felt the scrapes that were sure to pain her later.

At the edge of the road she stumbled in the rapidly accumulating puddles. He yanked her up and kept going.

Her teeth began to chatter, and she wasn't sure if cold, fear, anger, or excitement was responsible. Suddenly, she found herself face-to-face with a solid black wall—or, rather, horse. It was his horse, she realized, as he mounted and pulled her atop it. The beast's flesh and saddle were slick, but he held her so tightly there was no possibility that she would slip.

Seconds later they whipped through the rain toward she knew not where. He rode as if others were in hot pursuit, but the rain was falling so heavily she couldn't tell one way or another.

Fancy him turning up at the Boar's Blood at the same time she had. Had he been following her? Truly, she hadn't planned on stopping at the tavern or on taking Eliza's carriage until the last minute. How could he have known?

A low-hanging branch whipped by, inches from her face. Her attention returned to the present, and she ducked her head in time. She didn't know if it was the speed of the ride or the hand of the rider, warm through her wet dress, that caused her to tremble. As the horse slowed its gait, her nerves continued to prick lively. It was definitely his hand—flat against her belly and stroking rhythmically as if he weren't even aware of the motion—that stirred her inside.

They were near the Thames. She could smell it,

even through the rain. Up ahead there was some sort of warehouse. He urged the horse toward it. She could see the masts of ships over the rooftops.

"Looks to be deserted." He was shouting—she could tell by the way his chest strained against her back—but the sound was barely a whisper on the wind. "We'll hide out here for now."

Hide out? Here? Her pulse pounded. Never in all her dreams of the highwayman's kiss had she imagined they would be alone in an empty warehouse. She swallowed in apprehension.

He knew he couldn't keep her here for long. He had to return her before her friend had time to raise much of an alarm. Besides, he didn't want to allow her to get close long enough to guess at his identity. But, as he'd helped her down from the horse, she'd been so nervous and so trusting at once that it disarmed him. For a second, as she placed her hand in his, she was so timid, so sweet, so unlike the prickly creature he recalled from the first robbery, that he wanted to prolong his time with her.

Amelia Benedict intrigued him.

It was an admission he hadn't wanted to make—he was supposed to be interested in her fortune, not the woman who came with it! It wouldn't do to complicate matters by actually beginning to care for her.

He hadn't even planned on seeing her until later today, at her estate, when he could properly come to call on her. What games fate played, to throw her in his path again. He'd wanted to rob a coach to make a quick bit of coin, not to end up spending the afternoon alone with her in his warehouse. It had shocked the hell out of him to look up and see her amber eyes staring him down.

Indeed, he was fortune's fool.

"This should be comfortable enough for—"

"For how long? What do you plan to do with me? I want to go home. I'll pay you to deliver me safely."

He smiled. No one was after him yet, but they might be combing the streets. It wouldn't hurt to lay low for an hour or so before returning her, but he would have to pretend to be unfamiliar with the warehouse. If she caught on that he owned it, he could kiss his freedom good-bye. He hoped she would settle down and wait it out with him, but the way she paced, he doubted it was in her nature to be calm under pressure.

Perhaps he could find a way to settle her nerves.

"I plan to deliver you safely. Soon. For now we'll put in here until the storm passes."

"Until the constable loses track of you, you mean." She stood at the window, her back to him, but he knew how her nose wrinkled up when she employed her subtle brand of sarcasm. He was learning much about her already—it could only help his plans to know her well.

For now he acquainted himself with her figure from the rear. She had a gorgeous body. Lovely back, nipped-in waist, curving hips, and a backside rounded just enough to tempt him. Her wet dress clung so as to reveal her every curve to his hungry eyes. And his body responded readily to the sight, as would that of any man of sound mind. God, she was a vision!

And he had her all to himself.

"The constable isn't after me." He stepped closer to her. "I doubt anyone is yet. And I'm in no hurry to leave. I have nowhere in particular to go, nothing on my schedule of things to do."

He was upon her.

"Such is the life of a highwayman," she retorted. "No responsibilities, no—"

Her words stopped dead as she turned to face him and found herself staring straight into his chest. Clearly, she hadn't been aware he'd come up behind her. Her eyes met his. Her pretty lips opened in shock. And he could resist the urge no longer.

He closed her mouth with a kiss.

Chapter
8

His kiss was urgent, rough, consuming—and she couldn't help but moan from pleasure. It was the kiss of a man who wanted more than just a kiss. And heaven help her, so did she. The kiss deepened, and she felt herself rapidly losing track of time as the warehouse faded around her and she was left with the sensation of floating in her highwayman's arms, surrounded by nothingness. Only the scrape of his day's growth of beard against her cheek brought her back to her senses.

"Ow." She backed away and rubbed at her face.

"I'm sorry." He breathed huskily in her ear, his hands still grazing her back and roaming over her backside. "I wasn't thinking."

So polite, for a highwayman.

"I—" He didn't let her finish but mistook her opened mouth for an invitation to kiss her again, this time more ardently than the first. She got caught up in him all over again, though she struggled to keep her wits about her.

He pressed her up against the windowsill, his body solid and demanding. Perhaps he was not so polite after all. Her wet dress afforded her little security. Her nipples hardened and pushed against the thin fabric. How they ached for him. For his touch. He raked his hands across them and down lower, then seemed to change his mind. His fingers returned to stroke her breasts.

It was madness, this! She was insane to think that she could have him, could allow him—but did she even have the option to say no?

She flattened her palm against his chest and pushed him back a little. "Do you—" His eyes gave her pause, for they were warmer than ever, not at all hard as they had been the first time she'd met him. "Do you mean to ravish me?"

"Ravish you?" He threw back his head and laughed. The muscles of his neck tensed. She longed to kiss him there. "No, angel. I don't. I only meant to have some fun. Do you mind?"

Truly, she didn't mind. Not at all. In fact, she liked it. But how could she say so? What kind of lady would she be?

"I suppose I don't have much choice," she answered, though honestly she knew that she did. If she struggled, protested, or tried to push him away, she got the feeling he *would* stop. On the surface, he was a devilish rogue, but she sensed there was more to him. In her own way, she trusted him. It made no sense and she couldn't explain why she trusted him, but she did. He would not hurt her.

He kissed her again, and she felt the tingling between her thighs. What was she thinking? She had to put a stop to this. Unless . . .

She could use her body to bargain with him in order to recover her ring.

Revenge was quite out of the question—she didn't wish to hurt him now. She'd lost her taste to bring about a public exposition of his sins. Besides, her reputation was at stake. The longer he kept her alone with him, the worse the damage would be.

She may as well give him what he wanted and get what she wanted in return. But was it really her ring she wanted? Or was it him?

She pulled her lips away, gasped slightly in her quest for air, and allowed his mouth to blaze a trail down her neck and along her shoulders before she pushed him back again.

"Perhaps we can make a trade?" she suggested.

"A trade?"

"Mm." She smiled, trying to appear confident. But her body betrayed her as it began to shiver violently. It was cold in the warehouse, so cold she could feel it despite the heat that pulsed through her. And she was scared, not that he would hurt her, but that he would accept her proposition. "A trade. I offer you my body in exchange for the return of my ring."

Sharply, he sucked in his breath and stepped back from her. "That's quite an offer."

His eyes shifted left to right behind his mask, as if he considered her offer. So easily she could reach up and rip the mask away, discover the man who hid behind it. She thought about it for a moment. Truly, she didn't want to. The mystery made him all the more appealing. She didn't want to face the reality of whom he might be.

She wanted him to be her highwayman, her illusion. As it stood, he was whomever she wanted him to be. And at the same time it struck her as odd that the man in the mask was the one man she trusted—the man she could never really know. She was in love with a phantom.

Was it really love, she wondered? Of course not. It was a game of pretend. Going through the motions of being in love without having to take responsibility for her actions. It was a release, and it was exactly what she needed. With him she had no inhibitions, no boundaries to rein her in. No rules.

It wasn't like her relationship with Chadworth, where she had to be a lady and do and say all the right things. It wasn't like anything in her real world, and she would enjoy it while she could.

His lids lowered seductively as he drank in the vision of her before him. She could feel the heat of his gaze traveling from her sodden slippers, over the flat of her stomach, to finally rest on the swell of her breasts.

He smiled roguishly and stepped forward. She thought he would kiss her again. Instead, he chucked her under the chin with maddening impishness and said, "I think it's time we got you home."

"Home?" Her jaw must have dropped to the floor. She offered him her virtue and he wanted to take her home! "I don't want to go home. I want to stay here, with you."

She stood straight up and looked him boldly in the eye, as if to lend credence to her declaration.

He held up his hands and stepped back, laughing slightly under his breath but with no real humor. "Oh, no. No. This is not supposed to happen like this. You aren't supposed to—" He sighed heavily. "No. You're going home. Now. Before you catch your death."

"My death? I—" Oh. Yes. She was still shivering. She'd quite forgotten. It didn't feel cold anymore in the warehouse. For the first time she glanced around. It was a large, filthy space, with a few broken windows and many cobwebs. It was empty except for one desk and a crooked chair. Probably long-deserted. The perfect place to remain undiscovered. So why was he so eager to be rid of her? "I'll be all right. I could stay with you. If you want, you could hold me for ransom."

"Ransom?" He laughed heartily, then put his

hand to his chin, as if to mull it over. "No. Think of your reputation."

"What do you care about my reputation? You're damaging it as we speak. Besides," she crossed her arms over her chest, growing comfortably haughty with her masked man, "I don't care what they say. Bunch of ninnies."

"I'm surprised. You *must* care about what people will say. You'll be shunned. We can't have that."

We? Were they a team, then? Did he have a stake in her social success all of a sudden? And if he wanted money, kidnapping would ensure a better haul than robbing coaches.

"Let them talk." She became bolder by the minute.

"I'm no kidnapper. Too risky. No, you've got to go back to Br—to your home."

Wasn't there any convincing him? Didn't he want her? She thought he did, but now she was confused. Men were so very hard to figure. She wished her mother had lived long enough to warn her, or at least to give her some instruction in handling them. Her mother had never had any problem getting just what she wanted from Papa.

He began to pace, his boot heels pounding a hollow rhythm on the stone floor. With the flair of an aristocrat, he flicked his cloak over his shoulder to reveal a lining of crimson silk. She studied his body as he strode back and forth. He was lean but solid. She remembered the feel of his powerful thighs against hers and the evidence of his raging desire. Oh, yes. He *had* wanted her. But now he seemed determined to send her home. Why?

Suddenly, she began to sob. She was so embarrassed, and she took in large huffs of air to try to control herself. She wasn't one for tears, normally. Perhaps it was the rejection, or the cold, or—her ring! Yes, that was it. She wouldn't let him know how much his rejection hurt her. In fact, she wasn't sure how much it truly had. The ring was an easy excuse, and she became suddenly determined to cling to it. "I only want my ring!"

He looked up as if snapped to attention.

"Please? It was my mother's, and it's special to me. You can have anything else. I don't care."

His eyes narrowed to nasty little slits. "No. You can't have it back. I already told you, I'm no gentleman." In two strides he was at her side again, gripping her arm, his fingers digging into her tender flesh until she cried out. "Do you understand? I could have taken you so easily. You're lucky I decided to spare you, this time. Don't play games with a man like me, princess. You have no idea what you're dealing with."

"I—I—" For the second time today she was entirely speechless. He was right. She had no idea. How easily she could forget that she was attempting to bargain with a lawless rogue. Good God, he could have killed her and tossed her into the Thames. "I'm sorry."

"Sorry? You could have been. Very sorry. Now, stop whimpering and get back outside to my horse."

His voice was harsh. Her heart thundered, no longer from excitement but from fear. She turned quickly and started for the door. "Wait."

She turned back, but he'd already caught up to stand beside her. He wrapped his cloak around her shoulders with a gallantry that surprised her, considering his recent outburst. "Here. We can't have you getting ill."

Her head swam from trying to keep up with his rapidly changing landscape of emotions. Who was he? What did he want with her? And why did she want him so badly?

Maybe she would never see him again.

No. She would see him again. She knew it in her heart. He'd tried to keep his distance as he stopped outside the address she'd directed him to. He'd helped her down and stepped away. But she wouldn't let him go so easily. Boldly, she stepped forward. And when she'd held his face between her palms and kissed him so gently good-bye, she knew it was for now and not forever. And then she proceeded through the gate and into the Sloanes' town house, and he got back up on his horse and rode away.

She didn't look back to see him off.

Now she stood poised at the entrance of Kitty Sloane's parlor, ready to go in and let them all see she was well. She was ready to face their doting and their patronizing, the pitying glances and concealed tittering. Even the servants had been concerned to see her show up so disheveled. But she'd waved them off and insisted on presenting herself instead of being introduced.

Briefly, she listened at the door.

"Do you really think that's what he'll do with her?" Margaret Sloane gasped. Clearly, they'd been discussing her plight. She knew Eliza wouldn't be the soul of discretion, and who could blame her after what had happened?

"I can't imagine. You should have seen the way he kissed her," Eliza replied. "And she didn't exactly seem to mind."

"Oh, tell us!" Kitty said. "Tell us again how he kissed her!"

Amelia's gut twisted. Eliza had told everything, every little detail. And it bothered her that her kiss, something she treasured so privately, would be fodder for tea-table conversation. She swung open the door.

Kitty dropped her spoon and it clanged loudly to the plate. She was sitting at the table with her sister, Margaret, and her guests, Eliza and Lady Sarah Billings. Like hens, they nested in their chairs, pecking at biscuits and cackling out their gossip.

"Amelia, dear, how are you?" Eliza was first to get up and run to her. Kitty followed suit. The others stayed seated. "Did he hurt you?"

"What an ordeal!" Kitty added, taking Amelia by the arm and leading her to the corner sofa.

"I am perfectly well." Amelia shook them off.

"Just very wet and a little cold." She wrapped the cloak around her. His cloak. She hadn't even thought about it, but it pleased her to have retained some little part of him.

"Now, dear, you did nothing wrong. You should not be ashamed."

"I—what? Ashamed? I—" Amelia was rarely at a loss for words, but her shock rapidly overcame her.

"It is romantic, isn't it? I told her it was." Eliza was ready to press for more details. "Now, don't be cross with me. Please. We're all friends. It won't go beyond this room."

Kitty, a dear hostess, waved Eliza aside for now. "First things first. No need for Amelia to take ill. Come. We'll get you dry clothes. You can borrow one of my gowns."

"One of your gowns?" Margaret laughed and rose. "Oh, no. She'll have to borrow one of mine. Yours will be a tent on Amelia. She's more similar to me in figure."

It was true that Amelia and Margaret were both slender while Kitty was a trifle round. But Amelia knew the argument was more about who would get her alone to hear her story first than about getting her a more proper-fitting dress.

"I hate to interrupt your tea. Kitty, you must stay here and be hostess. Simply call your maid to help me. I'll be only a moment." Amelia tried desperately to keep the peace and maintain her privacy at once.

"Yes." Kitty welcomed the idea, which would

allow her to keep Margaret at bay, even if it meant losing her chance to hear the story first. She ran to the card table and rang a small china bell. "Jane! Jane dear! Come fetch Miss Benedict some new clothes," she called.

"She can wear my pearl-gray muslin," Margaret added.

The maid came and escorted her to Margaret's bedchamber and assisted her with a new shift and gown, but unfortunately, Amelia could not take long enough. Jane was much too efficient and had Amelia outfitted in no time. But she knew it was better to face her friends with the truth, or part of it, than to let them continue to imagine what had happened.

Amelia was quickly back in the parlor and taking a seat at the round table between Eliza and Margaret. She felt all eyes upon her, and she stared back at Eliza with her best look of hurt.

Eliza, clearly, felt no remorse. "I wasn't going to tell about the robbery, but my pearls . . . Margaret asked me about them. She knew I'd planned to wear them. And you weren't here. I couldn't lie, could I? Besides, I was worried about you. And it isn't as if it will hurt your reputation any. You've already been banned from Almack's."

"Of course I wouldn't ask you to lie," Amelia answered quietly. But neither did she have to reveal the whole truth. Well, it was done. There was no point in taking Eliza to task now, even though the biting comment about Almack's could have been left out.

It was true that she was no longer welcome at the ultimate haven for high society. Lady Jersey, the leading patroness of Almack's, didn't like Amelia's direct involvement with the orphanage and had seen to it that she was quite out of vogue and off the guest lists. Still, she couldn't stop Amelia's popularity from soaring among the *ton*, even with such a heavy-handed slight.

Most everybody liked Amelia. She knew it and was comfortable with the situation. She could stand being a little controversial, but she truly didn't want to be banned entirely from society. How would she ever fund the orphans without her contacts in high places? "We can tell Kitty, Margaret, and Sarah. But please, no one else should know."

"We are the very souls of discretion. Do tell." Margaret Sloane ran around to the back of Amelia's chair and hugged her gently from behind, as if to encourage her. "Start from the first one."

"The first—oh." Eliza *had* told all. Not only about this robbery but about Amelia's first encounter with the highwayman. There was nothing to be kept back.

"Very well, then . . ."

As she began her story, she knew by looking at her companions—the rapt attention, their fluttering eyelashes and sighs—that the "romantic" tale of her highwayman would be all over Almack's by tomorrow midnight. She would just have to hope that it wouldn't ruin her reputation before her ball. She certainly wouldn't tell them everything. A scaled-down version in which the highwayman had offered her one or two chaste pecks and brought her to the Sloanes' would have to do.

Her boys were in need of a new roof, and she had no intention of disappointing them over some highwayman's flagrant want of manners.

"Here's your whisky, love." Trudy set the glass and bottle down on the table and watched expectantly as Dylan poured. "I suppose you'll drink to the *ton* again?"

"To hell with the bloody *ton!*" he growled, then downed the shot and refilled the glass. He was in the mood to tie one on.

Trudy took her cue to leave him alone. He was in a vile mood now, brought on by deep disappointment, palpable dissatisfaction, and something else. Desire. Oh, yes, he wanted her. More than he cared to want anything.

He downed the second shot of whisky, not even giving the liquid heat a chance to settle before slamming his glass to the table so hard that it smashed in his hand. Dimly, the pain registered in his mind. Trudy looked over, alarmed. He was about to call to her to bring him another glass, but he thought better of it and waved her off instead. He wiped his bloody hand on the scarf he'd worn during the robbery to conceal his hair. He did not need more whisky in his system to cloud his judgment. What he needed was to take the time to reason through his earlier behavior.

Truly, the robbery had been a success. He'd made plenty of money from the Fairmont chit, which would aid him in carrying out his plan. So why the sharpness piercing his lungs every time he inhaled? Why the dull feeling of dread all through his body? Despite Amelia's protestations that she cared not for the opinion of her high acquaintances, she'd proven herself a spoiled princess who deserved to walk among them. When she didn't get her way, she'd cried. What further proof did he need that she belonged to them, to the *ton*?

I only want my ring!

Her precious ring. He fumbled for it in his pocket and withdrew it to study it over the candle's flame. It was nice, but not so dear. Yet she was willing to trade her body for it. It truly meant something to her. He would return it, eventually. For now, let her stew. Let her know what it meant to not get her way of things so easily. He smiled to himself, a wicked smile, as he allowed himself to enjoy the tightness that lingered in his groin. It wouldn't hurt if she couldn't get him out of her mind either.

Chapter
9

Briarwood.

As the barouche pulled up outside the vast and elegant structure, he let out a long, low whistle. He knew it would be grand, but he hadn't imagined just how marvelous her home would be. The horses led him through the ornate wrought-iron gates and up the long drive, which was expertly landscaped with lush greenery and flowers alternating in a matched pattern on both sides. He began to get an idea of the kind of fortune Amelia Benedict possessed. Still, seeing the house was no less of a jolt.

No wonder she preferred to make the thirty-minute drive to and from the city instead of taking up a separate residence inside London proper. Briarwood was worth the trip.

It was practically a palace. Surely, it rivaled some of the royal family's own lodgings, the extravagance of Brighton Pavilion be damned. The regent's London address, Carlton House, had nothing on Briarwood. Of course, Dylan still had no idea what it looked like from the inside. It could be gutted, for all he knew. But with the extensive maintenance the exterior required and clearly received on a regular basis, he doubted the inside could be wanting for much.

She was rich beyond his estimation.

Constructed of whitewashed brick, Briarwood shone like some sort of fairy castle, even under the gray skies. There were no turrets or ornate carvings, but it had the bearing of a castle just the same. With classic, simple lines and a definite symmetry to its construction, it was most pleasing to the eye. How Briarwood managed to be fantastical and realistic at once astounded him. It was an ethereal haven and a solidly built domicile all at the same time.

It struck him that his impression of the estate was entirely in keeping with his sense of the owner. She was the perfect blend of fact and fancy. Dreamy-eyed, but level-headed. Elegant, but never simple. As pretty as a princess, but sharp-tongued as a shrew. A good, solid mind and a body built for pleasure.

He whistled at the horses and got them going again, around to the back where a stableboy came out to greet him.

"G'day, sir. May I take your 'orses for you?"

"Indeed." He got down and handed the reins over to the boy.

"You have business with the lady? She ain't at home."

"No?" Now, that was a surprise. He'd hoped she would be at home, but maybe it was better that she wasn't, after all. He still wasn't sure of his ability to do or say the right thing to avoid her detection. And this way he got the advantage of taking away an intimate sense of the woman without her being present to cloud his senses. "Just hold on a moment, then. Don't release the horses. I'll leave my card and be right back."

"Very well, sir."

Running into her last week had been a fluke. But it was fate throwing them together, he decided. Destiny was showing him that he'd chosen the right path.

So where was she this afternoon?

He started to walk around to the front of the house, taking pleasure in the orderly beauty of the grounds.

At the door he was met by a butler. Obviously the man had been forewarned of his presence by the errant stableboy, who likely had hurried in the back way.

"Leave your card and I'll be sure she gets it."

Was he not even going to make it into the front parlor? He introduced himself, to no avail. "Miss

Benedict is expecting me, in fact," he lied, hoping to help his case.

The butler, a shrewd-faced little man with inky hair slicked down and combed over his pate, prevented his entrance, standing right in front of the door. Dylan let the butler sum him up with his beady black eyes. "I doubt it. If Miss Benedict were expecting you, she would be at home to welcome you herself. Hand over your card and I'll see she gets it."

He didn't *want* to be belligerent with the staff, but this fastidious little man was pushing him into a violent mood. Dylan raised an eyebrow in his most intimidating stance. The butler simply grimaced and itched at the base of his nose.

While he wanted nothing more than to flatten the man, Dylan came to his senses and simply produced a card. He wasn't about to play games and bolster the butler's self-importance.

"Very well. Here." As he handed over his calling card, he could see a young woman trying to get a look at him from inside the house, over the butler's left shoulder. "My," he said, raising his voice just a touch to be heard inside the house, "if the maids around here aren't as lovely as their mistress. I do hope Miss Benedict gets my card so I can have a better look."

He winked at the maid, who blushed and looked away.

She would make sure her mistress got the card, even if the butler didn't.

Dylan Marlow left Briarwood with the certainty

that he would hear from Miss Benedict within the week.

"What's this?" Amelia sat at the small round table on her enclosed patio, where she preferred to take her breakfast. The sun, shining through the glass panels, warmed her to the soul and made her forget that it had been a cold, and mostly rainy, spring. She fingered the torn edge of the card she'd just retrieved from the top of a stack of invitations.

"A calling card," Lettie answered matter-of-factly while she poured out a second cup of tea for Amelia. "Hodge usually throws them into the fire, but this one I managed to rescue in time."

"Why?"

"He was handsome. Charming. I thought you might want to know."

"No, I mean why does Hodge throw away calling cards?"

"He figures to save you the trouble. If he didn't do it, he thinks that you would. You did, actually, throw out most of them in the past."

"Yes, but what if Chadworth came to call? Bother! He may have already—"

"I haven't seen him."

"But he may have, and—well, posh! Just remind me to tell Hodge that all cards are to be kept and delivered to me henceforth."

"Yes, Miss Benedict." From the corner of her eye, Amelia could see Lettie's smile.

It was just what she was after, Amelia suspected—the chance to take Hodge down a notch. Lettie and the butler had never gotten along. "Were there any others?"

"No. Just the one calling card. The rest are invitations."

"Very well."

Lettie lingered on, even though she had already poured out the tea and brought a platter full of scones to the table.

"He was handsome, you say?"

"Oh, ever so!" Lettie jumped at the chance to gossip about the gentleman who had obviously taken her fancy. "Dark hair, brilliant eyes."

"Sounds promising." Amelia stroked the edge of the card and squinted to make out the lettering. The card was torn right in the middle of the surname. "What was his name, do you recall?"

"Marlow," Lettie added. "His name was Mr. Marlow."

"Oh—Marlow." She let out an unladylike grunt of disapproval. "Must he bother me at home too?"

"Bother? Pardon, miss, but I can't imagine Mr. Marlow being a bother to anyone, ever—those eyes!"

"Eyes? I'm supposed to admit him to my circle due to his extraordinary eyes?"

"So you *did* notice. I knew it."

"Lettie, no. He's just another rogue out to court me for my fortune. He is not worthy of notice, fine eyes or no. Hodge was right to throw this one away."

"But he has a Mayfair address!"

"Oakley Place. His uncle's house in town. Marlow is the Earl of Stoke's nephew."

"Oh. Well, nephew to an earl. Does Stoke have sons?"

Amelia could see where her maid was going with the conversation. "No. He may stand to inherit. He may not. And I don't care. Mr. Marlow is a tiresome man."

"But you would be a countess—only think!"

"I don't care for titles, Lettie. I have no interest—"

"But to be maid to a countess!" Lettie sighed in mock disappointment. "Well, he *is* handsome," she reminded Amelia.

"And what of Chadworth? I think Lord Chadworth to be the better candidate to wed, Lettie. He, too, is handsome. And charming. And titled."

"A baron." Lettie nodded. "It will do, I suppose. But I think you should investigate this Marlow fellow just the same. Keep your options open. Unless . . ."

"Unless?"

Lettie held her hands behind her back in the manner that suggested she was about to tease her mistress. Amelia braced herself. "Unless you've already made yourself fall so deeply in love with Lord Chadworth that you'd fail to notice any other man."

Lettie giggled mercilessly. She still disagreed with Amelia's argument that she could make herself fall in love. Amelia herself had her doubts. She'd been thinking of the highwayman far more than she'd thought of Chadworth of late. But she was determined to do her best.

It was time to change the subject. "Let's see what invitations we have, hm? Another garden affair. A tea. Another tea." She flipped through the stack of letters. "Oh, this one looks intriguing. A weekend in the country—just the thing to get away from annoying suitors."

"And Chadworth," Lettie added smugly.

"No, Chadworth should be present. A country weekend at the Abercorn estate. Chad hunts with Lord Abercorn on a fairly regular basis."

She felt her pulse accelerate. Yes, it had been so long since she'd indulged in a country weekend. Late breakfasts. Games in the drawing room. A hunt. Dinners. A ball. Perfect. And it would occasion the purchase of new clothes. It had been a long time since she'd ordered herself some new gowns, and she'd been meaning to arrange for one for her own ball later in the month. Amelia made her decision.

"Call on the seamstress, Lettie. We're going to order a new wardrobe!"

"Thomas! I knew I would find you here." Dylan Marlow emerged from a cluster of trees to see his friend surrounded by a small group of gentlemen. He'd been out riding alone most of the day, and now he welcomed the sight of company.

Riding in the open country was a rare treat for

Dylan now, and one he took full advantage of this afternoon. He'd arrived at the Abercorn estate too early, only to find himself surrounded by people he didn't know.

Amelia wasn't there. Yet. Dylan wanted to think she would be coming. After he left his card for her, he'd hoped to run into her. Another chance encounter in Hyde Park would have been just the thing, but he hadn't seen her there. Perhaps she'd been avoiding the park after the bit of unpleasantness during their last meeting near the river. So he'd looked for her at Drury Lane, the opera, and on Oxford Street—all to no avail. He even hovered around Almack's to see if she would be putting in an appearance, but no. No sign of her. It had been only a week, after all. But when the invitation to a country weekend came for him at his uncle's house, he knew it was his chance to see her again.

Now if she would only show up. When she hadn't been among the first to arrive, he became restless. To ease his discomfort and to avoid the annoyance of making small talk with strangers, Dylan had decided to explore the grounds.

At last Thomas had arrived. The men in Thomas's company looked at Dylan, looked at Selkirk, and looked at each other with glances of stupefied mortification. So they thought him a little coarse? To hell with it. He would mind his manners when there were ladies to impress. Otherwise, he would be himself.

Thomas rode a little ahead of the pack to greet

him more privately. "Marlow? I never expected to find you here."

He did seem honestly confused. "You didn't? I'd assumed you arranged for the invitation."

"No, I barely know Lord Abercorn myself. It was a stroke of luck, really, that I was invited at all. My father felt obligated, but he didn't wish to come, so he arranged for me to be here in his stead. Abercorn didn't care as long as I was an extra body to fill a dinner spot and agreeable to hunting at odd hours. But you? I wasn't aware you knew Lord Abercorn."

"I don't. I can't imagine—"

Thomas interrupted. "Wait . . . I think I can solve the mystery." He smiled wide, an impish grin. "Lady Melbourne is tight with the Abercorns, and she did take quite a fancy to you."

"Enough of a fancy to arrange for me to attend a country weekend, though? It seems odd."

"Delightful, nonetheless. She is richer than—"

"I tell you, I don't care how much she's worth. She is married. Quite out of the question."

"Perhaps you'll feel differently once you come to your senses about Miss Benedict."

"Miss Benedict has aroused all my senses, I assure you, and not for a moment am I ready to give her up."

"Suit yourself. I know your rival will be in attendance. The gentlemen have spoken of shooting with Lord Chadworth later in the day. And speaking of the *gentlemen*," he tossed his head back to the pack of them, causing Dylan to follow his gaze, "it's time we got you introduced."

"I suppose you're right." Dylan sighed as he looked them over. An unsavory lot, to be certain. He could handle street urchins and beggars and rogues well enough, but gentlemen? Just the thing to make his skin crawl. "Let's get this over with, then, shall we?"

Lord Chadworth was riding out by the gate, waiting for her to arrive. Amelia could only just make out his silhouette, but who else could it be?

"Look, Lettie, it's Chad!" She reached for Lettie's hand. "He's come to greet me."

"You sure that's him, miss?" Lettie squinted. The carriage hood was down, affording them a splendid view of the countryside as they'd ridden along these last few miles in Yorkshire, but the rider was still some way off, about a quarter mile down the road and drawing closer.

"I'm sure." She waved and he returned the gesture. "What fun we shall have. How do I look?"

Lettie took one glance at her mistress and laughed out loud.

"What is it, is my bonnet crooked? Is there something in my teeth?"

"No." Lettie paused and smiled, looking Amelia over with wide eyes. "I've just never seen you primp so to impress a man. Perhaps there is something to this making yourself fall in love after all."

"Oh, Lettie," Amelia scoffed. "He's coming. Now, hush."

"Good day, ladies!" he hailed as he approached and slowed his horse to a trot alongside the carriage.

"Why, if it isn't Lord Chadworth! Have you come for the weekend as well? What a surprise!" She pasted on a smile as large and delightful as she could possibly manage. She felt funny, lying so. But she couldn't very well own up to the fact that she had come in the hope of seeing him. She wasn't lying; she was flirting. Yes. That's what it was.

"Indeed, I am here for the weekend. I was going to set out for a ride, and then I heard your carriage from afar and decided to see who approached. I thought it might be you."

He'd been thinking of her? Expecting her? Her nerves tightened. What to say now? "I decided that a weekend in the country sounded lovely; just the thing for me."

"I'm sorry?" he cupped his ear with his hand. The rattle of the carriage combined with the clop of hooves made it hard to hear anything, and she hated to shout so.

"A country weekend sounds lovely," she called back.

"You do look lovely, Miss Benedict." He tipped his hat in parting and rode on ahead.

"Oh, Lettie!" Amelia felt the blood rushing to her face. "Did he think I was hinting around for a compliment? He must have misheard me. How embarrassing."

"Don't be embarrassed." Lettie squeezed her hand lightly. "You'll get the hang of it, dear."

Amelia had come out years ago, presented at St. James's Palace and to the regent at Carlton House. Yet at both occasions she'd remained aloof and unconcerned. Now her nerves snapped so tight they practically stung her. Why couldn't she calm herself? Why did it all suddenly matter so much?

Because she was thinking of changing her life permanently, of taking on a husband. And, for the woman who had rejected no end of suitors, the thought of being rejected herself was too shameful to bear. She'd always succeeded at things she'd set her mind to. But this time, success was not so certain. Could she win Lord Chadworth's heart? She wanted to think so.

Perhaps if her heart were in it she wouldn't be so intimidated. It was her great determination coupled with her desire that usually drove her to succeed. This time she had every bit of determination working for her. But the desire? She wasn't sure.

Did she want Chadworth because she felt she could love him? She certainly loved the idea of him. Of a man to marry, a companion for life, a father for her children. Or did she want Chadworth because marrying was the thing to do, and without catching the right husband she would be seen as less than a success? Or was it really boredom that drove her, as she first supposed? Chasing Chadworth had given her something to do besides minding the orphans with her uncle.

Right now she would give almost anything to be at Holcomb House with Uncle Patrick and the boys instead of facing a weekend of flirtation and drawing-room intrigues. But she was here now. The carriage was pulling into the drive and preparing to stop at the large French doors of the Abercorn's red brick country house. And Chadworth was down off his horse, waiting to help the footmen hand the ladies down from the carriage.

Once more she glanced back at Lettie and drew in a sharp breath. "I guess this is it. Here we go."

She watched her step as she prepared to exit the carriage. The stool that was placed for her foot was uneven due to the cobblestones beneath it. The last thing she wanted to do was trip and fall right into Chad's arms. His hand reached out to steady her. Without looking at his face she grasped the hand and stepped down to solid ground.

"Thank you, Lord Chadworth." At last she smiled up at him. The bright blue gaze that met her warmed her through. He had such nice—blue? Chad had brown eyes. Chad had been at the gate, truly, but he wasn't the same man who was greeting her now. "Mr. Marlow!"

"Yes, it is I. You sound surprised to see me, my sweet. And why wouldn't I come to enjoy myself in the country along with everyone else?"

"I'm not your sweet." She withdrew her hand from his. Realizing her tone had become a bit icy, she tried to lighten her voice. What offense had he caused, after all, but not being Lord Chadworth? He wore the same sort of brown riding jacket and similar boots, and that was all she had seen before she greeted him. "But of course you are free to enjoy the weekend. I—I just thought Lord Chadworth was helping me."

"Looks like I beat him here." He took her hand again and tucked it into the crook of his arm, the blackguard. Then he tipped his hat at the approaching Lord Chadworth. Chad was out of breath and without his horse. He must have stopped at the stables first. "Good day, Lord Chadworth. I've already helped Miss Benedict, but her maid could use some assistance."

With roguish charm Marlow turned back to Lettie and smiled wide. No wonder her maid liked him. No gentlemen took the time to concern themselves with ladies' maids, but now Chadworth would be rude to ignore dear Lettie. Actually, Amelia herself had to conceal a smile at Lord Chadworth's apparent disgust for the task.

"I'd be . . . delighted to be of assistance." Chadworth bowed low, the perfect courtier.

"Thank you, Lord Chadworth," Amelia said, and followed Marlow inside. She hadn't much choice but to do so, as he gripped her arm tightly in his and proceeded forward in haste.

Once inside, she wrenched her arm free of his. "That will be all, Mr. Marlow. I can find my own way from here."

"Are you sure? It's a large house. Rather rambling. Our hostess should be down in a moment. I will wait with you if you like."

Amelia sighed. Without being outright rude there was no way of getting rid of the man now. She would just have to suffer Dylan Marlow's company until her hostess could approach and relieve her.

Chapter
10

His instinct was to be as familiar with her as he'd like to be. He'd already kissed her, for God's sake; why not take her hand? But her icy demeanor reminded him that she had kissed the highwayman—she did not share such intimacy with him, Dylan Marlow. She was protective of herself, of her image, in public. It was only with the highwayman, alone, that she would throw off society's constraints and behave more naturally. With Dylan Marlow the shield was still in place. She had no idea who he was.

Relief and anger warred in his chest. Why didn't she know him? He knew he should be glad—a hint of recognition and it was over. One word from her could land him in prison. But it hurt to have to keep his distance, especially when he'd had a taste of the passionate nature she kept hidden beneath her cool society demeanor. He must take pains to be careful. And yet the urge to drop hints at her feet, the way a lover would leave a trail of roses, welled up in him.

Roses, of course, made her sneeze. He smiled. She had revealed a secret side of herself to Dylan Marlow too. Perhaps his complete success wasn't so far off.

She stood silent at his side, fiddling with the gloves she had just removed from her hands. He studied her long, slender fingers a moment. Lovely.

"I've been keeping myself in check." He spoke at last. "We're standing not far from a vase of freshly cut flowers"—he gestured to the round table at the foot of the grand staircase in the center of the hall— "and I've resisted the urge to come to your rescue."

"And I might give you credit for it," she smiled insincerely, "except that your pointing it out shows that you expect my praise, and so I shan't give it."

"You are too hard on me, Miss Benedict." He stepped forward, closing the distance between them.

"Perhaps you are too easy on yourself." She stepped back.

He was about to pursue the matter—and the lady—further, when Lady Abercorn started down the stairs with Lady Melbourne at her side.

"Miss Amelia Benedict." Lady Abercorn greeted her, ignoring Marlow. He'd already been introduced to his hostess, and she seemed to attach no significance to his attendance. "Lovely to greet you. Did you have a delightful journey?"

"Indeed. Fair skies; not a drop of rain. And the lilacs are in bloom, lending their heavenly scent to the country air. It is nice to get away from London now and then."

"Hm, well. Briarwood is far enough removed, no? I know you have it well apportioned, though I haven't been there in some time."

Dylan sensed some negativity to the woman's tone. Amelia must have sensed it, too, for she was quick to respond. "I do hope to remedy that situation shortly."

"With your ball this month, do you mean?" Lady Melbourne wasn't one to be kept out of a conversation long. "The invitation came a few days ago."

"That is what I mean, yes. I do hope you all will come."

The invitations had been sent and Dylan still hadn't managed to get himself on her guest list. He would have to work hard to impress her over the weekend. But for now Lady Melbourne had other plans for him.

"Mr. Marlow, so good to see you." She found her way to his side and looped her arm through his. "I heard you've been out riding all morning long. And here I've been waiting for you to escort me around the park, as you'd promised."

"As I—of course, Lady Melbourne." Clearly, she was stating her price for getting him invited this weekend. Likely, she also had news to share. While he wanted desperately to be with Amelia, he realized she would need some time to settle in. "Why wait any longer? Let's go. Good day, ladies."

But Amelia and Lady Abercorn had already started for the stairs and ceased to pay any attention to him at all as he made his departure with a grinning Lady Melbourne.

It wasn't until the dinner hour that Amelia was to learn the full spectrum of guests with whom she would be sharing her weekend, and Chad's attentions.

The Lambs were in attendance, with the ever-theatrical Lady Caroline seated directly across from her at the table, between Lord Chadworth and Mr. Marlow. Amelia herself was seated next to William Lamb, so much more cordial and bearable than his outlandish wife, and then there was the quiet Captain Terwilliger on her other side. The Viscountess Melbourne, William Lamb's mother, sat across from her son to Chadworth's right side and next to their host, Lord Abercorn, at the head of the table. Lady Melbourne's husband was not in attendance.

Amelia's gaze lighted on Thomas Selkirk. She knew his father, a most disagreeable man, and noted with pleasure that the son seemed a vast improvement on the elder Selkirk generation. Lady Sarah Billings and her parents sat near him, along with Lady Sarah's younger sister, Penelope, who had just come out last season, to Sarah's great shame. Oh, to have her sister out before she could marry! But

Amelia could see Lady Sarah stealing glances at the attractive younger Selkirk and wondered if there might be a connection made for Sarah after all.

A handful of smart and fashionable people that she could name if she cared to—but didn't—sat at the other end of the table laughing with forced gaiety at Lady Abercorn's dull attempt at lively dinner conversation. Amelia breathed a sigh of relief that the seating arrangements had placed her blessedly close to Lord Chadworth. As for Mr. Marlow, she would simply have to deal with him.

Dinner was served *à la française*. From the service of the very first course, it was apparent that Captain Terwilliger had bribed the footmen to increase his portions. His bowl was always filled; his plate was continuously heaped. William Lamb, on her other side, managed to get his share as well. But Amelia, though she struggled to catch the footman's eye, had to manage with what she was served from the start: a measly quarter ladle of pea soup, and none of the whitebait or stewed trout that was to accompany it.

Perhaps it was because she was a lady that they didn't expect her to eat much. But she had an enormous appetite for one of the fairer sex. It was largely for the food that she attended dinner parties in the first place, and not for the conversation or showing off. She looked on longingly as the plates for the first course were cleared and the second course was brought to table. Boiled capon, venison, ham, and meat pies. Again she was given small portions of only a few of the selections. By the end of the second course she determined she would be hungry through the weekend.

But she certainly wouldn't be in want of wine. Her glass had already been refilled twice, and now Dylan Marlow was lifting his glass to her again. She grimaced uncomfortably but followed his example to drink. It would have been rude not to drink when she had been so singled out. Then, as if not to be outdone, Lord Chadworth lifted his glass to her as well. The glasses were small, but if this kept up she would be in danger of slurring her speech before the final course was set to table.

Her only recourse was to try to avoid meeting the eyes of either man. She talked a little with Captain Terwilliger. When Lady Caroline's flirtation with the footman became a bit too obvious, she tried to ease William Lamb's embarrassment by speaking a little with him as a distraction. But as his eyes were drawn back to his wife, Amelia followed his gaze and found that it was Marlow who had drawn William Lamb's attention.

Apparently, the footman had grown tiresome and Caroline had sought more-successful game. Marlow locked glances with Amelia for just a second, and she prepared to grab her glass once again. But then his eyes turned from her back to Caroline, and in the end it was William Lamb's wife to whom he drank.

Delightful, she said to herself. Let him find a more suiting, if not suitable, target on which to pin his admiration. She did not want his attention. It was Chadworth she adored. But Lord Chadworth was engrossed in conversation with Lady Melbourne. He courted Lady Melbourne's importance perhaps. She was a woman of power and influence, and Chad was smart to ensure that she liked him.

William Lamb engaged Amelia's attention again by discussing the spice in the lobster curry. Apparently, the gossips had it right that he was growing tired of his wife's dramas and was beginning to ignore her outbursts more frequently than he acted upon them.

Amelia felt sorry for him, really. He was handsome, affable, everything a woman could want. There weren't many men like William Lamb, so why was his wife so indifferent to him? She thought about it for a moment, but at the same time she noted that she had been given more than her share of the lobster. Though she hated to admit it, especially given her sympathy for the Lamb's situation, she was eager for his conversation to end so that at last she could eat.

After dinner the gentlemen retired to one drawing room for a smoke while the ladies went to another for conversation. Dylan had the feeling that Caroline Lamb would have preferred to follow the gentlemen and may have done so had her mother-in-law not called her back to the parlor. William Lamb's wife was every bit as spirited as the rumors allowed.

Dylan had to own that she amused him with her frenetic style and her gift for effortless conversation. But she was nothing compared to Amelia Benedict.

Lady Caroline was clever and energetic, but she was of the sort that could grate on one's nerves before long. Amelia was a true woman of substance. She held her words until she really had something to say. Her wit was endless, but she used it sparingly. She felt nothing of the need to show off. Still, Dylan had noticed how Amelia had looked at him when he'd indulged Caroline's prattle. Perhaps he could use Caroline's interest to spark some fire in Miss Benedict.

He would think about it. Lord Abercorn's man came around with a box of cigars, which he declined. But he would not refuse the snifter of brandy passed not long afterward. Thomas joined him by the fireside, ending his quiet contemplation.

"I wouldn't advise setting your sights on Caroline Lamb," he whispered. "While her husband is likely to overlook it, she won't prove a promising mistress. She rather expects gifts more than she likes to give any."

"And you would know this how, exactly?" Dylan smiled as he watched Thomas blush at his insinuation.

"Word gets round. No, I haven't been with her. A friend of mine was one of her more regular lovers, though."

"And half of England, if you listen to gossip. After seeing the lady in action, well, I might start to have more faith in rumor." He tugged at his collar and looked over at William Lamb. The man couldn't hear them, but it made him uncomfortable to discuss Lamb's wife with him standing in the same room.

Thomas took a long draw on his cigar. "Still, you seem to be more successful with the married women than the single ones. Lady Caroline. Lady Melbourne . . . One might call you a shepherd."

"A shepherd? Why?" he asked, then sipped his brandy slowly, letting the heat spread through his chest.

Thomas's lips curled up slowly. His sole dimple, on the left side, cut a sharp wedge into his cheek. Before he even spoke, Dylan sensed a bad pun coming on. "The way the Lamb women flock to your side, of course."

Dylan rolled his eyes.

"So, it wasn't one of my better lines."

Dylan laughed. "Oh, no—you've had much worse."

"You couldn't have it much better, my friend. Two lovely ladies practically throwing themselves at you. As always, you have all the luck."

"I wouldn't exactly say Lady Melbourne is throwing herself at me, Thomas."

He thought back to their walk around the park earlier. She hadn't seemed interested in him in the way that Thomas implied, and yet he couldn't figure out for the life of him why she seemed to be frequently trying to get him alone. To help him? perhaps, but her pulling him away from Miss Benedict at opportune moments was hardly a help. What else was she after? A consummate player, she held her cards close to her chest.

"Hm," Thomas answered, taking another draw on his cigar. "Perhaps. But the interest is there should you wish to court it, unlike with Miss Benedict."

"Miss Benedict is perfectly interested, I assure you. I'm not nearly ready to give up on her yet."

"And neither is Lord Chadworth, from what I've heard."

Dylan eyed his rival, across the room. Chadworth's leg was up on the sofa. With the women he was all charm; however, once away from feminine influence Chad became graceless and decidedly male. He leaned over and discussed something with Lord Abercorn while William Lamb listened half-heartedly to the conversation. Dylan's eyes darted back to Thomas. "What have you heard?"

"More speculation that Chadworth is preparing to ask for Amelia's hand. He's having a ring designed in town. Rumor has it that it's for a . . . um, rather special purpose."

"Hm, yes. To lead her around by the nose, no doubt."

Sir Thomas laughed so hard that he spat his brandy into the hearth. The outburst called Chadworth's attention to them.

"What say you fellows?" Lord Chadworth was friendly, but Dylan had the distinct impression that he was being sized up as a challenger to his territory. "Are you up for hunting tomorrow, bright and early? We'll be gone all day. There's a ridge up to the north that Abercorn promises is loaded with pheasant."

Dylan was silent for a moment. He could have easily said yes. He enjoyed a good hunt as much as any man. But he also knew that he was out of practice. He hadn't had much time for such pursuits in the past four years. And Chadworth was eager for him to accept so that he could make a fool of him with his superior skills. Besides, if he declined and all the other gentlemen went out, he could be sure of having Amelia all to himself for hours.

"I'm afraid I'm not much for hunting," he answered, making Chadworth's mouth open in alarm. He obviously hadn't expected a refusal.

"Just as well. Lord Abercorn has informed me that while the ridge in question is stocked with pheasant, it is also overrun with wild boar. Wouldn't want to put you in any danger, lads. It's terrain for the most serious hunters only."

Thomas took the bait and asked to join the party. Any man fearful of losing his reputation would have done so. Dylan didn't give a hang. Thomas would enjoy himself—boar were child's play for him. They'd hunted and killed their share in their youth together. But this time Dylan had larger game to pursue.

"Thank you for asking." Dylan smiled. "But I'm

afraid it's best if I stay here and catch up on my reading."

He couldn't have said anything to give Lord Chadworth more delight—or a falser sense of security.

Chapter
11

When will the gentlemen be joining us?" Caroline Lamb stamped her slippered foot on the wood floor. Then, obviously displeased with the lack of noise to back up her tirade, she knocked a book off the shelf. "Oh, Byron." She stooped to retrieve the volume. "*Childe Harold*. Have you read it?"

"Yes," Amelia answered quietly. "I found it somewhat lacking, but I know it's all the rage."

"Lacking? Byron lacking? You obviously haven't met him, dear. He's perfection!"

"You haven't met him either." Lady Melbourne approached, snapped the book from her daughter-in-law's hands, and returned with it to the sofa. She didn't look to be interested in reading it, simply in getting it away from Caroline.

"Haven't met him *yet*. And she's not likely to make it easy for me." Caroline pouted at Amelia and rolled her pretty blue eyes. "Where are they?"

"Who?" Amelia found it hard to keep up with Caroline's chatter.

She didn't know why she indulged the woman at all. After dinner, with the departure of the men, Caroline seemed to latch on to Amelia as a coconspirator. She'd wanted Amelia to follow her to the drawing room to spy on the men, but Amelia would have none of it. Still, she had to own that Caroline Lamb, with her bursts of energy and drama, held some fascination, even for her. She began to understand why men flocked to her—at first. But Caroline Lamb wasn't the sort of woman one could take in large doses.

Still, she was fun to watch now and again. And Amelia didn't mind the company. At first she had supposed Caroline sought her out over the others because she was the only unattached woman present. Though Caroline was married and should have been as docile as the others, waiting patiently for their husbands, she seemed to want to pretend she wasn't wed. Lady Sarah and her sister Penelope weren't married, but they had their parents in attendance. Only Amelia had neither a husband to answer to nor guardians to check her actions. But that wasn't the sole attraction for Caroline, she soon discovered.

Caroline wanted to know about the robbery. She'd cornered Amelia almost as soon as dinner was at an end to ask her what it was like to be kidnapped by a highwayman. Was he handsome? Bold? Did he do anything besides kiss her? The rumors were rampant. Apparently, one or all of the ladies from Kitty Sloane's tea had talked, and Amelia silently cursed them before answering that she would rather not talk about her upsetting ordeal. Likely, her answer only fueled Caroline's sense of intrigue; however, Caroline was too interested in discussing the men present to think about it much longer.

The other ladies whispered about it for some time after Caroline had moved on, Amelia guessed. Her escapade with the robber had apparently been a prime topic of conversation among the *ton*. Still, it hadn't seemed to cause much damage to her reputation. She had been invited for the weekend, after all. Now she wondered at it and hoped it wasn't merely that she had become a curiosity. She was relying on her popularity to bring guests to her ball later in the month. She couldn't afford to be shunned.

Perhaps she should think about her uncle's request that she travel with more-visible escort. Only recently, with the robbery, did her uncle question the need for more-serious guardianship. And if he knew about the *second*—well, he just wouldn't know. That was why she'd avoided him for the entire previous week. She missed him and the lads at Holcomb House, and when she got back to town she would visit. By then she could probably prattle on without giving herself away or letting on that something was on her mind. The highwayman. He wouldn't leave her thoughts in peace.

Peace. She laughed. It was something she wouldn't have much of while Lady Caroline was around, and perhaps that was another reason why she liked her. If anything, Caroline was a distraction. From the way Caroline ruffled her blond curls loose from their arrangement and pranced to the center of the room, one could tell she was hatching a new scheme.

"Lady Cowley! You play so wonderfully. To the instrument with you!"

The lady jumped a little in her seat. She'd been involved in whispered conversation with the other married ladies, but she hardly seemed offended by Caroline's commanding tones. She quickly set her teacup down, and away she ran to the pianoforte, smiling wide. "What shall I play?"

"*Ach, du Leiber Augustin* will be perfect," Caroline ordered. Lady Cowley hastily obeyed.

Caroline began clapping her hands and ordering everyone out of their chairs. A few ladies were agreeable; the rest remained seated. "Very well," Caroline nodded at the dissenters. "But when the waltz is all the rage later this Season, don't blame me for not teaching it to you."

"Waltz!" Penelope clapped her hands. "We're going to waltz! I learned it last week from Minnie Draper. A delightful dance."

"If there is to be dancing," Lady Sarah spoke her part, "shouldn't we wait for the gentlemen?"

"Wait? For them? When they leave us sitting here lonely and bored? Oh, no. We'll show them what a good time we can have without them." Caroline smiled, satisfied with herself, as she began pairing up ladies to instruct them in waltzing. Caroline herself became Amelia's partner.

She held Amelia around the waist as firmly as any man might. Amelia laughed, a little stunned, when her "partner" even dared to pull her closer. Amelia stumbled over herself trying to remember the steps. It was an easy dance, really, but Caroline had her feeling flustered. After a while she began to catch on. They went round in circles, faster and faster, until all of them were wild with laughter. By the time the men arrived, not one of the women noticed.

"Ahem." Lord Abercorn cleared his throat. "We heard the laughter and came running."

"Yes, we wondered what we were missing," Lord Chadworth added, smiling as he met Amelia's gaze. She blushed and looked to the floor. The dancing had stopped, but Caroline held fast to her waist.

"Oh, go back to your bothersome smoking." Caroline waved them off. "We were doing just fine without you."

"Yes. So it seems," another man mentioned.

"Seeing you ladies so delightfully paired is an image that feeds my imagination, indeed." Lord Chadworth smiled. A few of the men laughed as if he might be making a joke, but Amelia couldn't see the humor at all. "In fact, it inspires me to dance now myself. What is this, the waltz? I'd like to try it."

But he stood back watching in admiration a bit

too long. Amelia had hoped he would step forward and claim her for the dance. Instead, the bothersome Mr. Marlow reached her first. Before she could bat an eye he was bowing to Lady Caroline and requesting to cut in and take her place with Amelia.

"I'll have to tell you what to do. Unless you know the dance?" Amelia stammered as the music began.

"I'm a quick study." He took her in his arms. "But I'm willing to let you lead."

Other couples paired up and began to twirl around them. Lady Caroline's husband had claimed her, to Amelia's surprise. But Marlow put an end to her study of other couples by pulling her closer and demanding her full attention.

"It is simple, really. Very easy to get the hang of this. I could do it all night." More secure in his dancing, Marlow reclaimed the lead, pressing his hand into her back to guide her.

"I find it all a bit tiresome," Amelia replied, and looked up into his eyes. Meeting his gaze was her mistake. He did have lovely, clear blue eyes. But she didn't want to like him. She struggled to look away.

"You miss the change of steps, likely, that our country dances afford. Dancing close like this is nice, but perhaps you want a little variation. You're not the type of woman to go for the same thing day in, day out, are you?"

"N-no," she answered thoughtlessly, growing dizzy. "I'm not."

"You'll have your chance to dance some line

dances at Abercorn's ball tomorrow evening. I'd be honored to be your first partner."

She looked up again, to be polite while he was talking. But those blue eyes—oh, they were too much to overcome. The eyes of an angel. How did he manage to get them, the annoying devil that he was? The circles of the dance, going endlessly round and round, coupled with the heat of his gaze were too much for her. Suddenly, she couldn't think. She just blurted out a yes.

Yes? Had she just agreed to have him for her first dance at the ball? She was reserving that for Chad.

Too late, Chadworth decided to put in his appearance. He'd waited on the sidelines for just a second too long before deciding to be gallant and ask Marlow away so he could have his turn with her. Have his turn with her? Oh, it sounded sordid. And her mind was spinning, spinning out of control.

But, to waltz with Chadworth—it was what she'd been waiting for, hoping for, wasn't it? And now she could hardly stand up, thanks to Mr. Marlow.

Chadworth stepped up to her and began to take her in his arms—in his arms, where she had been longing to be! Hadn't she? She saw two of him. And between him and him stepped her highwayman, laughing his merry head off. Oh, she was delusional, she was . . . dizzy. Perhaps she'd taken a cup of wine too many at dinner. Again she could blame Marlow for her plight.

Marlow, Marlow! Damn that man! Why did he have to spoil her weekend?

Before she could faint dead away in Chad's arms, she had to beg off. "I'm sorry, Lord Chadworth. Too much dancing. I must sit down."

"Oh, of course." Quickly, he escorted her to the sofa.

She sat back and tried to get hold of her senses. In a few seconds she was well again. Just in time to see Chadworth take Caroline Lamb in his arms for the next dance.

If she'd been at all envious of the attention he'd given Caroline Lamb at dinner, she was positively seething with jealousy that Lord Chadworth danced with Caroline. Marlow observed her as she watched them, her eyes narrowed to slits of golden fire.

He took a seat at the opposite side of the room from her, not ready to approach her yet. He needed a plan. The couples would tire of dancing soon, and what then? There had to be a way he could transfer Amelia's attentions from Chadworth to himself. For now, establishing a flirtation with another woman seemed to be the best way to catch Amelia's eye. At least, it was working for Chad.

Within minutes the dancers stopped, exhausted. They followed Caroline's lead and crashed to the cushions to catch their breath. Marlow didn't move in close to Amelia. Instead, he strolled over and took a seat at Caroline Lamb's side. Very close.

"I think we need to play some games." He leaned across the back of her chair to whisper to her. In doing so he'd captured William Lamb's attention, and Amelia's attention in turn. Perhaps she'd taken a liking to William. Enough to become protectively aware of the man's feelings.

"Games?" Caroline turned to face him, interested. She set her lips in a pretty pout and allowed them to rest dangerously close to his own. He could feel Amelia's gaze burning into him. The plan was working. "I don't much care for games. But how about charades? Charades, yes!"

Before he could even answer, Caroline bounded out of her chair and announced the game to the room. Charades. She would partner herself with Mr. Marlow. Full of vitality, she scurried from head to head, pairing people up as she chose. He'd given her an idea, and she had run with it. It took very little to inspire Caroline Lamb to action.

Unfortunately, the rest of the room was not as easy to please. Caroline had had her way once, with the dancing, and apparently once was enough for Lady Melbourne. There seemed to be some unspoken rule among society that Caroline was not to be catered to more than once an evening. Lady Melbourne simply looked at her son, and William stood up to declare his preference for cards.

A few of the gentlemen followed suit. Some of the ladies declared they were ready to go up to bed—among them, Amelia Benedict. Damn! He'd have to wait for tomorrow to charm her. And charm her he would. He was determined to make some progress this weekend.

Within a few moments all of the ladies had decided to retire for the night. Only Caroline declared her preference for staying up with the men, and again, Lady Melbourne would not indulge her. She took Caroline aside, spoke firmly under her breath, and soon both ladies were joining the others in finding their beds for the night.

Dylan Marlow was asked to join in the whist game, but he declined politely. He hadn't the funds to be gambling, and he suspected they played rather high. Chadworth opted out as well, but it seemed to be for the sole reason of cornering Dylan. To avoid him Dylan walked to the far corner of the room and took up a book, but Chad followed, determined to strike up a conversation.

"You don't play cards, Mr. Marlow?" He lit a cigar and blew a large puff of smoke into the air.

"Not tonight," Dylan answered tersely. A conversation with Chadworth could not prove productive.

"Cigar?" Chadworth offered.

"No, thank you."

"Hm." Chad walked around and leaned on the chair next to Dylan, looking over his shoulder to examine Dylan's choice of book. "You read. You don't smoke. Don't play cards. Don't hunt . . ."

"Reading improves my mind. You should try it. I don't much care for smoking, no. Now and again I'll play at cards. Not tonight. And I don't need to prove my superiority over trifling beasts by killing them. I set my cap at larger game when I have a score to settle, Lord Chadworth."

Chad seemed to think on Dylan's words for a minute while he chewed the end of his cigar.

"Well, let me tell you this, Marlow." He stepped forward, crowding Dylan as if to stake a claim. And he was. "You'd best not be hanging that cap on another man's rack."

Dylan chuckled. "Interesting analogy. Last I checked, Amelia's rack belonged to no man. Clinging a bit too tightly to the hat imagery, aren't we?"

Chad was angry now. He stepped even closer. "I mean it, Marlow. She isn't meant for you. Keep your distance."

Chadworth's voice grew louder. Loud enough for the others to hear. Glances whipped to the back of the room, and Marlow decided to play a little. He spoke in an equal volume. "I say, Lord Chadworth, calm down. I have no intention of pursuing Caroline. She's all yours. That is, unless her husband has something to say about it. Now, good night."

With that he turned on his heel and walked away. Only when he reached the stairs did he look back to see Chad's face, red and fuming.

Lord Chadworth was sure to be his enemy for life. Dylan sighed. He hadn't made his situation any easier by tormenting Chad, but he had certainly made his evening a lot more enjoyable.

Amelia was an early riser, just as he'd imagined. His instincts were dead on target once again. All alone she sat at the breakfast table. It was too early for any of the other ladies to be up. In fact, the men had gone out hunting only within the hour. Her plate was loaded with the leftovers from the hunters' breakfast feast. As he'd suspected, she hadn't managed to eat her fill last night. Though her figure didn't show it, she obviously had a healthy appetite. He hoped her appetites were enormous in other areas of life as well. The supposition made him smile to himself.

Quietly, Dylan entered the parlor. Amelia didn't even look up from her book. He crept up behind her.

Oblivious, she went on reading and nibbling at a muffin. He stood behind her for some minutes, studying the stray blond wisps that had fallen out of her chignon and trailed at the back of her neck. The skin there was delicate, so white. And her shoulders rose and fell lightly as she breathed. Occasionally, she sighed.

All at once he drew in close and wrapped his fingers around her face, covering her eyes.

"Oh!" She jumped and gave a little shriek.

"Hush, now. Guess who?" he whispered.

"I—I wouldn't know." She began to tremble wildly.

"Come on, you can guess." This time he didn't bother to whisper.

"Hm." She calmed instantly and sounded, in fact, a little disappointed. Then she guessed. "Chadworth?"

Chadworth! So that's who she was hoping for? He would chase the fop from her heart eventually, with persistence. He let go and peeped around. "No. It is I."

"Marlow!" Her voice was laced with disgust if he'd ever heard it. "It's only you."

"Only me, indeed. Yes, it is Mr. Marlow. Now, go back to your breakfast. I mean to join you, unless . . ."

"Unless what? Unless I beat you off with a stick?" Her nose wrinkled as she indulged her natural sarcastic bent, and he couldn't have imagined it would delight him so to see familiarity in the gesture. But it did. "I could, you know."

"I'm sure you could. I was going to say unless you'd secretly been expecting me and poisoned all the food." He smiled lightly, with no feeling behind it. "But we were thinking along the same lines."

"Hm." She'd gone back to her book with feigned—or perhaps real—indifference.

"The others have all gone out for a hunt."

She didn't answer until some seconds later. "But not you?"

"No. I didn't feel like hunting."

"Hm."

Again the indifference. But now it was beginning to sting. "What about you? Do you mean to stay indoors with a book for the whole weekend?"

"Perhaps." She may as well cut him for all the interest she showed.

Well, he would just have to issue a challenge. By now he knew that challenging Amelia Benedict was one way to get a rise out of her. But how? She did consider herself a charitable soul. . . .

"It's clear by now that you don't like me. Why?"

She dropped the book to the table, surprised by his direct accusation.

"What? What do you mean? I don't dislike you."

He stood, pretending to be enraged, and slammed the knuckles of both fists down on the table as he leaned over and glared at her. Then he spoke quietly. "But you don't *like* me. You hate me. Go on, admit it."

"I don't hate you, Mr. Marlow. I just . . ."

"Yes? Let it out. If you want me to leave you alone, state your case."

"My case?" She sat forward. He had her interest, anyway. "Really, Mr. Marlow, I don't hate you. I don't know that I could hate anyone. Hate is such a strong word."

"And you, Amelia Benedict, are a woman of strong emotion."

"Me? I—really, no. You have me all wrong. I—"

"Oh, no. I can see it in your eyes. You are a woman of passion. And you hate me passionately." He drew back from the table and did his best to look hurt. Sighing loudly, he went on. "I understand. And I shall keep out of your way for the duration."

"Mr. Marlow, have a seat." She rose, all affability. "I know there has been some misunderstanding between us. Somehow." She looked puzzled, as if trying to pin down an exact instance that he could be drawing from. "But I don't hate you. Truly. Accept my apologies for anything I may have done to mislead you so, and please, sit down. Sit and have some breakfast."

"With you? Are you certain?"

"Absolutely. I insist."

"Very well." He returned to the sideboard and loaded a plate. She sat down at the table and picked up her book again, nimbly fingering through the pages as if to find her lost place, eyeing him all the while. He took the seat across from her and began eating his fruit and bread.

He could tell she remained at the table now merely to prove that she wouldn't be the first to leave. It suited him. Perhaps he would try for more. "I've found a delightful grotto just around the back of the garden. Would you join me in exploring it after breakfast?" Amelia looked up as if surprised by his attempt at conversation. But after her insistence that she did not hate him, she didn't dare say no.

Chapter
12

Dylan Marlow, she observed to herself as she followed him to the outer recesses of the garden, was a peculiar man. She didn't know quite what to make of him.

His sudden outburst at breakfast surprised her greatly. His presence had been a surprise in itself. At first, when he'd covered her eyes with his hands, she'd thought—well, it was silly. She blushed slightly that she had even thought it. But she did for a moment think that her highwayman had come for her. She trembled just thinking of him, burning with the idea that he had come to find her here, at the Abercorns' of all places.

Of course it was not the highwayman. Her ridiculous suspicions just proved to her how far she'd let

her little fantasy go. It was time to rein in her imagination. The highwayman was a depraved robber. She
was a civilized lady. There would be no joining of
their worlds, no magical transformation to make him
acceptable to her. She probably wouldn't even like
him, if she could see beneath the mask. But still she
thought of him. To the point that she imagined him
popping up in the Abercorns' parlor.

She laughed out loud.

"What's so funny?" Marlow turned back to her.

"Nothing. Carry on. I'm following."

He shrugged and continued on. Mr. Marlow.
Well, perhaps he wasn't such a bad companion after
all. She'd hoped it would be Chadworth's hands
over her eyes, but Chad was out hunting. Mr. Marlow would have to do. Running off in search of his
little grotto certainly had it all over sitting around
reading Byron again while she waited for the others
to wake up. And she'd had enough of Caroline
Lamb in one night to last a month, let alone the
remainder of the weekend.

But . . . well, they were going on an awfully long
time. It seemed they were starting into the woods.

"Mr. Marlow?"

"Yes?" He looked back again.

"Isn't that the garden we left some minutes
back?"

He shielded his eyes with his hands and stood
tall to peer into the distance. "Yes, I guess it is."

"Well, where is this grotto of yours? You said it
was just beyond the garden."

"A little farther off. Through this next row of trees."

He turned and continued on. She sighed, exasperated. He could at least wait for her, help her. In her thin slippers it was getting increasingly hard to climb over brambles, branches, and the occasional unearthed tree root.

At last she caught up with him in a clearing. She supported herself by leaning on a tree trunk while she caught her breath.

"There you are, finally." He turned to look at her.

"Here I am." She continued to breathe heavily. "I might have made it sooner had I assistance."

He laughed. "I might have assisted you, but I know how you detest heroic types."

"I should have known that would come back to haunt me."

"You aren't the sort that needs rescuing." He brushed off his hands and ruffled them through his thick, dark hair.

He really was a handsome man. She hadn't bothered to notice earlier. And those eyes . . . he raked them over her, reminding her that she was very much alone with a man who could be seeking her hand. Earlier, when they'd set out, she hadn't considered the possibility that she was putting herself in a compromising position. Now, as he drew nearer, she began to wonder if she didn't actually want to be compromised, just a little. . . .

Madness, this! She wanted Chadworth, not Marlow. Chadworth was a baron. Respectable. Admired. She didn't know a thing about Marlow, hadn't even heard of him until a few weeks ago.

He continued to approach until he stood at her side. He leaned against the same tree and gestured around them.

"This is my grotto. What do you think? Worth the effort, no?"

She looked around her for the first time. Lush trees giving wide berth to a gurgling little stream. Wildflowers growing up all around. Yes, it was lovely.

She glanced back at him. The sun, shining through a break in the leaves, kissed the top of his head, making his black hair appear almost blue. His profile was sharp and majestic, almost aristocratic in the power it projected. The hint of a beard made itself apparent on his chin. She followed it along the line of his strong jaw and for a moment wanted desperately to taste him. She wouldn't. But how tender would his skin be there?

"Beautiful," she answered at last, not taking her eyes off him.

Her heart pounded as his aquamarine eyes narrowed on her. They seemed almost colorless in the shade. The effect was rather striking. There was something about his eyes that took her breath away, just as soon as she'd caught it again.

He placed his hand on her cheek and stroked

gently. He leaned in—she supposed to kiss her—when a loud whistling made their heads dart up at once. Hot searing pain shot through her foot not an instant later. She froze in place.

"What the bloody—" Marlow's glance had followed the missile on its path. "Lord!"

She had to muster the courage to look down. Yes, it was as she supposed: An arrow had been shot at her. Already the ground was soaked with her blood. The arrow was lodged just beside her foot in the base of the tree. The point had just grazed her, thank the good Lord, and was not embedded in her skin. It hurt like the devil, nonetheless. And she wondered for a moment if it had taken off one of her toes.

"Got it!" A voice rang out. "I've got you now, beastie! I know I—" The trees parted to reveal a triumphant Lord Chadworth. Abercorn and Cowley followed close behind.

"Oh, Lord! Amelia! Tell me it isn't so!"

If Marlow hadn't been holding her up, she thought he would charge forth and take Chad's head off. "You've hit her, you whoreson! You have injured Amelia with your tomfoolery."

"Tomfoolery? I'm hunting, you imbecile. I was shooting at a doe, not at Miss Benedict. What the hell did you think, bringing her out here in the first place? You knew we were hunting," Chadworth fumed.

She'd never seen him in such a rage. And it was

all because of Marlow's accusations. But he had hit her with an arrow, no matter his intentions.

And he had yet to check on her well-being.

Marlow stood at her side, supporting her, though she knew he was dying to get to Chad. Cowley and Abercorn dashed forward as soon as they grasped the situation.

"Are you hurt?" Lord Abercorn asked. "Is the arrow—" He stopped his own inquiry when he got close enough to see that the arrow had not penetrated her foot but only grazed the skin. She began to feel awfully weak. Her knees were shaking, and she couldn't stop trembling. Truly, though, she no longer felt pain in her foot. Perhaps it wasn't so bad after all.

"She's ghostly pale!" Marlow shouted, his voice full of concern for her. "Help me lower her to the ground. Let's have a look."

"*I'll* look!" Chad bounded forward and jerked up her skirts, unconcerned with how much of her he might expose to all gentlemen present. Marlow at least had the presence of mind to tug her hem down a little. She smiled at him by way of thanks. He hadn't let go of her hand the entire time. "Hm, yes, it's bad."

"How bad?" Marlow pressed him. "Will she need a surgeon? Does she have all her toes?"

Chad jerked her slipper off roughly. "Five toes."

"Hfft." She bit her lip at the pain. "Ow."

At least she still had some feeling in her foot. If

she were surrounded by women or her uncle Pat, she might have cried. But in the woods, here, with all the men? No. She would be as tough as any of them.

"Back off, now. I can get up." She shooed them away.

"Not likely." Marlow laughed a little. It was a nice laugh, husky and low. It brought her more comfort than all his coddling had, though she did appreciate his concern.

"Cowley, fetch the surgeon. Abercorn, bring round the horses. Let's see if we can get her home." Chadworth took charge admirably, though he'd been slow in starting to care for her.

"She'll need to be carried."

"We won't get a cart through those trees."

They spoke of her as if she weren't there. Her eyelids were heavy, and she allowed them to close all the way, since they didn't need her opinion anyway. Marlow still supported her head, and she could hear the leaves rustling as Chadworth paced at her feet.

"You blasted fool!" Chad yelled. "You brought her out here on purpose, didn't you?"

"What do you mean, on purpose? Yes, we came for a walk. Is that a crime?"

"It was when you knew we were hunting in the vicinity."

"You were supposed to be over the ridge, with the boar. What happened to that plan?"

"The others are still there. The birds were sparse, so we decided to flush out some larger game."

"Well, bravo." Sarcasm from Marlow. She smiled, though she doubted anyone saw. "You *are* a crack shot."

"Don't get snide with me, upstart!" Chad's wrath again. "Who the hell are you, anyway? I've seen the way you've looked at her. You've been itching to get her alone. Is that what this little jaunt was about?"

Outrage struck in Amelia's breast. She hated the loud, angry voices, and she trembled under her skin. "Don't fight. Why are you fighting? I'll be well."

She thought she'd said it aloud, but the arguing continued back and forth. She wanted to follow the conversation, but she lost track of which voice belonged to whom. And she lost track of her own feelings as well. Who did she love? Who did she hate? Someone talked of her hating . . . whom? She didn't hate anyone. But she might be in love. With whom?

Marlow was going to kiss her. Chad said Marlow had tried to get her alone on purpose. And did Marlow know that he exposed her to such danger? Chad didn't even think of her at first. . . .

Chad, Marlow. Marlow, Chad.

And as she drifted off to sleep, she heard the voice of her phantom highwayman telling her it was going to be all right.

She woke in Chadworth's arms as he hoisted her up into the saddle. The stirrup had caught at her foot, and though her wound was wrapped in cushioning fabric, she felt it and winced from the pain.

"Be still now. We'll get you back quickly."

She welcomed his attentions, let herself be soothed by his low voice. He gripped her firmly. The only thing she needed to worry about was protecting her foot on the way home. She tried to look at it but couldn't see. Marlow must have wrapped it. She didn't remember. She wondered why Marlow didn't carry her and if they had fought over the privilege of taking her home. But, then, Marlow had told her of his back problems that day in Hyde Park. He couldn't have carried her if he'd wanted to, she recalled with a pang. Perhaps it was just as well she was with Chadworth. Chad would take care of her now.

And Lord Chadworth was most attentive of her on the ride. She leaned against him and closed her eyes. He was a good man. A capable man. It was nice to have someone to dote on her for a change.

Marlow had taken care of her, too, while he could. The thought jarred her like an invasion to all her senses. Marlow. Must she think of him? She was with Chadworth now. Would Marlow spoil everything for her, even the peace she could find in Chad's arms?

In a flash they were back at the house. Chadworth had a groom hold on to her while he hopped down from the horse, so that he could attend her himself. Apparently, he thought she didn't have the strength to hold herself up. It had occurred to her to protest until she realized it was true. She should have eaten more breakfast. Then she would be strong enough and not wilting like a flower. After not eating much last night and then letting Marlow get to her over breakfast, she'd never gotten enough nourishment in her system.

Marlow, again! Always Marlow!

Chad's arms were firm and strong as he lifted her down from his mount. She held tight around his neck and leaned against him. A tremendous fuss had risen up in the house. Ladies came running from everywhere. Lady Abercorn was first on the scene.

"My dear, what's happened? I saw you riding in from the upstairs window." Lady Abercorn's tone reflected her concern as a hostess that someone should have been hurt on her grounds, but nothing more.

Chadworth mumbled something about Amelia having been shot. He didn't go into detail. It wasn't his fault, really. She would have to let him know she didn't blame him.

"Amelia!" Lady Sarah Billings had some genuine worry in her voice. "Is she—will she be all right?"

Amelia managed to lift her head from Chad's shoulder and smile. "It's just a scratch."

"The surgeon is on his way," Chadworth added. His voice was a comforting rumble in his chest as she leaned against it. "Lord Cowley went to fetch him."

By the time he made it up the stairs with her,

Chad was winded, breathing heavily. Still, he'd carried her all the way without complaint. Lady Caroline dashed forth as soon as they started down the corridor. Her chamber was next to Amelia's suite.

"My dear Amelia!" No formal "Miss Benedict" for her. And by the distress in her voice, one would think they'd been childhood friends, not recent acquaintances. "Look at you! What has happened? Fetch the surgeon! Why is he not here?"

"He's been sent for." Chadworth nudged Caroline out of the way to get Amelia into her room. He stormed by Lettie without explanation and didn't bother with questions of propriety. He would see her straight into her bed.

She collapsed against the pillows when he finally set her down and commanded Lettie to come take charge of her. Lettie was all fuss and concern, of course.

"The surgeon will be in shortly," Chad said from the doorway before leaving her. "And I'll be back to check on you. Take your ease now." He bowed sharply and left immediately after his speech.

Chapter
13

Dylan Marlow wouldn't have his first dance after all.

It was, indeed, just a scratch on her foot. A rather deep scratch, the surgeon had told him. More like a gouge, really, was what he'd said. But she would be fine in a few days, as long as she avoided infection. She simply had to stay off her foot. But Amelia Benedict, he was learning from his frequent visits to Lettie to check on her condition, did not make a very good patient.

She wouldn't admit him for the whole first day. She refused to take the laudanum that Dr. Phillips had left to ease her pain and help her sleep. And when she'd heard him at the door, she'd cried out.

"Lord Chadworth? Has Lord Chadworth come to see me?"

"It's Mr. Marlow, Miss Benedict."

"Marlow!" A pause. "I'm not well. Send him away."

He'd swallowed his wrath at Lord Chadworth and had worked on Lettie to try to find out how his rival had turned her against him. He'd been making progress until the arrow struck. And now the tide had turned most unfavorably.

Lettie was a darling assistant. He'd been wise to get the maid on his side. She let him in every time and slipped him all the information she could manage to wheedle out of her mistress. So far he'd learned that Chadworth hadn't been to see her at all and that she was convinced Marlow himself had carelessly put her in danger by bringing her into an area where she should not have been. Chadworth shared none of the blame. None at all. But Amelia *was* tired of waiting on him to visit. It was something.

Even now Chadworth was off having a grand time without her. Marlow had put in a quick appearance at the ball, to see how everyone was dressed and how the room was done up in order to give Amelia an accurate description should she want to know what she was missing. Chad had danced his first with Lady Melbourne, all deference to the esteemed matron. When Marlow left, Chad had moved on to Caroline Lamb, who was pouting about something new. She'd been quite out of sorts since

Miss Benedict came home wounded. Nothing like an invalid to claim all the attention.

But, really, Amelia wasn't getting her share. She'd become the accepted conversation starter, stealing that honor from the weather. Instead of "Do you think it looks like rain?" people would ask, "Do you think Miss Benedict will be allowed to come down today?" But while everyone had spoken of her and had put in the requisite visit—almost everyone, he corrected himself—no one had spent any length of time with her since the accident.

She had to keep off her foot for only one more day, according to Dr. Phillips. At that rate she'd be walking just in time to get in her carriage and go home.

The sprightly strains of music in the ballroom echoed even in the upstairs corridor. It was sure to make her peevish by reminding her what she was missing.

He stopped outside her room and knocked on the door, balancing his tray in one hand.

Lettie answered.

"Mr. Marlow!" she spoke in a high-pitched whisper as she stepped out into the hall. "I thought you'd be down enjoying the ball."

"I was, for a moment. It's rather dull. How's our patient?"

"As usual." Lettie grimaced. "She didn't touch her broth. Went on about needing real food, whatever that's supposed to mean."

Marlow lifted the silver cover off the steaming

plate of roast venison, duchesse potatoes, and tarts. "Do you think this will do?"

"Mr. Marlow! But the doctor said she needed to keep to a liquid diet!"

"Doctors? Rubbish! She needs some hearty nourishment. Enough with the 'liquids to restore her good humors,' as Dr. Phillips said."

"Good humors, yes. I begin to wonder if she had any to begin with." They both laughed.

"So you'll let me bring it in to her?"

Lettie nodded wildly, a willing coconspirator.

"And while I'm there, why don't you run down and take a peek at the ballroom? I'm sure no one will notice, and if they do I doubt they'll mind. And then she won't be able to blame you for my intrusion."

"A lovely idea." Lettie clapped. Dylan knew she was eager to have a look at the dancers. "Go on, then. And good luck to you."

Lettie scrambled off. He steeled himself for Amelia's wrath and went in through the parlor to pause outside her chamber door. She was at the edge of the bed, trying to stand up despite doctor's orders. He set the tray down on the corner table and watched.

Her shift was sheer, revealing her lovely body almost as effectively as her wet gown had that day in the warehouse. He had to control his groan, as well as his arousal at the sight. She managed to walk from the bed to a side table with only a slight limp. It must have hurt to flex her foot, but he doubted there was any other difficulty. The bone and muscles hadn't been touched. Having her keep to her bed was a mere precaution to keep the wound closed and free of infection.

"Try to keep me from the ball, will you!" She swore and headed for the cupboard in the opposite corner of the room. Did she mean to go down, then? By the time she reached the end of the bed, though, she stumbled slightly.

Without thinking he dashed forward and caught her in his arms. She looked up, alarmed. Then her eyes, alight with golden flames, narrowed in rage.

"May I have this dance?" He smiled, not letting up on his hold. "There isn't much room to waltz, but we can try our best."

"What are you doing here? Get out! *Lettie!*" she called. "Lettie, why did you allow him—"

"Lettie isn't here. She must have stepped out for a moment."

"Oh! How convenient." Amelia tried to pull away from him, but she wasn't strong after two days in bed with little more than broth to sustain her. As she struggled, her body pressed against his and it became more difficult to keep his arousal in check. He let her go as soon as he was certain she had her footing.

"Indeed, I thought so. You've been avoiding me."

"Not this again. I haven't been avoiding you,

Mr. Marlow. I just . . . well, let me get into bed, will you? It isn't proper, your standing there looking at me like that."

"Like what?"

"Like you're about to eat me alive."

"That's your own hunger talking. Get into bed, then. I have something for you."

"I'm sure you do, and I don't want it." She sat back down on the bed and tried not to wince as she brought her foot up to tuck it under the covers. "No offense intended, it's just that I haven't wanted any visitors since I've been hurt."

"Except Lord Chadworth."

"What?" Her eyes narrowed again.

"I heard you call for him. I suppose you'll let him play the hero while I've been relegated back to 'annoyance.' "

"Back? Oh, no. I assure you that you never really moved up from there. You are an irritating man, Mr. Marlow. There. I've said it. Be vexed if you wish." She pulled her covers up over herself and smoothed them.

"I'm not vexed." He stepped forward until he stood at the edge of the bed, then he sat down and looked into her glowing amber eyes. "In fact, I'm rather pleased you think of me as an irritant."

"You are?" Clearly uncomfortable with his proximity, she shifted back into her pillows.

"It means I'm under your skin, Miss Benedict." He let his hand stray to the lace trim of her covers and he rested it there. She stared at it, uncertain.

"And once I'm under your skin, well, you'll have a devil of a time getting rid of me."

"Mr. Marlow." Her nose wrinkled up when she said the name, as if to make apparent her level of disgust. She knocked his hand away. "I shall scream for assistance if you get any closer. . . . No, actually, I won't. And you know I won't. You already have them talking. I've heard the gossip. Caroline Lamb's voice carries marvelously through these paper walls."

"Gossip?" He batted his lashes in an attempt at innocence.

"You and I in the woods alone? You know how people talk. We shouldn't have been there in the first place."

"I didn't force you to come along."

She paused to consider her words, refusing to lift her eyes to his. "Nevertheless, I've been paying for the rumors. You knew exactly what you were doing, luring me to your grotto. Honestly. I was such a fool. And now Lord Chadworth won't come near me. See what you've done to my reputation!"

"Your reputation?" he scoffed, and stood, indignant. "What of *my* reputation? That you've made everyone think I had to stoop to subterfuge to get a woman alone? Ha! If I wanted you as badly as you seem to think, Miss Benedict, I'd have you eating from my hand."

"Excuse me?" She sat up, forgetting to hide her beautiful, barely concealed breasts under the sheets.

He stepped closer and leaned over the bed, speaking with drawn-out deliberation. "That's right. If I wanted to I'd have you begging for me, darling. Pleading. On your knees. Until you couldn't stand it any longer."

She couldn't even find words to speak. She simply gasped. He spun on his heel and returned to the parlor to fetch the tray he'd left there. He brought it into the chamber and left it on the table beside her bed, his blue eyes blazing.

"And if Lord Chadworth hasn't been in to see you, it's because he's feeling guilty since he's the sot who shot you and he's not man enough to come apologize." Again he spun on his heel and made for the door. He'd been learning a thing or two about dramatics from watching Lady Caroline in action the past few days. Sharply, he turned back to her. "Besides, he's having too much fun in the ballroom to bother coming up here. And I believe, since my services here are neither necessary nor appreciated, that I will go and join him. Good evening, Miss Benedict."

On that note he stepped through the door and swung it closed behind him, not even giving her a chance to reply. He didn't have to see her face again to know that in the other room she was stunned into silence.

He laughed a little to himself, pleased with the role he'd played. That should do it. He would leave her with that last impression and stop coming after her for a time. She would realize, perhaps, what she was losing. Or at least she would no longer think he was in pursuit of her.

He felt slightly guilty for playing with her a bit. But, he assured himself, he shouldn't feel bad in the least. He'd seen to it that she was quite all right. He'd even brought her some food. Now the only thing left to plague Amelia Benedict was her own nasty little temper.

Feeling better, he trotted off toward the stairs. Lettie passed him on her way back to her post.

"How's our patient?"

"Same as ever." He smiled.

"Did she eat anything?"

"I don't know. But there is the distinct possibility that you'll be cleaning the remains of venison and potatoes off the back of the bedroom door."

Lettie didn't stay for more polite conversation. "Oh, dear!" she cried, and ran at a mad dash to tend her mistress.

"I'm sorry, Lettie!" he called after her. She looked back for a second to wave and smile. If only her mistress were as constantly good-natured.

Marlow went right to the parlor where the men were gathering to smoke. Selkirk was there, already puffing away. He looked startled when he caught sight of Dylan.

"A brandy. That's what I need. Ah, yes." Dylan grabbed a glass from a nearby tray and sipped, savoring.

"Where have you been?" Thomas asked.

"Visiting Miss Benedict."

"She let you in? Are you truly making progress?" Thomas spoke quickly, a blush spreading over his already ruddy cheeks.

"She did, in fact. And I am. I do believe I am." He sipped at his brandy again and observed Thomas through narrowed eyes. "Out with it, Thomas. What have you done?"

"Done? What makes you think I've—"

Dylan raised his left eyebrow. "How long have we known each other? No hemming. Tell me."

"All right." Thomas sighed. "Lord Chadworth was down here, drinking. He's absolutely miserable over having hurt Miss Benedict, you know."

"Yes, I saw him dancing earlier." Dylan tried to check his sarcasm, to no avail. "And he surely looked to be all broken up."

"Seriously, Marlow, the man is upset."

"And your good nature kicked in again, hm?"

"Well, the poor man, Marlow. I couldn't just watch him suffering so. I gave him a few tips to help him go and apologize."

"You advised him to go see her?" Marlow tried to control his anger. Selkirk couldn't keep him away, after all, but did he have to be so encouraging?

"Yes. He should, don't you think? And he seems to really care for her."

"Care for her, my—" Temper, Dylan, temper. "He doesn't care for her, Thomas. I assure you. But you were only trying to help. Your true nobility will earn you recognition one of these days. Not today, mind you, but someday."

"Thank you, Marlow, for having sense in the matter and not being angry with me."

Marlow took his last sip, nodding. It had taken him more than a little effort.

Selkirk, pleased with himself and growing bold enough to go on, added, "Now I feel comfortable enough to mention that I also recommended he bring her flowers."

"You did what?" Marlow nearly spit the brandy all over his friend.

"I insisted he bring her flowers. Ladies like flowers. I thought it would soften her heart toward him. So she'd at least consider his apology."

"Flowers?" Dylan started to laugh.

"Yes, flowers. I told him the more the better. And though it's dark outside, he's gone to pick them fresh."

"Fresh. Yes!" Dylan threw back his head and laughed wildly. Flowers! Of all things for Chadworth to bring her. In trying to cheer her up he'd make her more miserable than ever with her sniffling and sneezing. It was a classic move. Top drawer. "Let me get you a drink, Selkirk, to celebrate. You're a genius!"

As soon as Marlow had left, Amelia was all curiosity to see what he'd brought her. She leaned over and lifted the silver lid.

Food. The man had brought her food! And she'd been so ornery to him.

A twinge of guilt battled with her pangs of hunger until hunger clearly won out. She would face her guilt later. She needed food *now*. She lifted the tray onto the bed and started on the haunch of venison. Oh, it was scrumptious! Food. Actual food. She took a second to inhale the fragrant aromas and went back to eating, using only her fingers. She was alone. What did it matter?

The door creaked open and she dropped her venison abruptly.

"Miss, I'm so sorry I left you alone, please, I—" Lettie. It was only Lettie. The maid paused in the door, smiling. "Oh, thank goodness, miss, to see you eating instead of . . . instead of . . ." Lettie looked behind the door and back at the bed, clearly relieved. "Never mind."

"What did you think?"

"Well, Mr. Marlow was just here, yes? I passed him in the hall and—"

"Passed him, my elbow, Lettie! You two have been conspiring against me all weekend. You like Mr. Marlow. Admit it."

Lettie bounded to Amelia's bedside and sat down, careful not to upset the tray. "I do, miss. Truly, I do. He is a fine man. And he's been here so often, showing such genuine concern for you."

"Genuine?" Amelia lifted her knife and fork and started on the venison more delicately. "Can you be sure he's genuine about me, Lettie? Perhaps he's more genuinely interested in my money?"

"Listen to you go on. I pity you sometimes, miss.

Not everyone cares so much about money, you know. One day a real prince is going to come along and your suspicions will drive him clean away. Mr. Marlow acts and dresses as if he has money. And he lives in a Mayfair town house."

"His uncle's, as I've told you."

"And how truly wanting can a man be when his uncle is the Earl of Stoke?" Lettie raised a brow.

Perhaps she was right. Perhaps Amelia was being far too hard on the man. The twinge of guilt returned, higher than her stomach this time. Closer to her heart. She'd nearly kissed him in the woods. She wondered now what might have happened if their lips had met instead of the arrow connecting with her foot.

He had been to see her. Lord Chadworth hadn't taken the time of day. And he'd brought her food. It showed a fair amount of insight to know what would please her most at the moment. In a temper she'd sent him away. She had been rude. Accusatory. Now he was enjoying himself at the ball. Dancing—with whom?

"Lettie, perhaps you are right about Mr. Marlow. I don't know." She dropped her fork and sighed. She wished she could dress and go down. But no. Her foot was too tender. If she couldn't make it to the ball, though . . . "Were you having fun downstairs?"

"Oh, yes. It's lovely. All done up like a wonderland. I stood with the other servants at the patio just off the kitchen, and I could see it all in the windows.

Such beautiful dresses. Yours would have been a hit. Only Lady Caroline's is anything to it."

"Caroline, hm?" Her stomach roiled. "Why don't you go down and watch again? I'll be perfectly all right up here. I'm only going to finish my dinner and go right back to sleep."

"Are you sure you don't mind?"

"I don't mind." Without another word Lettie started for the door. Amelia called her back. "And Lettie? Do be sure to tell me with whom Mr. Marlow and Lord Chadworth dance."

Lettie smiled. Likely, she knew the request would come. "Aye, miss. I'll keep an eye out for those two."

As soon as the door closed, Amelia started back to her food. It was wonderful. She'd been so hungry. And she was almost full now. But there was room for perhaps one more of the tarts. . . .

She bit into one and sighed aloud, nearly in ecstasy from the creamy sweetness inside.

"Have I—have I come at a bad time?" Lord Chadworth stood in the doorway.

Amelia nearly jumped out of her bed. Goodness, how embarrassing—that Chad should see her so enamored of a tart! Again she cursed Mr. Marlow. But this time she softened toward him a little. He'd meant well. It wasn't his fault that Chadworth should walk in as she was making a glutton of herself.

She put the sweet down, dusted her hands, and

moved the tray off to the side. "No. Never a bad time. Please, do come in."

He fidgeted, embarrassed. "I did knock. Several times. I—no one answered. I thought I'd come ask the maid for permission to see you."

"Oh, Lettie's stepped out. But here I am. You have my permission."

He hesitated in her chamber door. "I—I'm not sure it's proper. You know how people talk."

Her heart fell to her stomach. Lord Chadworth was concerned with propriety after all? She recalled him stomping wildly through the pansies, risking Lady Melbourne's wrath. She'd thought him beyond all of that, at least enough to have a private conversation. But now she wondered.

"We don't really care what people say, do we, Lord Chadworth?" She wanted him to say he didn't care. So badly.

"Well, one must consider one's reputation." He looked shocked. "They're already talking so about you and that highwayman. Then there's Marlow—ahem."

Of course, he wouldn't go on. That would be indelicate. Damn! She so wanted him to be willing to throw caution to the wind for her.

He remained in the doorway, refusing to enter her boudoir. Heavens, the impropriety . . . Her nose wrinkled up. She was about to sneeze. At last he revealed what was behind his back. "I've brought you flowers. But I'll just leave them here for the maid to take care of. I wouldn't want to stay too long."

"Stay!" she shouted. He was here. He'd brought flowers. Flowers made her miserable, truly, but he didn't know that. He'd thought to bring her flowers. There was still hope! "Stay, please. I'm so bored. Have a seat. Tell me about the ball."

"No. I'd—I'd best get back before the gossips start at it, hm?" He bowed slightly. "You do look lovely, though, Miss Benedict. Even while unwell. I hope to call on you in London."

"Please do." She smiled.

"Good night, then, for now." He left quickly. Did it matter so much to him that the gossips would know they had been alone together? How silly!

But the flowers. They were beautiful. Two big bouquets of wildflowers. All for her.

Chadworth brought her flowers. Marlow brought her food. And all she truly cared to think about was the man who took what he could away from her.

Had the highwayman stolen her heart so that she no longer had it to give freely elsewhere?

Chapter
14

Within a week Amelia's foot was in perfect condition.

She'd left the Abercorn estate on Tuesday with the rest of the guests, quite against doctor's orders. All of his medical knowledge considered, Dr. Phillips didn't know as much as she did about the management of her own body.

There was no chance she would overstay her welcome and prove a burden to her kind hosts. Yes, she'd been sneezing and a little shivery. But it hadn't been due to an infection, as the doctor had surmised. She knew perfectly well it was because of the flowers that Lord Chadworth had delivered to her. The flowers that, despite Lettie's protestations, she'd insisted on keeping in her room, beside her bed.

It was sweet of him to bring her flowers. She wouldn't reward his generosity by tossing the bouquet into the fire. And she still didn't know what she intended to do about her plan to fall in love with Lord Chadworth. Over the weekend she'd seen a slightly different side of the man.

He cared entirely too much about propriety, for one thing. Honor in a man was a good thing. Certainly, she wished a lover to have pride. But when his concern about what others might think came before his regard for her . . . well, that would never do. She wanted to be the most important thing in the life of the man she chose to love. Her husband, when she took one, should think of nothing before he thought of his dear Amelia. That's how it was between her parents. That's how it should be for her.

Lord Chadworth hadn't even been to see her until the very last day of the weekend. And when he had finally come to visit it occurred to her that he had never once attempted to apologize for having wounded her in the first place. Oh, she didn't blame him. It was an accident. Truly, no one was at fault. But she would feel better if he had even once tried to explain or offer his regret for having involuntarily injured her.

She had once been so sure of Lord Chadworth's suitability as a mate, but now she began to wonder if he would be a good match for her. Did she truly want to encourage his affection? She would reserve judgment until next Tuesday, the eve of her own ball. How he acted toward her at her own celebration would determine her future course of action with Lord Chadworth. Certainly, he would attend. The invitations had gone out, and of the extraordinary number that had come back in the affirmative, Chad's had been among the first. He couldn't get out of it now. She would just wait and see what to make of him.

And then there was Dylan Marlow. She hadn't invited Mr. Marlow, but to think of him still gave her a twinge of remorse. While she was injured, Mr. Marlow had shown her great regard. But what did she really know of him? There was no time to investigate his character more thoroughly before her grand event. True, the Abercorns had invited him for a weekend; however, she suspected their only interest was in pleasing the influential Lady Melbourne, who seemed pleased by Dylan Marlow in turn. No one else had asked him anywhere. No one even seemed to know who he was.

Not that she cared what anyone thought . . . but she did have to think of the Holcomb House lads. The ball was to raise money for them. If she offended guests—potential donors—enough to keep them away, the boys would never have a new roof. Her uncle, who was also in charge of her inheritance until her marriage or her twenty-fifth birthday, would not allow her to finance the enterprise herself. She would need that money, he always said, "in case . . ." and they both knew he meant in case she didn't marry well or marry at all. He allowed her to set up a small annuity for the benefit of Holcomb House, but if she wanted the boys to have more, she had to raise the money herself. He would not let her just give them her own.

And the boys needed more, of that there was no doubt. If her ball was a great success they would have their roof. She wouldn't have them learning, playing, or, for goodness sake, sleeping under leaks anymore if it was in her power to help them. For no man would she risk not helping her boys. Even if the mere sight of his extraordinary eyes had the power to make her knees go weak.

Did Dylan Marlow make her weak in the knees? It had never struck her before, though her heart did race just to recall their last encounter, when he'd leaned over her bed and whispered those cryptic words.

That's right. If I wanted to I'd have you begging for me, darling. Pleading. On your knees. Until you couldn't stand it any longer.

There was something about the man, about his eyes, his voice. Begging for him? Honestly! She would beg for no man. She found him physically attractive, perhaps. That was all. She wasn't falling in love with Dylan Marlow, for pity's sake. Or with Lord Chadworth.

Perhaps she'd been wrong to think she needed a man at all.

She closed her account books with a slam, which

elicited a shriek from Lettie. "Lettie," she sighed, "I'm done with going over the figures for the day."

"But it's Thursday," Lettie said, matter-of-factly. "You always go over the books on Thursday, to make sure everything balances out. What if Hodge is cheating you out of tea again?"

"The hang with Hodge, Lettie. If he wants to reuse all my tea in order to pocket the money with which he should be purchasing fresh, let him. For now. We'll catch him later. I'm simply too peevish to go over numbers now."

"Peevish?" Lettie looked puzzled. "In the middle of a Thursday afternoon? You haven't even been making social calls."

It was the tedium of social calls that often left Amelia feeling out of sorts. Going over accounts was something she usually enjoyed. "I know. But I can't help the way I feel. I'm going for a ride."

"A ride? But it isn't on the schedule."

"I know. I'm going to do it anyway." She rose from her chair and stretched, feeling quite pleased with herself.

"I'll—I'll tell Foster to bring around the carriage," Lettie stammered.

"The carriage won't be necessary. I mean to go out on horseback alone."

"Very well, miss." Lettie bit her tongue, Amelia could tell, so as to not say anything to curb Amelia's sudden burst of spontaneity. But her eyes blinked rapidly in shock. Amelia Benedict was going to do something on a whim!

Poor Lettie. In all their years together, she had never known her mistress to do something that hadn't been meticulously planned in advance. Amelia's parents' spontaneity was what had cost them their lives. They weren't supposed to leave for Italy until the following week, but there was an opening on a ship and they'd left early—and drowned in the storm that wrecked the boat. Amelia had been quite against doing anything on a whim ever since. But now . . . well, if she didn't take a chance at doing something unusual, she'd go stark raving mad.

If her life was dull she had only herself to blame. Only she had the power to liven it up. To hang with the notion of needing a man and planning every action, every moment.

She alone was in control of her fate, and her plans were hers to change as she saw fit.

He needed to do something drastic.

She had no interest in him as Dylan Marlow. Only as the highwayman had he been able to capture her imagination, to encourage her to want him. What could he do to transfer the excitement she felt for the robber into real admiration for the man behind the mask?

To find a clue of how to win her heart, he had to don the disguise once more. As the highwayman he might convince her to tell him things about herself that she wouldn't share with anyone else—with Dylan Marlow, most especially. What was it that she liked about Lord Chadworth? Why did she seem to dislike Dylan Marlow so? Had he really ever had a chance? Or would she marry Chadworth after all?

Before leaving the Abercorns, he'd heard how she'd insisted on keeping Lord Chadworth's bouquet at her bedside.

"Chadworth brought her flowers." Caroline had practically swooned with envy at the breakfast table. "It looked to be a whole roomful of them. Isn't it sweet? And just yesterday we'd all thought she would run off to elope with you!"

Caroline Lamb had a way with exaggeration. His excursion into the woods with Amelia had been a topic of conversation, but no one had assumed they would marry. Chadworth still retained the chief honor of being her supposed future spouse, more so after bringing her flowers.

And then Lady Melbourne's cutting response to her snippy daughter-in-law: "With Dylan Marlow? No, Caroline, you're mistaken. The rumor everyone took to heart—the one I believe you started yourself—is that Mr. Marlow is *your* latest lover. But perhaps I have that wrong. It's so hard to keep track of the men you take to your bed these days. I only know it isn't my son who is keeping you warm at night."

"No? And how do you know that? Or perhaps you can account for his nighttime presence better than anyone. I've always said he was his mother's son."

Dylan had blushed to be sole witness to such an intimate and spiteful conversation, but that was the way of it, he supposed, in the Melbourne family. Lady Melbourne despised Caroline for the shame her careless actions had brought to the family name. And Caroline would do anything to get a rise out of her mother-in-law, or anyone who would pay attention. He didn't wish to get caught in their argument.

He knew what motivated Caroline—the simple desire to hear herself talk. He had no idea what drove Lady Melbourne to help him and hurt him by turns, but her motivations weren't important to him now. Winning Amelia was his only immediate concern.

He tied the scarf around his head, over the edges of his mask, and swung the cloak—borrowed from his uncle's closet to replace the one that he'd given Amelia that day in the warehouse—over his shoulders.

It was time for the most important robbery of his short-lived career. Time to steal the key to Amelia Benedict's heart.

It had been ages since she'd been out riding.

As a girl she used to charge all over her grounds on the back of her favorite gelding. Somehow it no longer seemed suitable to be so wild and free. She'd selected a tame little mare and had her outfitted with the sidesaddle, to ride as befitted a lady of her station. And instead of flying off in a frenzied gallop, she kept the mare to a civilized trot.

How she really wanted to let loose, to feel the wind in her hair and billowing through the fabric of her dress. She wore one of her new gowns, even though she had no special plans. Her injury had prevented her from wearing her beautiful new clothes at the Abercorn estate, so she figured she may as well make use of them now.

The gown she'd put on this morning was really too fancy for riding—golden satin overlaid with filmy ivory crepe. The dress had a wide scooped neck, short puffed sleeves, and a trim of seed pearls right under her bosom, from which the skirt fell in voluminous folds. Her hair had been done up perfectly as well, but it didn't feel right. Too restrained. She took it down and fingered through the silky-straight strands, which, when unfettered, fell almost to her waist.

"Come on, Rosamonde, old girl. We can do better than this!" She clucked her tongue and tried to encourage the horse to pick up the pace. Rosamonde trotted a little faster but not fast enough to suit Amelia's mood. She sighed and gave in to the respectable gait. Even her horse seemed determined to make her keep up appearances.

At least she was out of the house, away from her account books and her various responsibilities. She seldom took time to indulge in recreational pursuits, but riding alone—especially at such a slow pace—wasn't quite the escape she'd been looking for. It did afford her the opportunity to view her estate and to think, however.

Viewing her estate was perhaps something she should do more often, she thought, surveying the handiwork of groundskeepers. The grounds around the house were well tended, but the men had been neglectful of the surrounding acreage. Clearly, they knew the paths she kept to more regularly and didn't bother with the rest. The grass had grown up so tall. And the shrubs and trees had gone unchecked and had taken over some of the space she preferred to have kept clear. A few years ago the space she rode on was all wide-open meadow. Now it was hard to get through, a mass of tangled brush and weeds without an established path to follow.

As she navigated her way around fallen tree trunks and unruly grass, she thought about her life. Her loneliness. Her uncle Patrick and the boys of Holcomb House could provide her with some diversion, yes. They helped to ease her pain, her longing for a family. After her parents had died, her uncle was all she had. As she grew older and needed less of his attention, Holcomb House took up more of his time. If she wanted to see her uncle, she had to share him with the lads. And truly, she didn't mind. The orphaned boys were troublesome, and often exasperating. But they were also genuine and as giving as they were needy. They were a welcome change from the self-centered crowd she kept company with day after day. But were they enough—enough to fulfill her for the rest of her God-given days?

No. She knew they weren't all she needed in her life to be happy. Love. Marriage. Children of her own—these were all things she wanted so badly, things she'd dreamed of having since her childhood. Why couldn't she fall in love at least with someone she could realistically marry? Lord Chadworth was most suitable for her station. His wealth was rumored to match her own. He had property. A title. He was received in all the best houses. She could get back into Almack's. . . .

But what did all that matter in the end? Did she care if she ever supped at Almack's again? Did she give a hang about titles, convention, propriety? About Lord Chadworth? When she thought of him she felt no reaction. Her heart was perfectly empty with regard to Chad—it was time she faced the fact. Oh, this thinking business was far overrated. No wonder she always did her books on Thursday. With her head in the ledgers she didn't have to worry about matters of the heart.

Then there was Mr. Marlow. Dylan Marlow. She did feel her skin prickle when she thought of him. There was something about him that excited her, but there was also something that didn't seem right, and she couldn't put her finger on what it was. It was queer, really, as if the very things she liked about him were the same things that made her feel uncertain of him. His eyes, his voice, his sudden shifts in temperament. Strange.

As intriguing as he was, though, a mystery would never do for a husband. However Dylan Marlow made her feel, she simply didn't know enough about him. And if she wished to marry, she'd better do it soon. Not only was she getting a bit old for the marriage mart, she was also risking her reputation over the fact that she had been linked in the rumor mill with three different men in the past month—Lord Chadworth, Dylan Marlow, and her phantom highwayman.

A flock of birds rose up through the trees all at once and startled Amelia and her horse. Rosamonde began to snort and rail.

"Only birds, Ros. Calm yourself." At least the distraction had served to make the horse trot faster and to call Amelia back to attention. She'd been so deep in thought that she had lost track of her way. She was still on her own grounds, but she had already reached the fringe of trees that bordered the meadow and led out to the main road.

A wary horse, Rosamonde increased her speed as they rode by the dense little patch from which the birds had risen up. Amelia tried to rein her in, but Rosamonde would have none of it. Of course, now that she wished for the animal to slow down, it began to move faster and faster.

"Rosamonde, whoa!" she shouted, to no avail. It was a few minutes of gripping tight and riding straight on ahead at increasing speed before Amelia realized that Rosamonde wasn't running because of the birds. She ran because they were being pursued.

Amelia whipped her head around to see the muzzle of a black horse drawing up on Rosamonde's rear. So close! He'd come so close before she even noticed him! How dare he!

Oh, she couldn't see the rider. She didn't need to see him to know who he was. Her highwayman had come for her again.

"Steady, Ros!" She pulled on the reins, trying to force the horse to stop at last. But Rosamonde kept on going.

The highwayman seemed to know she was in distress. He charged his mount into action. His horse, a superior beast built for speed, was upon them instantly. Her heart raced from fear already, but it beat out of time to see him again, riding beside her, his hat lost in the wind, the damnable scarf on his head.

He took hold of her reins and jerked Ros to a stop. Amelia didn't think it would work, not so easily, but it did. Rosamonde slowed to a halt.

"There. That's better," he said. "I didn't mean to frighten you."

"Ho, no, frighten me? You're only a bloody *highwayman*! Whyever would you wish to frighten me?" She was furious now, though she wasn't certain why. He hadn't meant to spook her horse. She knew he hadn't. "How could you rob me if you scared me off?"

"I don't want to rob you."

She wasn't listening. Agitated, she dismounted and tugged at Rosamonde's reins, walking faster than the horse had trotted at the beginning of their ride.

"Come, now," he pleaded, his naturally gruff tones growing softer. "I only wish to talk." He, too, dismounted and walked around to the front of his horse to try and keep up with her.

She stopped and jerked around. "To talk? Now you've come to rob me of words?"

He laughed. "Well, you would have to admit it's as much as I usually get from you, angel."

She laughed too. He was right. Except . . . well, he had her ring. Perhaps he'd come to give it back. Her eyes must have revealed her hope, for he answered her as if he'd read her mind.

"No, I don't have your ring."

"Oh." She didn't try to conceal her disappointment.

"Not with me, anyway."

"You do have it, then? You haven't sold it?" She dared to hope.

"I'm not at liberty to divulge."

"You mean, you won't," she said crossly.

"No. I won't. I'm entitled to my secrets."

"Says the man in the mask." She harrumphed and walked on.

"We all have our secrets, don't we, Amelia?"

She paused and drew a sharp breath. It was the first time he'd said her name. Amelia. It sounded lovely coming from his lips. Usually, he called her princess. Or angel.

"I suppose we do," she answered at last. She knew her secret—that she was in love with a wild fantasy. What secrets did he keep hidden behind his mask? She didn't want to know, she reminded herself. She really did not wish to spoil her dream.

If she was dreaming now, she didn't want to wake up. She'd longed for him, and he was here.

"What did you wish to talk about?"

"About you, your secrets." He paused now. She did the same.

"You want to know my secrets?"

"All of them. I wish to know everything about you, Amelia."

"Like where I keep my fortune or why I never carry any valuables around?"

"No, nothing like that. I can get money from the others."

Her nerves tightened when he mentioned others. Other women. She knew he must have robbed others. Countless others. But somehow she'd taken to thinking that she was the only one. Eliza Fairmont didn't count. She only happened to be with Amelia. Did he kiss the others? Kidnap them? Hold them close enough to feel his desire?

God, how she wanted him now!

"The others?"

"Never mind that. From you, I want more. I want to know you, Amelia." He walked around her horse to stand directly in front of her, so close. He placed his hand over her heart, flat against her breast. Her every nerve whipped to taut attention. She felt a throbbing down low, between her thighs. And her nipple rose up as if to meet his palm and beckon it even closer. Was it possible to want a man so badly? "To know your heart."

Her heart? It raced against his palm. He must know what he did to her.

"To know your soul. To know every inch of you." He drew closer still, his mouth lowering until his lips almost touched hers. "Inside and out."

"Inside and out," she repeated, her voice a breathy whisper. "I want it too."

Before she could finish her words, he caught her lower lip between his lips and sucked lightly. She groaned. His arm slipped from her breast to grasp her around her waist, and he pulled her closer with one sharp tug. Her legs opened slightly around him and her knees nearly gave out from under her. He was hard against her. Hard, throbbing, masculine, devastating. He kissed her, deeply and intimately, his tongue rubbing erotically against hers.

She would have given him anything—*anything*—just to finish what he started with that kiss.

Chapter
15

Her kiss was one of the most satisfying experiences of his entire life. He could only imagine what making love to her would be like. But here, now?

He hadn't planned on seducing her in the wilderness.

His goal had been to find out if he, as Marlow, could oust Lord Chadworth from her heart. Clearly, he could accomplish the task as a masked robber. What was it about the highwayman that she liked? How could he transfer her affection to Marlow?

With her in his arms, her sweet lips not an inch from his own and begging to be kissed again, he could scarcely think. Even when he'd just glimpsed her riding across the open field, her golden hair trailing behind her, his body told him he had to have her. She was a vision. His angel. By God, her unbound hair reached to her waist. And it was so soft. He tangled it in his fingers, ran his hands through it, couldn't help himself.

To hell with being himself. To hell with Chadworth. She was here, now, in his arms—his for the taking. She wanted him; she'd said so herself. He gathered her up in his arms, and she did not protest. Her mouth blazed a trail across his neck, pausing to nibble the base of his jaw. He groaned and once again sought her mouth with his own.

It was an extraordinary stroke of luck finding her out here so soon. He thought he would have to watch the house for a few days and catch her coming or going. Today he'd simply been exploring the surroundings, and there she was, placed in his path again by chance. Fate kept throwing them together.

When he'd carried her far enough away from the horses to a little patch of overgrown grass protected by the shade of surrounding trees, he lowered her gently to the soft ground and sat beside her.

"Here. A good place to . . . talk."

She smiled, drawing closer to him. "What shall we talk about?"

"You." He slid his arm over her shoulders as she leaned into him, allowing her to get as close as she wished. She'd chosen to practically sit in his lap, and that was fine with him. "Your secrets. Have you ever been in love?"

"In love?" She batted her lashes coyly. "No. But I'm beginning to think I might be soon."

The loveliest blush spread over her cheeks and down her neck and shoulders. She had beautiful, creamy white shoulders. A slender, long neck. He longed to see more of her, to tug her dress down and reveal her to him fully. She'd said she hadn't been in love, and that meant she didn't love Chad. She may as well have thrown up the flag of surrender. He could proceed—and how he wanted to go on!

He reached for her, nudging her hair off her shoulders. It fell in one smooth wave down her back. Gorgeous. He stroked her neck, allowing his hand to reach under her sleeve to caress her bare skin. She didn't stop him. Instead, she rolled her head back, wordlessly urging him to go on.

And he did. He eased her dress off her shoulders and replaced the cloth with his hands, with his kiss. He pulled her close in one sharp tug.

She was on top of him now, her legs around him. She could feel him under her, and she wanted to move. Her hips bucked lightly. She could hardly keep still. He'd ripped her shift a little when he pulled it down, but she didn't care. All that mattered was that her breasts were in his hands, where she wanted them. She'd dreamed of this, of his hands rubbing her, his fingers plucking at her nipples. His mouth—no, she hadn't dreamed *that*.

He sat up a little under her and his mouth closed around her breast, his tongue circling round and round with a silken speed she never could have imagined. She quaked to her very core, and she felt as if she'd melted completely. As if she were liquid pouring through his hands.

"Don't stop," she panted, moving rhythmically against him. "Don't stop."

Stop? He would sooner die. He didn't think he could stop if he wanted to at this point. Her breasts were more perfect than he'd imagined. Full, round, tipped with tender peachy buds. She was like nectar in his mouth. He could have suckled her all day. All night. Forever.

She'd been more willing than he'd ever dreamed. He thought he might have to convince her, teach her a few things, but she'd taken to making love with a natural finesse.

"God, yes!" he groaned aloud as she ground into him. He'd explode if he let her carry on. He urged her off him, rolling over her so that her back was planted in the soft grass. Her lips opened as if she were a little surprised by the sudden movement. He covered her mouth with his, ready to devour her.

She wrapped her legs around him, urging him into her. But he wouldn't. Not just yet. He backed away to study her, his mask a bit of a hindrance. He wished he could rip it off, wondered what her reaction would be.

Her dress fell in voluminous folds around her, a cloud for his angel to perch on. She still wore it, but it hardly did its job to conceal her glorious body.

Her breasts, swollen from his caresses, were completely exposed to him. Her long legs stretched out. He ran his hands up them, feeling the soft skin of her thighs and the damp heat between them.

She moaned. If she knew his name, she might have said it.

But she didn't. She didn't know who he was. And it didn't matter.

You're nothing to her, Marlow, a voice inside him cried out. *She doesn't know who you are. She wants the highwayman, a phantom, not* you. *She wouldn't let Dylan Marlow touch her like this. . . .*

He tried to ignore the voice, to forget it. He rolled on top of her and kissed her again. And again. If he kissed her enough he might forget. She drew his tongue into her mouth and sucked on it. He wanted her as he'd never wanted before.

And she wanted him. He felt so good on top of her, so solid, so masculine. She wanted to feel all of him. To be bare under him. She reached her hand into the collar of his shirt and stroked his hard chest, tangling her fingers in the soft curls there. She pushed him up, so that he sat astride her once again, and undid the buttons of his shirt. Perhaps she ripped one off; she didn't care. She'd never known such physical longing. Lust was wrong, she knew. Wrong, right, nothing mattered. No wonder the world was full of sin.

Sin felt *incredible.* She'd always been such a good girl, but now she felt free as she tugged his shirt out of his breeches and rubbed her hands over his solid chest and his taut, rippled abdomen. A patch of hair rose up just over his belt, teasing her. She wanted to see him. To touch him.

Her hands reached for him.

His mind rebelled again. His body had never been so aroused, but his mind—it wouldn't leave him be. He backed away.

Amelia sat up, stunned. "What—where are you going?"

She was an angel—all gold silk and billowing folds of gossamer cloth, her breasts bared to him, her fair hair spilling over her shoulders and down her back, the sun framing her from behind. A Renaissance artist would have sold his soul to paint her thus.

"Don't you see, princess? I can't make love to you. I'm not real."

"If you're not real, then what's the harm? Let's continue with my fantasy, shall we?" She reached for him, to tug him back down to the grass.

He pulled away. "I can't mislead you like this, Amelia. You must know that I can't love you."

"You're not real, so what does it matter? Tell me you love me and it will be real for now, and then it will fade away on the wind. Like you afterward."

Her logic was dead-on. He *would* fade away. "It matters."

She paused, smiled, and continued to move toward him. She reached out to fumble with his breeches. "For a man who can't feel, you're doing a wonderful job of reacting. I think you feel more than you let on. Come. Let's not worry about all this now. I give myself to you willingly, aware of all the consequences."

"No," he said, pulling away, the sharpness again in his lungs. He may regret what he was about to do for the rest of his life. "You may be right about my feeling more than I let on. I seem to be developing a bit of a conscience. I can't do this to you, Amelia. I'm going to let you go."

"No, please!" She reached out for him, a sob in her voice.

If he'd planned on backing away before he hurt her, it was already too late. Still, he'd left her something. If he had made love to her, he would have destroyed her. Once she got hold of her senses and realized what she'd done, who she'd given herself to, there would be no saving her. It was better this way.

"Please? I tell you, I don't care—"

"But I do. Too much. Good-bye, Amelia." He bounded to his horse, determined not to look back. But he had to, just once. She was a vision. Disheveled. Nearly naked. Straw in her hair. What man could walk away? But he did. And he knew he was a better man for it. "Good-bye."

"Your jewels, your money, now!" This time he was certain he'd gotten the necessary tone of evil in his voice. Another robbery would be just the thing to ease his wild temper, and when he'd spied the Melbourne livery on the carriage as it passed him, he hadn't been able to resist the urge to strike. Lady Melbourne, for her snide manners and all the games she'd been playing with him, deserved to be brought down a notch or two.

Ah, but it wasn't the Lady Melbourne he saw trembling behind the door as it opened. It was Caroline Lamb.

He was in no mood to fool around. He'd left a dream behind. *A dream.* And now, though he had perhaps done the right thing, he was feeling empty inside. Devastated. How could giving up Amelia make him feel so incomplete?

She was only a woman. He'd had enough of them. And he was in it only for the money. He would make his fortune from robbery after all, instead of from cheating Amelia Benedict. What was the harm? What did it matter?

Damn if he wasn't falling in love with her!

It was why he couldn't swindle her out of her money, why he couldn't marry her simply for her wealth. She was an angel. His angel. And he could never hurt her.

Caroline Lamb, on the other hand . . . He couldn't physically hurt any woman, but he was aggravated with Caroline's flirting to the point at which he could feel his anger rising. Would she try to tempt even a highwayman to her bed? She wasn't throfting forth her jewels but sitting forward in her seat, batting her lashes as if awaiting his physical response.

If Lady Melbourne had been in the carriage, he would have his pockets filled and be on his merry way. Why did it have to be Caroline? But as he thought it over he realized that Caroline would boast of the robbery to all who would listen. Amelia would likely hear of it and know that she wasn't his only victim. Perhaps she would begin to think that she wasn't special to the highwayman, that he would rob and kiss just anyone. Perhaps it was what she needed to know in order to put aside her longing for the highwayman at last—to be struck with the knowledge that she wasn't special to him.

That she wasn't special to him.

The mere thought cut him like a dagger, but it would serve her well to learn her lesson now. Loving a phantom was a dangerous thing. She was too precious a gift to hand out to some masked ruffian. She deserved so much more than he could give. For now. But maybe one day . . .

"Why don't you take off that mask and show me what you look like, hm? I'll wager you're handsomer than the devil." Foolishly, Caroline tried to take the flirtation one step further.

"You won't have money enough left for wagering when I'm through with you," he assured her, doing his best to sound intimidating. "And I keep company with the devil, my lady. I assure you he is far from handsome."

"Oh, you rogue!" Caroline fanned her face as if

she had a genuine case of the vapors. "Keep it up and I shall swoon. You are *too* dangerous!"

"Your jewels, all of them, or you'll taste the danger firsthand when I cut out your tongue." He leaned across the seat and pressed the dagger's blade to her lips. Spying a bracelet on her wrist, he changed his mind about wanting *all* of her jewelry. "But not that. That one I caution you to keep."

It looked to be made of woven human hair. He guessed it came from one of her numerous lovers. Such a token he didn't want. And he was itching to make haste, for he hadn't hit the driver nearly hard enough and the man was beginning to groan as he woke.

"I can think of some better uses for my tongue," she replied as she stripped her fingers of rings. "Oh, you bad, bad man."

Caroline was enjoying her role of victim all too much. If she kept on any longer, he would end up giving *her* what *she* wanted instead of the other way around, just to be rid of her.

"Done." He ripped the last jewel—a necklace—from her himself. There was no possibility that he would be able to sell Caroline's jewels before she bragged about the robbery all over the city, so they were worthless to him. Why did he bother, except to make it seem authentic? He had her cash, and it was quite enough. "Good-bye."

Before he could make his exit she grabbed him by the lapels and kissed him hard on the lips.

"That's what you were really after, isn't it? I've heard about you, my friend."

"No. I've got what I was after. Your kisses are so frequently reproduced that they have lost all value on the open market, madam. Now, that will be all. Adieu."

And as quickly as he had made the decision to pull the carriage over and rob it in the first place, he was off.

Word would be back to Amelia before midnight, if he guessed correctly.

She wasn't sure why she'd gone straight to her uncle Patrick. It had been two days since she'd last seen the highwayman, and still, she feared Patrick would guess at what she'd almost done. He was the last person she would want to know about her wanton behavior.

Still, being with her uncle made her feel better. He knew when she was hurting, even if she'd rather he didn't know exactly why. And perhaps she was seeking absolution. Patrick was not only her uncle, after all, he was a priest. He was not the most conventional of priests, but he'd raised her well enough to know that she'd been on the verge of sinning.

Carrying on as she did without benefit of marriage, and with a complete stranger, was wrong, so very wrong. But it hadn't *felt* wrong. Somehow she'd felt she belonged with her phantom highwayman.

The first day after he'd left her in the meadow, she'd thought she felt bad not for what she had done but for what she had not. But now she knew the truth. The story of Caroline Lamb's robbery was all over London.

The highwayman had decided he didn't want her, and he'd gone after someone else. She didn't matter to him. He was merely a rogue playing games. He'd been on the verge of becoming special to her, but to him she was just another pretty girl with a fortune at her disposal. It ached a bit, but it was better to face facts now.

"Why don't you bake us some treats, muffin? It's been so long since you've spoiled us with your macaroons."

"Now I know you're only trying to make me feel better, Uncle Patrick. When you start *asking* me to bake, I must seem pretty pathetic indeed." She forced herself to laugh.

"Something is not right with you. You don't often come to see me unannounced. And the boys weren't counting on a visit until after the weekend, for your promised story hour. What is it that's troubling you, child?" It was the same tone he used to get the boys to confess their misdeeds.

She would not confess. Her uncle meant the world to her. After her parents' deaths he'd become her rock, her foundation. Not only had he helped her through the pain of losing her parents but he'd helped her learn to laugh again. It was Patrick who taught her to go on after mourning, who instilled in her the knowledge that her parents were dead but she'd been left to go on. To live. And that's all she was doing with her highwayman, after all, wasn't it? Living. Enjoying her life to the fullest. She could share almost anything with Patrick, but not this. Her moments with the highwayman would remain her secret.

For the past two days she'd felt as if she were in mourning again. Her phantom wouldn't have her. The daydream was dead. But now, being with Patrick, she was starting to recover. She was beginning to realize that he hadn't taken anything from her this time. This time he'd left her a gift—the gift of realization. Life was passing her by. She had only to grasp it and see where it would take her. Instead of a dull trot through her days, she could have a glorious ride.

"You know, Uncle Patrick, nothing is troubling me," she decided. "I feel quite well after all."

"You do? So easily?"

"Yes." She nodded violently in the affirmative, and she meant it.

She'd had a grand afternoon. What wonderful feelings her highwayman had given her! She never knew she could feel so deeply, so wonderfully. Truly, he *had* given her a splendid gift.

Besides waking her up to the fact that she was in control of her life, free to follow her desires, he'd helped her to see what love was like. That feeling she'd had—the tickling inside, the heat spreading through her, the frantic, tumultuous need—*that's* what it was to love. Maybe he wasn't the lover for her, but now at least she knew what she needed. What she wanted. She simply had to find the man who could make her feel that way again.

And he was out there somewhere. Without a mask. Waiting to love her in return.

Chapter
16

He waited for her on Oxford Street.

Marlow had word from Lettie that Amelia had planned to shop today, and he set about bumping into her quite by well-planned accident. If he'd been pursuing her for the same underhanded reason he'd begun to court her in the first place—for her fortune—he would feel guilty. But now it was for love's sake alone that he chased her. He needed to explore the feelings he had for her, and he hoped he might inspire her to feel something for him as well.

Forgetting her was something he'd already tried, to no avail. It was too late to pretend he'd never wanted her. *She* was under *his* skin, and he would go quite mad if he didn't at least try to find out if they had a chance together. He would get his ship on the ocean again. He would make a tidy fortune. And then, only then, would he be worthy of her. God willing, she wouldn't marry anyone else in the meantime.

His new plan was to stay afloat in her social circle so that he could remain close to her until he was solvent. It was imperative that when he finally came into his own, she would know him, remember him well, maybe even want him a little in her own right. And the need to be near her was strong. He craved Amelia Benedict like an addict craved his opium. He needed an invitation to her ball, and he was running out of time. Thus the quest for Lettie's advice and the desperate search for Amelia on Oxford Street.

And there she was. He finally spied her stepping into the milliner's shop. He strolled across the way and waited for her outside. To impress her he'd dressed in new clothes. A black riding jacket, frippery ascot, form-fitting breeches—if it hadn't been for the mud, even his Hessians would have been spotless.

As if on cue, a passing carriage sent a puddle spraying in his direction at the same time Amelia Benedict emerged from the shop. He missed her in trying to save his jacket from certain ruin. Damn! But he saw her going into the dressmaker's shop up the road. He ran after her and waited outside a second time.

Ladies could take an ungodly amount of time at dress fittings, he was well aware. He waited, then grew tired of waiting and started forward, only to bump into Amelia as she exited the dressmaker's shop.

"Mr. Marlow!" She ran smack into him and promptly dropped the box she held.

"Miss Benedict. I—oh, I'm so sorry. Let me get that for you." It couldn't have happened more naturally, more perfectly. He was in delights. But her box had opened and her poor bonnet had tumbled out. It now sat in a puddle, likely ruined. She would be angry with him, perhaps.

She looked at her ruined hat, her mouth open in surprise. He wanted to kiss her pout away, but instead he told her to stay put so that he could fetch her bonnet. It was the least he could do.

Carefully, he crept through the mud to the edge of the puddle and reached across for the bonnet. He lost his balance at the very edge and nearly slipped in. As he wavered, comically flailing his arms, she laughed.

A genuine laugh from Amelia. It warmed him through.

"Here you are, fair lady." He bowed low to hand her her bonnet, only to lose his hat in the same puddle. Now she roared with laughter. He only waved the hat off and said, "Oh, forget it. I hated that hat anyway."

She smiled. "Well, Mr. Marlow, now I feel I owe you something. You've been so kind, and I still haven't repaid you for the wonderful meal you brought me when I was hurt. You'll have to stop being so chivalrous."

"Or you'll have to start being more generous."

"Such criticism." She blushed, still wearing the lovely smile. "I suppose I deserve it."

"Perhaps you could allow me to accompany you to wherever you are going. That should gratify me enough to leave you alone for almost another month."

"Mr. Marlow." She seemed to truly feel remorse. It was an astonishing development in her relationship with Dylan Marlow as himself, and not as the highwayman. "I don't require you to leave me alone."

"Really? I seem to recall on our last meeting, you said—"

"I was a shrew, Mr. Marlow. And I'm sorry. I assure you I'm changed. My foot is well, and my disposition has improved along with it."

"No need to apologize, Miss Benedict. I believe we both said things upon our last meeting that we might blush to recall now. It's forgotten. In fact, let's start over, shall we?"

"I'd like that." She stopped walking and even took his hands as she smiled up at him. "I'd like it very much. And you may accompany me if you like. I'm going to Holcomb House to see my uncle."

Amelia never would have imagined that she would run into Mr. Marlow today, nor could she have guessed that it would please her so very much to see him. She felt a stirring down low in her belly, the kind of feeling she hadn't had since . . . well, since the last time she'd seen the highwayman.

As they ambled along she was at a loss for words, but she occasionally stole glances in Marlow's direction. Had he grown more handsome since she'd seen him last? There was certainly something different about him. Perhaps his hair had been cut. Or his eyes seemed much bluer. Was he taller than she recalled? No, she couldn't place just what it was about Mr. Marlow that struck her, but she was glad that she'd run into him.

"You look lovely, all flushed from the heat." He spoke at last.

She didn't know how to take compliments from Mr. Marlow. In the past she would have suspected an underlying purpose. Now it seemed he was simply being nice. "Don't be silly. I'm all winded."

"Winded should come into fashion, then. I rather appreciate it." He looked at her, a crooked smile on his face. She used to think it cocky. Now she found it charming. "But I don't mean to embarrass you. I shall change the subject. Your uncle is at Holcomb House?"

"He's in charge of the lads. He oversees their education and keeps them in order."

"I see."

"I was orphaned myself as a young girl," she said quietly. "Uncle Patrick became my legal guardian when I was only ten."

"I'm sorry." His face showed real remorse. She didn't know why until he added, "I lost my parents as well. My mother at birth, actually. My father sometime later, but he was lost to me years before his death, just the same. It's a complicated story."

"Perhaps you will tell me sometime. I find it helps to talk about loss. It helped me. But for now, here we are."

"Oh, yes. Holcomb House."

"You've probably left your carriage at the other end of town all for my sake. It will be a bit of a walk back. Would you come in and take some refreshment? Lemonade, perhaps?"

"I am parched." He seemed a little hesitant to take her up on the offer, but he followed her to the front door.

When she walked in she never expected to have an audience to greet her; however, Patrick himself was in the entry hall with about ten of the lads gathered around him, all sitting on the floor. As soon as they caught sight of Amelia, there was no keeping them calm. But once they saw that she was with a man, well, their wildness increased tenfold.

She introduced him. "This is my friend, Mr. Marlow." There was no point in rattling off the names of all the boys. He'd never remember. But she did blush when her uncle rose to shake Marlow's hand, his eyes growing round with interest. Amelia, with a young man? She could hear him going on about it already.

"Mr. Marlow?" Patrick stood about a head taller than Marlow and was a good deal stouter. Still,

Marlow showed no trepidation at meeting her uncle—at first. "Mr. Marlow. Yes, I recall. Good to see you again, lad."

"Father Patrick Benedict." Amelia continued the introductions, though Dylan's face was a mask of shocked recognition, turning ten shades of red, from dark to light, and then starting on new shades of pale. They must know each other, she thought, but how?

"Yes. And you," Marlow stammered, still blushing. "You're here at Holcomb House now? Quite a trick to keep the lads all in order, I would wager."

"I have a way with keeping wild boys in line, as you may recall." Uncle Patrick's eyes twinkled as he spoke, as if he imparted some hidden meaning. It drove Amelia mad with curiosity. "It's not so difficult, actually, when you're built as big as a bear and can roar as loud."

"But how do you two know each other?" Amelia asked, her curiosity getting the best of her.

Mr. Marlow went pale. Patrick laughed aloud and offered up the answer. "Oxford, Amelia. Dylan Marlow was a student there at the same time I was an instructor."

"Oh." Was that all? Amelia thought she was missing out on some elaborate tale, and here it was only that they knew each other from Oxford. "Well, why are you here in the hall, Uncle? Shouldn't you be in the schoolroom about now? Oh, don't tell me . . ."

"More problems with the roof. We'll manage. Sister Hortense took half the boys out to the garden to study. I've got the rest in here going over their Latin lessons."

"What about their beds? Are the chambers holding up?"

"We had leaks over our beds last night. We got to sleep in the parlor," a young boy named David piped up.

"Oh, dear! Sleeping in the parlor?" Amelia was upset. The condition of the roof was worse than she had thought.

"It's all right, really. We've slept in worse. It's fun to camp out in the parlor. But Latin is ever so dull, Miss Mellie." Andrew, the youngest of the boys and her favorite, tugged at her skirts. She hadn't even realized he'd left his place with the others. Apparently, neither had Patrick. "Can you tell us a story instead?"

"Back into place with you!" Patrick roared. Andrew obeyed, but not without a groan of disappointment.

"Perhaps some other time. We don't want to interrupt. Shall we go fetch that lemonade now, Mr. Marlow?" She took his arm to lead him away to the kitchen and to let Patrick and the boys get back to their studies.

As the kitchen staff was busy with preparing the noon meal, Amelia poured out the lemonade herself and escorted Mr. Marlow to the back parlor.

"So you were at Oxford when my uncle was still teaching?"

"Yes," he answered curtly, raising her suspicions.

She smiled. "My uncle doesn't usually have such a good memory, Mr. Marlow. If he remembers you at all, I can only imagine it is because you were an impressive scholar or"—she paused and examined his expression—"or that you were intolerably wild. Which is it?"

"I'll leave it to you to guess." He seemed to relax now, his lips curving up in that sly grin she was getting so accustomed to seeing.

If she'd been told a day ago that she would be having an easy conversation with Mr. Marlow—a pleasant time, in fact—she would never have believed it.

Standing so close to Dylan Marlow, looking into his clear blue eyes, her heart began to pound. She had the sudden, overwhelming urge to get to know him better.

"Mr. Marlow, have you heard that I'm having a ball—"

Sister Hortense's shrieks interrupted Amelia.

"No, Andrew! You'll be killed!"

Amelia's face went pale as ash. Midspeech, she stopped everything to rush out and see what was wrong with the boy. Dylan himself didn't even think to curse the lad's bad timing; he ran as fast as he could after Amelia to see what had happened.

They came to a stop in the front hall, but nobody was there.

"The common!" Amelia shouted, and took off in the other direction.

Once in the common they could see the cause of the commotion. Little Andrew, who was no more than six if Dylan pegged him right, had climbed to the top of a very tall tree. Sister Hortense stood at the base, waving her arms hysterically.

The lad had simply climbed a tree. From the way the sister was carrying on Dylan had assumed the boy was in grave danger. Apparently, Amelia still thought so as well. She covered her mouth with her hand, and her eyes opened wide with concern. He'd never seen her look so scared, not even when he was robbing her. She obviously cared for the lads a great deal.

"Andrew!" He walked to the base of the tree and shouted up. "Andrew, are you well?"

Andrew didn't answer at first. The poor lad was too frightened to even open his mouth. He'd climbed up without a problem, but once he got to the top and looked down . . . well, looking down was the mistake. Dylan remembered the day he'd done the same thing, as clearly as if it had been yesterday.

He'd scampered up the old oak on his uncle's country estate. Once he hit the upper branches and looked back down, he'd become frozen too. Just like Andrew was now. So well he recalled praying that his uncle would come up and get him. Peter, one of the stableboys, had begun to retrieve him, but his uncle had ordered Peter down.

"If he's going to act like an ape and climb trees," his uncle had said, "let him live like an ape and stay up there."

Panic had gripped him hard. Live like an ape? His uncle couldn't mean it.

"Or he can be a man and climb down on his own, just as he climbed up." His uncle had left it at that.

Dylan had climbed down. Not right away—it took him half the day to build up the courage to move. But he had done it. And afterward? He learned to think through his actions more carefully, this was true. But he'd also learned that the person he'd counted on most—his uncle—would turn his back on him when he got in a tough spot. It was a horrible lesson for such a young lad to learn. One he didn't intend for little Andrew to have to figure out for a long time to come. If ever.

"I'm—I'm stuck," Andrew shouted down at last. "And the branch beneath me keeps creaking!"

"All right, then, sit tight. I'm coming up." Dylan shed his coat and tossed it to Amelia. She caught it, her amber eyes wide and staring at him gratefully.

It had been years since he'd last climbed a tree. He wasn't exactly certain that once he got up there he wouldn't freeze up like Andrew. No, of course he wouldn't. Andrew needed him. And it felt good to be needed.

"Patrick stepped out for a moment," Sister Hortense was explaining to Amelia. "I brought the boys out here for a quick breath of air, and—well, when we went back in and counted heads, I realized one was missing. Little Andrew—"

"The others are inside?"

"I told them to stay put. Oh, but—"

"Not to worry, Sister Hortense." Amelia calmed her. "Mr. Marlow will get him down."

Her voice was unwavering, full of confidence in him. How long had it been since anyone had relied on him for anything?

He made it to the top. Andrew was so scared he was shaking, and indeed, it made the branch crack beneath him. Another minute and it would snap clean off.

"That's it, Andrew." Dylan found a solid footing, lower than he would have liked, but to go any higher would leave him on a weaker bough. "Lean down and take my hand."

"No." Andrew still shook. "I can't."

Andrew had been whimpering softly, but he began to cry harder now that Dylan was nearer and his rescue was imminent. Being rescued meant that he would have to come down, and coming down meant facing his fear.

"It's all right. Close your eyes."

Andrew shook his head ever so slightly, his green eyes growing wider, his lips twisting in a funny way that was so common to young children and dreadfully adorable. It must have been his paternal instincts kicking in, making him want to just reach out and grab the boy and hold him tight. Dylan didn't even know he had paternal instincts until now.

"I know an old trick from India." He let those instincts guide him now. "Close your eyes and think about floating."

"Floating?" Andrew had closed his eyes, but he peeped one open to check with Dylan.

"Floating. On air. If you think about it hard enough, you can make it happen."

Andrew's little face screwed up tight. He was thinking too hard. It wouldn't work. Dylan had to give him something else to think about, a distraction. "Oh, yes. I almost forgot. It doesn't work unless you chant. You must repeat the words *Humma Sesame* over and over."

"Humma Sesame?"

"Shh, now. I think it's working. Keep your eyes closed. Keep saying it."

Andrew began to chant. "Humma Sesame. Humma Sesame."

"Good," Dylan said. Now what? He had to get closer, and that meant putting himself in danger. But he needed to get a solid hold on the boy. It was the only way.

He spread his weight between two branches, lifting himself up with his arms and spreading his legs wide between the two nearest, most solid boughs. Now he was close enough. He let go of the upper branch gradually so that he could scoop up the lad.

Andrew flinched when Dylan's arms closed around him. "Humma Sesame. Keep saying it," Dylan cautioned. The boy continued to chant, but he instinctively wrapped his arms tight around Dylan's neck at the same time.

"Stop chanting now. Just hold tight to me." Andrew did. The extra weight and curve of the boy's body clinging to his own made his climb down treacherous. He couldn't see where he was stepping or what branch to hold on to, but he felt his way around and made it down at last.

When only a few branches remained between them and the ground, he decided to let Andrew reclaim some of his manhood.

"My arms are giving out," he said. "Do you think you can make it the rest of the way down by yourself?"

Andrew looked. "Oh, yes! I can!" He let go of Dylan, clung tight to a branch, and leapt, springing without a care down the few lower branches.

Dylan dropped to the dirt, where Amelia and Sister Hortense fussed over Andrew. The boy was in Amelia's arms, and Dylan was just a little bit envious of the loving attention.

But he didn't have to be jealous for long. Amelia handed the boy back to Sister Hortense with instructions to get him inside, and before Dylan could speak he found himself in her arms. She embraced him without even a hint of reservation.

He breathed deeply of her clean lavender scent,

the fragrance that still clung to the dark clothes he wore as the highwayman.

"Thank you." She pulled back to look at him. "Thank you so much. But look at your clothes! They're ruined. And your back! How are you? I didn't even think—"

His breeches had a small tear, he noticed now, but it could be mended easily, and he hadn't even thought about his supposedly bad back. "My back has been feeling much better. I'm perfectly fine. And my clothes aren't important. The boy's all right. That's what counts."

"That's what counts." She nodded. "Exactly."

"Well, I must be going."

"Oh. Yes." She handed him his jacket. She'd draped it over her shoulders and had nearly forgotten about it, apparently. "And one more thing."

"Yes?"

"What I was saying earlier about my ball. A ball and auction really, to benefit Holcomb House. It's late for an invitation, I realize, but would you care to come?" Her eyes held such warmth. Her cheeks blushed a faint pink. "Please come, I mean to say. I'd really like for you to attend."

"I'll be there, Miss Benedict. Thank you."

He wouldn't miss it for the world.

"I'm going to Miss Amelia Benedict's ball, Thomas. What do you think of that?"

Thomas Selkirk waited for him in the parlor, Freddie had informed him. It was his first visitor at Oakley Place, but Dylan didn't take time to fret that the furniture was still covered under sheets or that the house was dark because they were saving on candles and only lighting them in certain parts of the house at certain times of day. He didn't even bother with hello. He strode into the parlor, delivered his news, and waited for a response.

"I say, Marlow, how did you accomplish that?" Selkirk managed, after he finished blinking back the shock.

"I've made her fall in love with me, that's how." Dylan strode to the window and pulled aside the draperies. Dust flew everywhere, catching the light of the sun as it fell.

It didn't matter. It was only Thomas, after all. His friend knew his financial state. Dylan hadn't even used the parlor since moving into his uncle's house. To keep evidence of his sojourn there to a minimum, he'd taken one room for his own and kept to it, except for his visits to Freddie and the staff in the kitchen for an occasional meal. The rest of the house was still shut up as it had been when his uncle left, and he intended to keep it that way. He hadn't planned on having visitors. Thomas was an exception.

"In love? With you? Someone ought to tell Lord Chadworth. He seems to think he'll be marrying her by Michaelmas."

"Ha, the blasted fool! He *would* think so. Is that what you've come to tell me?"

"Indeed, that is why I'm here. I've just come from White's, where I dined with Lord Chadworth and some other fellows. Chad was going on about how he means to propose to Amelia at her ball. He has no expectation of failure."

"He will fail, I tell you. I've just come from an afternoon stroll with the lady herself. I've never seen her look at Chadworth the way she was looking me." He gripped his lapels and puffed out his chest, filled with genuine pride.

Selkirk sighed. "I was afraid you would keep after her."

"And since when have you become Lord Chadworth's champion over mine? You encouraged me after her in the first place, and you've been doing nothing but trying to undermine me since the Abercorns' weekend. Explain yourself."

"Oh, Marlow." Selkirk sunk down onto the sheet-covered sofa. "That's just it. I'm feeling like a regular blackguard. I only wanted you to have some money. I've got my obits to draw from, but what have you got? Nothing. At first I thought it was a fine idea to encourage you to court some heiresses. But, well, Miss Benedict is top drawer. I hate to see her heart get broken. We shouldn't use her ill, Marlow. Highway robbery seemed the more dangerous pursuit at first, but now I see that chasing women for their money is in poor taste, very bad form. If she can love Lord Chadworth as I'm convinced he must feel for her, well, we should let the two of them find happiness."

"Aha, you've developed a conscience, have you?" Marlow sat in the chair across from his friend, rubbing his hands with pleasure. "Well, for once I beat you to it. I'm no longer after Amelia Benedict for her fortune."

"No? Then why—"

"I'm in love, Thomas. I'm in love with Amelia Benedict, and I aim to see that she feels the same about me."

"You? In love?" It was a good thing Thomas was already sitting down, because he looked shocked enough to have fallen if he wasn't.

"Is that so surprising? A man has to experience love sometime. I wasn't certain until today, of course. I'd thought that I could be falling for her, but seeing her today at Holcomb House . . . I know I love her. At one time I'd thought her spoiled and hypocritical. I was wrong. She's nothing like the rest of them."

"Them?"

"The *ton*. The hollow, moneyed, self-centered—"

"Easy, now. That's my crowd you're talking about. *I'm* one of *them*."

"Out of necessity, to please your father. But Amelia—oh, Tom. She's loving, and giving, and . . . she doesn't give a hang what the *ton* thinks. She simply courts their favor to save her boys."

"Her boys?"

"The orphaned lads at Holcomb House. The entire purpose of her ball is to get people to take part in her auction to raise money for their new roof. Is that not delightful? Is she not the soul of generosity? And you should see her hair. Unbound, it reaches past her waist!"

"But you—Marlow, I'm astounded. I always thought that I would be the first to lose my heart. I never imagined that you—well, you're a rake!"

"Hm. I was perhaps. A man can change. I aim to be worthy of her, Thomas. I mean it. There is nothing I want more than to be deserving of her love."

"And for her to stay unwed until then," Sir Thomas added. "Chadworth is a formidable opponent. Don't underestimate him. If he means to have her—"

"I have faith, Thomas, that she will choose the man who is right for her in the end. Chadworth could never be that man, but I will be. In time." He nodded his head, determined. "In time."

Chapter
17

The time had come, at last, for her ball.

She was in grand spirits. All week she'd been preparing—arranging furniture, decorations, giving orders for roasts and sauces, wine punches, and negus. Now everything was ready.

Amelia herself was done up like a princess from top to toe. She wore her new silk gown, a confection in the barest of pinks trimmed in pearls and coral with matching beads twisted into her coiffure. Lettie had spent hours on her hair. Never had Amelia felt so beautiful.

Any minute now her guests would begin to arrive. Who would arrive first? What would Marlow wear? She imagined him in a midnight blue waistcoat to set off his brilliant sky blue eyes. She was so relieved she'd seen him in time to invite him. He'd been such a darling with her boys at Holcomb House. And so charming with her afterward, sharing lemonade and genuine laughter before they'd rushed outside to save Andrew. He'd been such a hero! He hadn't worried a thing about himself, his bad back, or ruining his fine clothes. That Andrew was frightened was all that mattered.

She'd been thinking of Dylan Marlow ever since.

And then there was Chadworth. She knew what Chad would wear. It was a formal event, so he would appear in black tails and a burgundy velvet waistcoat, predictable black silk ascot neatly knotted round his neck. At least Chad was dependable.

She heard the door and nearly jumped out of her seat, but she decided to stay put in her sitting room until more guests arrived so she could make a grander entrance. Hodge was downstairs to usher in guests, and there were plenty of maids to show the ladies where to hang their cloaks and footmen to bring the gentlemen to the conservatory for a smoke. Her uncle Patrick had come to play host, though she wasn't certain how long he would be comfortable in the role without her by his side.

Lettie came by to see how she fared, and Amelia immediately started asking question after question about what went on downstairs. "How is it going? Who has arrived? How do I look?"

"Relax, miss." Lettie smiled. "It's going well. Admiral Whyte and his wife were the first to arrive.

Lady Fairmont was next, accompanied by her nephew and niece."

Amelia bristled. She was glad she hadn't gone down yet. Charles Fairmont, Eliza's brother, had made her her first offer of marriage, and she'd been uncomfortable with him ever since she'd turned him down. And Eliza . . . well, she hadn't seen Eliza since Kitty Sloane's tea following the second robbery.

The robbery.

Her heart gave a lurch. She'd been recovering nicely from her experience with the highwayman, but she hadn't gotten over him entirely. She still looked for him on dark nights and on cloudy afternoons, and she thought of him almost every time it rained and when she looked out over the grassy fields beyond Briarwood. Would she see him again? Did she wish to? She was no longer certain. Reality became more and more appealing all the time. Perhaps there existed a man she didn't wish to change, a man who was perfect just the way he was. A man for her. And if there wasn't, so be it.

She couldn't wait any longer. "How do I—"

Lettie interrupted her with light laughter. "You look like a dream, miss. A fairy princess, if I do say." Lettie had spent hours on Amelia's hair, making the stick-straight strands hold a glorious curl. She looked on Amelia with pride. "Now, go on down and see your guests. You know you want to."

"I do. I'm going. All right." She started to leave and turned back. "Is he—is he here yet?"

"Lord Chadworth has not yet arrived."

"No, I—I meant Mr. Marlow." Amelia blushed and studied her fingers so as not to meet Lettie's knowing eyes. The maid had long been hoping for her to get together with Mr. Marlow, and Amelia was far too embarrassed to mention that her heart was leaning in his direction, that Lettie had perhaps been right all along.

"Mr. Marlow." Lettie beamed. "In fact, he arrived before anyone. He came too early and ended up helping in the kitchen so as to stay out of the way."

Amelia couldn't quite believe her ears. Helping in the kitchen? She could hardly imagine Lord Chadworth rolling up his sleeves and pitching in with physical labor merely to bide his time and keep out of the way! She was astounded and thrilled beyond measure. Plus, the image of Marlow removing his jacket and working up a sweat was not an unappealing one. She imagined what his chest might look like. Did he have curling black hairs, as her highwayman had? And was his stomach as tight and rippled? She liked a muscular stomach on a man. She hadn't known that either, of course, until she'd glimpsed the highwayman with his shirt undone. . . .

"Miss? Miss Benedict?" Lettie waved her hand in front of Amelia's eyes as if to break her from a spell.

Amelia snapped to attention. "Oh, oh, yes. I'm

going. I'm going down." She wrung her hands to contain her excitement, but her heart beat out of time just the same.

She wanted to be lovely, elegant, universally adored. Well, at least adored by the two men she'd set her cap to impressing. Lord Chadworth and Mr. Marlow. Really, the more she thought of the rest of her guests, the less they mattered.

Marrying to impress the *ton* was no longer on her mind. She wanted to be happy. That was all she wanted—to experience all the joys that life could offer.

Her ring used to remind her to avoid spontaneity at all costs. Since her ring had gone missing, she realized, she'd ceased to let caution rule her judgment to a fault. She'd let herself go, let herself live. And through living, she did greater service to her parents' memory than through holding back. Her parents had always embraced life, taken chances, followed their hearts. But it had cost them in the end. Or had it?

They'd died together doing what they loved, cruising the world. They'd been happy people. The happiest she'd ever known. But when they died, she'd taken the wrong message to heart—to be careful. There was nothing wrong with caution, surely, as long as it didn't hold one back. And she'd held herself back for too long. Now she followed her heart, and she let it lead her right to Mr. Marlow, who waited out in the hall.

———

"Mr. Marlow—what are you doing here?"

He simply stared at her, unable to speak for a moment. "You look . . . exquisite." She did. He needed to catch his breath. "I . . . came to see that you are well. Guests are arriving. I expected you would be—I'm sorry." He blushed and turned to leave.

"No, Mr. Marlow. It's all right. I was just going to join my guests. You may—that is, would you do the honor of escorting me?"

"I would love nothing more." It was exactly what he was hoping for. When Chadworth saw Amelia enter on *his* arm, he was sure to be put off. He couldn't allow Chad to get her alone, at any costs. If Chadworth secured a private audience with her, he might have a chance of success. Dylan needed more time.

He'd come early for the sole purpose of keeping her away from Chadworth, but once he'd arrived he realized a new danger. Her uncle Patrick. Her uncle remembered him, and Dylan felt awkward around the man. He'd been so foolish in his youth. That one mistake had cost him so much more than he'd ever dreamed it could, and Patrick was the one man left—besides his own uncle and Thomas—who was well acquainted with Dylan's errant past.

When he'd first heard Amelia's uncle's name, he hadn't made the connection. But when he saw Patrick Benedict face-to-face at Holcomb House, he knew he was the same Father Patrick Benedict who'd officiated his case at Oxford, and knew of his expulsion, and on what grounds. Patrick was a bit more lenient in attitude than the other priests had been on Dylan's expression of atheistic principles, which was why Dylan had chosen him to make his confession to, but he still knew all the details of Dylan's dismissal.

What if he protested Dylan's involvement with his niece? Dylan's own uncle had disinherited him. Why should Amelia's uncle, a priest, accept him?

He had to avoid Patrick until he could be certain that he had half a chance at winning Amelia's love.

And if Amelia knew of his expulsion and disinheritance, she would know that he was staying at the Earl of Stoke's house against the earl's wishes, and she would realize that his interest in her had started out as a less than honest cause. It ate at him deep inside. He wished more than anything to be honest with her now, to tell her everything about him. And he could—he would—in time. But first he had to be certain she could love him as much as he loved her, without condition. It was too soon to reveal all.

As he entered the ballroom, a radiant angel on his arm, he knew how fortunate he was. Every eye was on them. Every mouth began to whisper. They were saying that Miss Amelia Benedict had never looked so beautiful, so ethereal—so in love.

In love with Dylan Marlow.

And how he hoped it to be true!

She opened the dancing with Mr. Marlow.

A waltz was out of the question, of course. It hadn't been danced at Almack's yet, and though Lady Jersey was not present and would not have deigned to attend one of Amelia's events, Amelia had enough respect for her detractor to leave the introduction of new things for parties other than her own. Smiling gaily, she took Mr. Marlow's offered hand as he led her down the line. She had never felt so free, so happy.

He looked wonderful tonight. His eyes shone bluer than ever. He gazed at her as if she were the only woman in the room, and in fact she hadn't yet looked around to see who had come and who had yet to arrive. She had eyes only for Mr. Marlow. She was sad when the dance required her to separate from him and felt her heart race when he was again in her sight.

He'd chosen a silver waistcoat to complement his black jacket, and it turned out to be a more perfect choice than the blue she had envisioned. His eyes did have a shimmering, silver quality. Her breath caught as she returned to him, took his hand, and met his gaze, which was silver in the dim light. Silver like *his* . . .

No, that was ridiculous. Only because she was becoming attracted to Marlow did she think of her highwayman. The highwayman's eyes were mocking and cruel. Marlow's eyes were kind and approving. Just because they were such a similar shade didn't mean they belonged to the same man. She'd loved the highwayman—at least her fantasy of him. She was beginning to feel stirrings for Marlow.

And that was all.

She breathed easy again, free of suspicion and able to smile at him with a clear conscience. As their part was over and the dance continued down the line, she had nothing to do but look at him. His fine-fitting trousers, his nipped-in waist, his powerful chest and wide shoulders. His charming smile. The way his dark hair fell forward now, spilling a little into his eyes.

When it was their turn to move again, he reached for her hand. His grip was firm yet gentle. On some level she had begun to get very comfortable with Mr. Marlow, as if she had nothing to fear from him, nothing to doubt. On another level she felt anything but comfort. Her nerves skittered uneasily, and a tingle had taken up residence low in her belly.

"Whoo!" The final move of the dance involved a spin, but he held tight and spun her round at least three more times than required, leaving her giddy. She finished the dance winded and exhilarated.

"Shall I go get us some punch?" Mr. Marlow asked.

Amelia nodded and watched him leave her. He looked as good from the rear as he had looked from the front. He had a fine build. She'd noticed it on the very first day she'd met him, but she didn't want to acknowledge the stirring he'd created in her then. She'd been far too intent on the signals of her doubt.

Now she was listening a bit more closely to the signals of her body.

On his way to the refreshment table Dylan noticed Lady Melbourne off in a corner alcove. Her gestures were sharp and filled with anger; she was arguing with someone he couldn't see. As usual, she looked imperious—and he was glad that she was occupied and hadn't seen him. He was in no mood for Lady Melbourne's games.

But just as he got to the table, the punch bowl was being refilled, making it necessary for him to wait. Lady Melbourne's companion came out from the alcove, revealing himself as none other than Lord Chadworth. Upon emerging, Chad wore the look of a henpecked husband; however, a second later, as they made their way into the room, he resumed the role of passing acquaintance, bowing cordially and leaving Lady Melbourne to head off in the opposite direction. Lady Melbourne became engaged in conversation with Lord and Lady Cowley, but occasionally she looked up as if to keep tabs on where Chad had gone.

"Lovely, isn't she?"

Dylan looked up to see Chadworth himself by his side. He followed Chad's gaze but grew confused. "Who? Lady Melbourne?"

Clearly, she wasn't the lady Chad meant to point out. Lord Chadworth's mouth gaped, and he blushed, and stammered, "N-no. Miss Benedict, of course."

"Oh. Indeed, she is. And a wonderful partner." Dylan smiled, feeling the upper hand. If Chadworth meant to intimidate him, he was off to a bad start. "We opened the dancing."

"I saw." Chadworth seemed to gain confidence as he spoke. "I hope you enjoyed it, because it's the last time you'll be so close to her."

"I don't think so." Dylan was not at all put out. "In fact, I'd say we'll be getting much closer before the evening is out. She's already accepted my invitation for a second dance."

Apparently, Chadworth didn't take well to the news. He became red-faced again, but this time Dylan guessed it was from anger. "Who the hell are you, Marlow? You show up from nowhere and act as if you belong. Upstart nephew of an earl? It doesn't make you one of us. She'll see right through you."

Chad had struck a chord of truth, but Dylan was careful not to tip his hand. "See through me? I wish she could. Then she would see how much I care for her, how deeply I value her."

So what if he was nobody? He could be just what she needed. He cared about her, that was the difference. Dylan would never hurt Amelia, and he would make sure that no one else could either. He knew what motivated his affections for her now, and it wasn't fortune or greed. It was honest regard. What prompted Chad's interest in her? He'd never suspected Chadworth's motives for pursuing Amelia before, but after seeing him with Lady Melbourne his suspicions were raised.

"Value her, do you? Value her fortune, perhaps?" Chadworth spat the accusation. "She's too smart to fall for it, Marlow. She knows a fortune hunter when she sees one."

"And what's your game, Chad? Do you think she hasn't seen through you by now? Perhaps it's why she's avoiding you."

"Ha!" Chad became cocky. "I don't need money. Ask anyone."

"Then what do you need? Why are you courting Miss Benedict?"

"I'm telling you to keep your distance from her." Chad drew threateningly close.

"Fortunately, you have no say in Miss Benedict's social calendar."

"Not tonight, perhaps. By the morning I fully intend to see that the situation changes to my advantage."

"Then, Lord Chadworth," Dylan took Chadworth's hand and pumped vigorously, "I wish you the best of luck."

Dylan smiled widely and walked away, all confidence. He would return for the punch in a moment. For now he couldn't pass up the opportunity to walk away from Lord Chadworth and straight back to Amelia, who eagerly awaited his return.

Unfortunately, he didn't get halfway across the room before Lady Melbourne latched on to his arm.

"Good evening, Mr. Marlow. How delightful to see you again."

"The pleasure is all yours." Dylan responded curtly, shaking off her grasp. No longer was he afraid of offending Lady Melbourne. He had no idea what she was up to, but he suspected it was nothing good. She'd placed herself in his path, but he stepped around her and kept walking. She caught up.

"Peevish, are we? Have I neglected you, is that it? I didn't know you cared." She latched on to his arm again to prevent his walking away.

"What I care about is that you seem to have some sort of need to manipulate people. What kind of game are you playing with *me*, Lady Melbourne?"

"Oh, you're angry." She pouted.

"I'm quite serious." He took her hand and escorted her across the room, into the same alcove she'd used to have a conversation with Chadworth earlier. "What are you up to? I've seen you with Lord Chadworth. Are you two carrying on?"

"Why, do you wish to warn your little heiress away from Chad?" She laughed. "She won't believe you. I know who you are and where you come from, and I can ruin you in her eyes if I like. It won't take much. A simple word or two of your origins and how nice her fortune must look to a man who has nothing. She's very suspicious of most men, you know. That's how it is for rich girls. They learn early on that their chief appeal is their money. For many it isn't a problem. They're so desperate to marry, they don't care how it comes about. But Amelia is different."

"Yes, she is. That's why she won't listen to you. She'll know—"

"What? How you feel, just by looking into your eyes? Oh, Mr. Marlow. You are a romantic. How sweet. But we both know you're in a spot."

He did know. Bile rose in his throat. It was going to be deucedly difficult to prove himself worthy of her, and Lady Melbourne's speaking against him wouldn't help. But he couldn't let her marry Chad.

Lady Melbourne smiled smugly. "You need me. Just like Chad needs me." She ran her hand up his arm and squeezed lightly at his bicep. "And I find I like to be needed. I'll bet you're a real stallion in the bedroom, Mr. Marlow. . . . Oh, but I'm getting carried away. Forget about Amelia. Even if she would have you—which isn't likely—she couldn't satisfy you as I could. What is it you fancy, Marlow? Money, power? I could offer you a wealth of opportunities, so to speak. . . ."

He tugged his arm away, disgusted. "Is that how you took in Lord Chadworth? Seduced him with your ability to feed his desires? What was it for him?"

She looked hurt. Suddenly, he felt for her. Underneath her lofty social position she was just a lonely old woman, using whatever means she could to draw people close to her. In her crowd she was celebrated and adored, but it was her wealth they cheered, not her.

"I'm sorry, Lady Melbourne, but my heart is spoken for and I shall be true to Amelia. Which is not to say I'm not flattered. You're a beautiful woman."

"An *old* woman." She cast her eyes down and ran her hand down her face, pausing at her slightly wrinkled throat.

"Your age doesn't matter. If anything it lends a certain loveliness, a softness to your features."

She smiled and looked almost girlish. "You're very sweet to say so." She sighed. "Ambition. It's ambition that drives Chad. He wants grand political success. I can help him, if I choose to, and he knows it. We've been seeing each other in secret for more than a year now, and I believe that in that time, in his own way, he has truly come to care for me. And I love him. I want to keep him with me always."

"Chad's interest in Amelia must have been a great disappointment to you, then." He took her hand, all sympathy. "And that's why you've been helping me to court her?"

Lady Melbourne shrugged him off and gave a little laugh. "Amelia Benedict was all my idea. Chad needs a wife. How can he be seen with me if he isn't safely married? I can't afford to let my husband find out. Besides, Chad's getting too old to be a bachelor. People talk."

His sympathy faded, leaving only a scornful distaste. "But why Amelia?"

"Why not? She's lovely. Oh, I see. You're thinking I should have chosen an ugly girl, someone he may not be so attracted to. But really, she's just the thing to satisfy any need he may have for a younger woman in his bed. I've seen him looking. I know he's had urges. He is a man, after all."

Dylan couldn't speak. He was stunned.

"And besides, she can't do a thing for him. That's why she is absolutely perfect. She isn't even accepted at Almack's, you know."

He didn't know, and he didn't care. But it explained why he'd never seen her show up to attend an Almack's event.

"Lady Jersey, among others, doesn't like her. Her involvement with those orphans—"

"Because she actually works with them and doesn't just send money to aid them, is that it?"

"Indeed. Some people forgive her foibles as endearing, but others—"

"They judge her for it. How typical." A sick feeling rose up in his stomach, to think that he'd once judged her too. He'd thought she was one of them, the hypocritical nasty lot who shunned her because of her caring nature.

"At any rate, she's just what we need. She'll provide a diversion, so no one will think Chad's having an affair with me."

"You're horrible." Dylan was truly shocked.

He'd thought himself low enough for trying to win Amelia for her fortune, but Lady Melbourne's scheming went beyond his comprehension. "How could you? And how can you tell me all of this? You don't really think I'll let you do this to her."

"You can't stop us. I have the power to destroy you, and you know it. Besides, it's too late—"

"Too late?"

"Look." Lady Melbourne drew Dylan out of the alcove. "She's with Chad now. He's going to propose."

Dylan felt like a fool. He'd allowed Lady Melbourne to draw him into conversation, diverting him from Amelia and letting Chad move right in. Damn! What if she said yes? He had to stop Chadworth before it was too late.

Chapter
18

Didn't see fit to wait for me?" Lord Chadworth came up beside her and took her by surprise. Her thoughts had been on Mr. Marlow as she awaited his return.

"Lord Chadworth, good evening." At first she had thought he was funning about waiting for him, but his defensive tone put her on edge. And his eyes—how he glowered at her.

He laughed with no apparent warmth. "I'm playing with you, of course, Miss Benedict. Forgive me for my tardiness." He bowed.

"Forgiven." She smiled with reserve. Had he changed course to hide his anger, or had he meant to be lighthearted from the start? She wasn't so sure of Chad all of a sudden.

"I do hope you've saved me a dance or two."

"The night is young, Lord Chadworth." It was an evasive answer but the best she could manage. "For now I need a rest."

"I saw you"—he sounded almost accusatory—"dancing with Marlow." Even Marlow's name was a distasteful drawl on his lips.

"Have you a quarrel with Mr. Marlow?" She leaned against a column.

Chad drew in close to stand beside her. "Only that he spends too much time with you."

"Oh? I'm surprised, Lord Chadworth. I had no idea you were the jealous sort."

He moved to stand in front of her, blocking her view so that she could not see if Marlow was returning. "Please, don't judge me harshly." He took her hand and played with her knuckles, looking down instead of meeting her gaze as he admitted his guilt. "Jealousy is an ugly emotion. But I can't help myself when it comes to you."

For weeks she'd been craving this sort of attention from Lord Chadworth, and now that she had it she didn't know what to do. Did she want his love, or didn't she? Was she flattered or distressed by his admission?

Panic rose up in her throat. She choked it back. "I see." She searched the crowd in vain for Mr. Marlow. Would he not return? It was then that she spied him across the room. He wasn't at the refreshment table as she'd expected. He was emerging from a corner alcove with Lady Melbourne. What business did he have with her? And though she knew it was silly, she felt a tightening in her chest. Jealousy was an ugly emotion, indeed! Surely it was an innocent flirtation at worst; likely they were simply making conversation. But she was jealous of his attention to another woman, an older married lady, in fact. It could mean only one thing: She was falling in love with Mr. Marlow!

How could she? Perhaps she'd been in love with him all along. She'd certainly felt strongly about him, but each time she'd convinced herself the response was simple aggravation. She recalled his words when he'd visited her after she'd hurt her foot. She had called him an annoyance, and he'd replied that he was glad to be one: *It means I'm under your skin, Miss Benedict. And once I'm under your skin, well, you'll have a devil of a time getting rid of me.* Lord, he was right! She couldn't stop thinking about him, and what a mystery he was. Could she be in love with a man she hardly knew a thing about?

"I'm sorry, Miss Benedict. You're growing pale. Would you like to take a walk with me? Fresh air may do you some good."

Fresh air. Yes. What a good idea. Without thinking ahead or realizing fully who had spoken, she agreed. Only when she stepped out into the night air and found herself alone with Lord Chadworth, who grinned like the court fool, did she realize what she had set herself up for. He was going to propose— and she had no idea what to say in response.

They walked farther from the house than she

had intended. Her legs kept going, going on as if the faster she walked, the harder it would be for Chadworth to speak. At last he took hold of her arms and swung her to face him.

"Oh." She was startled.

"I need to speak with you, Miss Benedict. It's urgent."

"Urgent?" Panic rose. Her mouth went dry. "Let me catch my breath, I beg you. What could be so urgent that it can't wait for me to get my fill of air?"

"Pardon." He let go immediately. "Let's go to the bench there. You may have a seat and rest."

He took her arm and led her to a bench overlooking the garden. She sat, hoping for some divine intervention to interrupt what she suspected was about to take place. How strange to think that only weeks earlier she had hoped for just this sort of scene . . . but now?

She waited, breathing deeply in and exhaling loudly. Nothing happened. After a few breaths Lord Chadworth interrupted. "Better?"

"Yes." There was no more putting it off. "I am."

"Good." He cleared his throat uncomfortably. "For some time . . ." he began, then paused to get down on his knee at her feet.

Oh, no. Her fears had come true. She hated to turn him down, though she knew she must. She wished she could find some way to stop him from asking at all. But she'd encouraged him too much in the past—he was the one suitor she never dismissed, never avoided. He had every reason to think that his suit would meet with success. And she would dash all his hopes, all because she had changed her mind. Now she fancied herself in love with Mr. Marlow. How fickle could she be? Would she change her mind about *him* next week as well?

Deep down she knew she wouldn't. She'd never felt for anyone the way she had begun to feel for Mr. Marlow. The constant yearning, the way her heart beat out of time just at the thought of him, and the tenderness she sensed in his every touch. Not even the highwayman had inspired her to such tender regard, though she had wanted him with a fierce passion.

"For some time I've been attracted to you, Miss Benedict. I've come to—to be a bit in love with you, actually, and—"

"A bit?" His wording snapped her mind to attention. She couldn't help interrupting.

She'd been proposed to before, many times, and somehow she'd imagined Chad's proposal would beat all of them for romance and eloquence. Apparently, she'd been wrong. Never before had a man requested her hand because he was "a bit" in love. Violently in love, yes. Ardently in love, of course. Hopelessly, desperately in love. She'd heard it all. And all of her would-be lovers, no matter how painfully gripped by the throes of their affection, had managed to walk away and forget about her almost as soon as she'd refused them. Now Chadworth admitted to being only "a bit" in love? It didn't encourage her to respond quickly, and he seemed to realize it as he stared at her.

"Love—it's so new to me. I need to learn to express myself better, perhaps."

He was all humility now. And she did appreciate his honesty if expressing himself was difficult. She could work with honesty, if not ardor.

"I understand." She waited for him to continue.

"I would—that is, I—I want for you to—"

Her panic returned. In a moment he would be done, and she would have to give him her answer. She'd turned down so many proposals before, and each time she'd felt bad, but nothing compared to the way she felt watching Lord Chadworth try to stammer out his. Since she'd never encouraged the others in the first place, it made it easier to say no. But she *had* encouraged Chadworth. What was he to think? She closed her eyes and prayed for rescue.

"There you are! I've been looking all over for you."

Mr. Marlow? Could it really be? She opened her eyes to check, thinking she may have dreamed him. It *was* Mr. Marlow. He'd come between her and Chadworth before, and she'd always cursed him as an annoyance. Now she was ready to kiss him for his interruption. He'd come! He'd saved her from answering, and she couldn't think of a more worthy hero.

"Mr. Marlow! Oh, what a surprise."

"Marlow!" Chadworth rose instantly, the name a curse on his lips.

"I'm sorry, am I interrupting something?" He was a little out of breath. Clearly, he had run all the way from the house.

"No, not at all," Amelia blurted out, a bit too quickly. "I mean, can we continue our conversation later, Lord Chadworth?" She smiled sweetly in attempt to spare his feelings.

"Indeed." Lord Chadworth bowed politely. "I will come to you later. Now, Marlow, what is it?" The second he turned his attention to Mr. Marlow, the tension thickened. Clearly, Chad was angry and would take his wrath out on Marlow if he could. Amelia clenched her teeth and prayed they wouldn't come to blows as Chadworth started toward Mr. Marlow, a menacing look in his eyes.

She stepped between the men. "Yes, Mr. Marlow. What is it?"

Marlow looked from one to the other, hesitating a moment so that Amelia wondered if he truly had a reason for being there. At last he smiled smugly. "The bidding. Your uncle is eager to start the auction, and everyone is looking for you. Shall I escort you inside?"

As Marlow took one arm, Chadworth stepped up to take the other. In silence they walked back to the house.

———

Once inside, it was obvious there was no hurry for the auction to take place. It had all been a ruse. But why? Had Mr. Marlow seen her leaving with Lord Chadworth and guessed the reason for their departure? Did he have a reason of his own to stop her from marrying Chad, or—was she being far too hopeful, reading her own thoughts into the situation?

She looked at him, hoping for some sign.

Marlow smiled, placing his hand warmly over her own, a furtive action that was lost on Lord Chadworth.

"I don't see my uncle anywhere," Amelia said.

"Yes, Marlow." Chad released Amelia's hand and turned angrily toward Mr. Marlow. "Are you sure he was looking for Miss Benedict? You best have a good excuse for bringing us inside."

"There you are, Lord Chadworth!" Lady Melbourne came in from the hall, interrupting the conversation before it could take a turn for the worse. Amelia felt a great sense of relief. "Lady Cowley and I have been looking for you to settle an argument between us."

"An argument? Settle it yourselves! I—I mean, I'm sure any one of a number of gentlemen can help you in my stead." Amelia was surprised. Chad had always treated Lady Melbourne with deference, and now his voice held a hint of rebellion.

"Would it were so, Lord Chadworth." Lady Melbourne flashed an ironic smile. "Only you can solve this little crisis between us. You are an authority on claret like no other. Lady Cowley says that Miss Benedict's claret is better than any she has had, and—begging your pardon, Miss Benedict—I strongly disagree. We need your opinion."

"You want me to taste the claret?"

"Yes. Come along."

Without so much as taking the time for polite dismissals, Lady Melbourne took Chad's hand to lead him from the room. He followed obligingly, looking back only long enough to tell Amelia he would return shortly.

Dylan Marlow smiled after the departing Lord Chadworth, then he took Amelia's hand and addressed her in a conspiratorial whisper. "Come, let's sneak off. I wish to speak with you alone."

"Alone?" Her heartbeat picked up speed. She felt none of the dread that she'd felt when Chad had whisked her away. In fact, she was suddenly giddy. Would Marlow propose now? She hardly knew a thing about him, and it didn't matter. She hoped with all her heart that he was going to ask her, and she knew that she would say yes. Yes! What else was there to say?

"Hm, where can we go?" He led her down the corridor, away from the ballroom.

"In here." She gestured toward the study. It was perfect. Her uncle would be in the ballroom tending her guests. She, too, should be playing hostess, but—well, no one would miss her for a few more minutes. Why did Marlow need to get her alone? A tingle of anticipation danced in her belly.

He nudged open the door. "Perfect."

She walked in ahead of him. He was right. It was the perfect setting for romance. Only one candle was lit, and it burned low.

She paused in front of the sofa. Should she sit? Would he get down on one knee, as Chadworth had? So long as he didn't profess to be a "little bit" in love. . . . She took a deep breath, preparing herself.

He stood in front of her but didn't encourage her to take a seat. He showed no signs of dropping to his knees but moved in closer to her, forcing her to step back. She could feel the curve of the sofa against the back of her knees, and he stepped forward still, so that they were practically pressed right up against each other. It thrilled her, feeling him so close. And when he gripped her gently, his fingers stroking her bare upper arms, the flutters in her stomach went wild. Was he going to kiss her?

"Yes?" Her breathing slowed. She turned her gaze up to meet his.

"I have something to give you." His voice was hushed and low, almost gravelly. Most unlike Mr. Marlow. More like—no, she was being foolish again. He let go of her and fished around in his pocket, pulling out a small, shiny object. She couldn't speak. She wanted to cry.

It was her ring. The very one that the highwayman had stolen from her.

At last she found her voice. "Where—where did you get it?"

She trembled with emotion as he took her hand and slipped it on her finger, the same finger it had been taken from.

He looked at her, his eyes telling, his voice steady. "It's a little something I picked up. I thought you should have it."

His words revealed nothing, but his gaze dared her to reach her own conclusions. She looked at her ring, blinking back her tears. She looked back up at him, trying to imagine him in the mask, the cloak, his dark hair hidden under the gypsy scarf. Lord, it *was* he! Mr. Marlow. Clearly, he wanted her to know. In his own way he was telling her who he was. And what did he expect her to do?

What did she *want* to do? She was filled with relief, and excitement, and rage all at once. Yes, she was angry. He'd tricked her. Did he think she would run to him with open arms once she knew the truth? He'd *lied* to her. Bad back? Balderdash!

And yet—she had kissed him passionately. She had let him stroke her breasts. Her bare breasts. There was so much she had let him do as the highwayman. Embarrassment made the blood rush to her cheeks. Lord, what did he think of her? He knew how willing she had been, how much she'd wanted him!

He'd had every opportunity to take her too. She would have given him her virtue that day in the meadow, and he had walked away. Now he was giving her back her ring. But if he was trying to express his love, she wanted him to say it. Confessions were well and good, but now he seemed content to leave the next step up to her, and she resented it. He'd given her the ring and now he looked at her expectantly, ready to take his cue from her. Would she rail and scream? Would she throw herself into his embrace? He'd played it all to his advantage, and now he sat back in wait to see how to proceed. She'd always loved to be in control of her life, but how she yearned for him to take the initiative now, to speak up and tell her how he felt about her, why he'd done it.

Instead, he said nothing. And neither would she. She would play him at his own game.

"Mr. Marlow! It's lovely. My mother used to have one like it. Wherever did you find such a treasure?" She pasted a warm smile on her face.

His eyes opened wide with shock. Amelia's failure to recognize him as the highwayman was the one response he hadn't counted on. And now he didn't know what to do.

"I—I picked it up. I knew you'd like it." He blinked, puzzled. She enjoyed watching him wonder what to do next.

"Well, *thank you.*" She stood on her toes and kissed him chastely on the cheek. "I do adore it, Mr. Marlow. You knew just the thing to impress me, indeed." She studied the ring once more and stepped slowly away from him. "Now, if you'll excuse me, I do have to start the bidding. Good evening, Mr. Marlow."

"Wait, I—"

Before he could stop her, she dashed from the room. If he wanted to explain himself he would have to seek her out again and try to go about it more properly. If he, as Dylan Marlow, possessed any of the daring he'd shown her as the highwayman, he would go to any lengths to win her over, and she was more than willing to watch him prove himself.

It seemed fitting after everything he'd put her through.

She ran toward the ballroom but stopped just outside. She wasn't yet ready to face her guests. She wanted to duck into the front parlor to compose herself, but she heard voices coming from the room. Someone was in there.

She drew close. The door was open just a crack so she listened for a moment, trying to identify the speakers. From her vantage point she could see only the woman's shadow playing on the wall in the candlelight, and she couldn't make out the voice, but the gentleman was none other than Lord Chadworth.

"Then she won't have you?" the woman said.

"I tell you I never had the chance. That damnable Marlow interrupted us. What have you learned about him?" Chad paced, agitated.

"He's nobody, just as we suspected. Why would she choose a nobody over a baron? You have a title to your credit, Chad. Not to mention your numerous other charms." She spoke in a flirtatious whisper.

Amelia was shocked. They were talking about her! Perhaps Chad wasn't even a little bit in love with her. It seemed more as if he was in cooperation with the woman he spoke to and that Amelia was a means to an end, a necessary part of a plan. To think that she'd truly considered marrying him at one time!

"She has been welcoming to my advances up until this week. I need only ask and she'll be mine." He spoke with confidence, but his tone held less assurance than his words suggested.

"You must convince her, Chad. You must, or— it's off. I can't run the risk. My husband is most serious this time. If any more of my affairs are exposed, he'll cut me off."

"He bluffs, surely. How many infidelities has he endured? Why, half his children aren't even his own."

"Enough! My children are Lambs." It was Lady Melbourne! Amelia nearly gasped aloud. Lady Melbourne and Chad, together? "And they are none of your concern. You need only worry about my husband. He mustn't find out. I tell you that you must have a wife or I can't risk being seen with you in public. It's one thing if we're two married people seen about town at the same functions. It's quite another for me to be seen constantly in the company of a confirmed bachelor. People talk. I won't have them talking thus about *me*. My son's wife is doing enough to tarnish the family name. I certainly won't contribute. I've worked too hard, and William is on the verge of particular success."

"Your son will come before me at every turn, won't he, my sweet?"

"I'm a mother. What do you expect?"

"Hm, yes. Well, if I marry Amelia I'll be a husband. And my lovely wife may end up being first with me. How would you like that?"

"Posh, I don't care what you do with her. You need me, Chad. I'm an influential woman. With my help you can achieve the ultimate political success. With her—posh. Amelia Benedict has a certain amount of charm, and marriage will lend you a particular respectability, but she can't do for you what I can. She doesn't have the kind of acceptance that will get you any power. I can help you rise above. She'll be a pretty little toy, but I'm the one you'll always need, the one who can help you get to where you are going, where you belong."

Amelia felt ill. All this time Chad and Lady Melbourne had been having an affair. She'd never caught on. Never in a million years would she have thought that her chief rival for Chad's affection would be a married woman, for goodness sake. And they had planned to use her to conceal their affair so they could continue without arousing gossip. Well, if Amelia Benedict had ever had an ego, it was effectively dashed to her fancy polished floorboards now.

She squeezed her eyes shut to block the tears from falling down. She'd certainly learned a thing or two tonight.

Chad wanted her, but for the sole purpose of providing him with a diversion.

Amelia made her way back to the ballroom just in time to hear Caroline Lamb suggest a tune. A waltz. And why not? So what if Lady Jersey would bar her from Almack's eternally? Amelia had nothing left to lose.

Oh, yes, she did. She changed her mind, stepping faster toward the podium she'd had constructed at the far end of the room. She couldn't afford to be ostracized—not yet, anyway. She needed the *ton*'s money for the boys. Her uncle Patrick and the Holcomb House lads depended on her. They were her family. She could want for nothing as long as she had Pat and the boys.

Her heart throbbed, aching.

She could want for love.

She recalled the way he'd kissed her, Marlow—as her highwayman. It was a feeling she would never know again, and one she would never forget. Even if he had been a blackguard, using her for his own amusement. Even if he was an infernal cad.

Before all the couples could pair up on the dance floor and the music could swing to full lilt, she made it to the podium and raised her arms.

"Good evening, friends." Her voice rang out loud and clear, stronger than it ever had before. She hadn't agreed to marry Chad. Her precious ring was back on her finger. And Marlow? She looked around but didn't see him. Perhaps he'd left. Perhaps she would never see him again. Perhaps it was for the best. "It's time for the auction to begin."

But as Dylan Marlow entered the room, quietly walking across the floor to join in at the back of the crowd, she felt her heart skip a beat. He'd stayed! Maybe there was hope for him after all.

Chapter 19

He watched her conduct the entire auction.

Her voice was clear and strong; only once did she waver—once, when she'd looked up as he had entered the room.

She had raised a lot of money for Holcomb House. Hundreds of pounds. It was a large house, though, and many repairs were needed. She still hoped to come away with enough for a new roof. Her voice held increased hope and fervor with every item on the block.

Watching her, he was filled with awe and respect. She appeared before these people, ignoring the loudly whispered criticism of her caring so much for the orphaned boys. She would spend hours in a dilapidated house, in a horrible part of town, cooking and cleaning for them despite the gossip and scorn of her peers. She'd built up a reputation after doing it for years. And people still adored her, still came to her balls and invited her to theirs. Most of them, anyway.

Lady Melbourne sat at the back of the room, keeping careful distance from Chadworth, who had made his way to the front and was raising his arm to bid. He'd been wrong to worry about Amelia with Chadworth, he realized. She was an intelligent woman, able to judge for herself. She would never have consented to marry the man. Even if she didn't know he was having an affair with Lady Melbourne, she knew enough not be deceived by such a heartless cad as Chadworth.

And how long had she known about *him*? As soon as he gave her the ring he could see it in her eyes, that she knew he was her highwayman. He was hoping for her love, but what did he expect? That she would throw herself into his arms and forgive him for robbing her, for lying to her? He'd even anticipated her anger. She should have been angry at him. Furious! Anger he could have handled. If she'd yelled at him he might have been able to gauge what he needed to do to earn her forgiveness. Instead, she'd said nothing. All of the warmth they had established between them over the past two weeks was gone. In an instant she had become distant to him. And it was a distance he was none too sure he could cross.

Amelia's voice called him back to attention. It

quavered with a note of desperation—she was still several hundred pounds short of the total needed for a roof, and there was one last item to go: a gold platter. It wasn't much. The ladies in attendance had their share of platters at home, he was certain. This one was fine but not extraordinary. He thought about bidding, but it would take everything he had, and he needed the money to repair his ship. He had enough to get one ship seaworthy, and one ship was all he needed to start making money to buy more.

The bidding rose. Going once, going twice, Chad saved the day by putting in an extra twenty, but he wouldn't go above forty-five. In the end the platter went for little more than fifty pounds, and that had been a stretch.

Chad and Lady Melbourne. He and Amelia had been their dupes all along. Suddenly, Dylan was more determined than ever to win her heart. Earlier, when she'd been so cold, he'd felt so low. He certainly hadn't been good enough for her before; what if he never could be?

The money burned in his pocket. He wouldn't have it at all without having resorted to robbery. He glanced again at Lady Melbourne. She was an evil woman. Vain. Destructive. Far too powerful. She had all the money he would need, but even the thought of robbing Lady Melbourne irked him now. As much as his heart cried out that she deserved to be brought down a notch, he simply didn't have the heart for swindling anymore, for cheating, for stealing, for lies. His heart belonged to Amelia, whether she chose to accept it or not, and her goodness had spread to him, making him a better man for having known her, for having loved her.

Amelia's uncle Patrick stood in the hall, watching the festivities from the entryway without coming in to take part. This was her world, not his. Dylan understood Patrick Benedict too well. His father, too, had been a second son—a witness to the splendor but never an invited guest. This glimmering wonderland was a thing of beauty to behold but never meant for them.

Sweet Amelia fluttered between the two worlds, but instead of feeling like a stranger in either, she'd made a place for herself in both. She possessed an innate courage he could never hope to have. So instead of fighting for his place in her world, he'd left it altogether.

He would leave it again, but this time not for lack of course or strength. This time he'd leave it for a far more noble purpose. He may as well do one thing right in his life. As he strode toward Patrick Benedict, he pictured the orphaned lads all gathered around the hearth in the front hall of Holcomb House. They were good lads. He could clearly recall little Andrew's face, looking up at Amelia. *It's all right, really. We've slept in worse.*

He, too, had slept in worse. It wasn't a life for anyone, least of all young children.

Her boys deserved their roof.

"You wish to see me?" Patrick approached Dylan before he had crossed the room.

"Yes." Dylan attempted to blink back his amazement. "I do. How did you know?"

"I knew you wouldn't let her down. Come, let's adjourn to the study. We can speak privately there."

Dylan followed wordlessly, still uneasy. Patrick Benedict was well acquainted with his past, and yet he didn't seem to mind Dylan's involvement with his niece. Perhaps he would mind if he knew what Dylan had once intended for her.

Patrick walked across the room to the other side of the desk. Dylan paused in front of the sofa, lost in the recollection of the scene that had taken place there earlier, when he had returned Amelia's ring.

"Come. Sit." Patrick gestured to the chair across from the desk. "Your face—it reminds me of when you were a boy. You don't have to look so awed by me now. I have no power over her heart."

"Excuse me?" He took his seat.

"You may ask me for her hand, but it will be her decision in the end. Amelia is very much in control of her own life."

"Her hand?" Patrick thought he had come to propose. Dylan's throat constricted. "You misunderstand my intentions."

"You don't intend to marry Amelia?" Patrick's face grew stern as he leaned across the desk.

Dylan rose, agitated. "Forgive me. I feel like a lad again—now you remind me of when I was young and foolish. My intentions toward Amelia are honorable, but I have nothing to offer her."

"Do you love her?" Patrick raised a thick silver brow.

"With all my heart." He answered honestly, meeting Patrick's gaze.

"Then you have all she needs."

"I aim to be worthy of her. The reason I wanted to see you is—" Dylan reached deep into his waistcoat pocket and pulled out his money, all he had. "Here. This is for Holcomb House. With what she has made tonight, it should be enough to fix the roof and maybe even some extra for other minor repairs."

Patrick didn't reach for the money but allowed Dylan to walk all the way to the edge of the desk and place it there himself. "God bless the boys, Father. They deserve any little bit we can give them. I only ask that you don't tell her. I don't want her to know it comes from me."

"I understand."

"Thank you. Then we're all settled. Good night, Father—"

"Wait. I must ask one more thing of you."

Dylan turned to face Patrick. "Yes?"

"The atheism papers at Oxford. Did you—"

He didn't have to finish. Dylan knew what he was getting at. "No. I never meant it as anything more than a prank. I never lost my faith, Father Benedict."

Patrick nodded, looking pleased. "Very well. As

you've kept your faith in God, may you keep faith in yourself, young man. Good evening to you."

"But I don't understand." Amelia looked at the pound notes in her palm, the ones her uncle Patrick had just given her. The ball was over and she was alone with Patrick in her study. "Where did you get this? The auction's over. There is no more to bid on. We didn't get the roof. Or so I thought, but this will be just enough. It puts us a little over our goal, in fact."

"Let's just say it came from an anonymous donor. He left it in my care to give to you. I'm sure there's a reason he'd prefer you didn't know it came from him."

"Him?"

"*God bless the boys, Father. They deserve any little bit we can give them.* That's what he said when he handed it to me. I always knew he believed."

"He believed? Who believed? Believed in what?"

"In God, of course."

"Uncle Pat—" She blew her hair out of her face. Her curls had fallen hours ago. "Tell me. Was it Dylan Marlow who gave you this money?"

"I promised not to tell."

"Can you tell me who it wasn't?"

"If you ask properly—we'll see."

"Did Dylan Marlow not give you this money?"

"I can't say that he did. But I can't say that

he did." Patrick smiled wide, his blue eyes dancing. "I do like that Dylan Marlow, though. Much better than your other suitors. Has it all over Lord Chadworth."

"Don't speak to me of Chadworth." She grimaced visibly.

"Oh, so you have come to your senses? Good. Marlow's the one. Let me know when to add it to my schedule."

"Add what, Uncle Patrick?"

"The wedding, of course. I'll need to arrange for Sister Hortense and Father Martin to handle the boys so I can have the morning off to officiate."

"There will be no wedding." Dylan had left without saying good-bye. His position was clear. She wasn't worthy of an explanation. She took a seat at her desk and began to add the figures again, just to make sure she'd raised enough to pay for the roof.

"Hm. I'll keep June open. Just let me know. For now I'm off to bed. It has been an exhausting night just watching all the dancing and carrying on. Don't stay up too late now."

"I won't, Uncle Patrick. Good night." She finished adding her last column of figures in time to watch him go up the stairs and on to bed. Don't stay up too late? How did he expect her to sleep?

So many thoughts spun in her mind. So much had changed. Chad. Marlow. Her highwayman. They'd all been phantoms, in a way.

Lord Chadworth, with his air of respectability, would have used her as a cloak to shield his sordid affair. A little bit in love, indeed. He'd never loved her at all.

And Mr. Marlow. Those twinkling blue eyes had almost fooled her. She was used to dancing eyes and a charming smile. He had seemed so good, so true. And all the while he'd let her believe his lie.

Why had he robbed her? Did he need money? It hardly seemed to be the case when he'd given so much to the lads. With his contribution she would be able to provide their new roof. It touched her heart and softened her toward him. How truly bad could he be inside when he could do something so kind, so generous?

She didn't know what to think. There was no denying the fact that she was attracted to him. There was no doubt that he had been physically attracted to her when he'd worn his highwayman's guise. She blushed when she recalled the evidence of his desire.

She had begged for him to make love to her. At one time, as Marlow, he had said that he could make her beg. And she had.

He could have taken advantage of her, used her to satisy his needs, and left her, no questions asked.

But he hadn't.

He could have exposed her, destroyed her reputation.

Instead, he'd walked away.

She paced the halls, thinking, until she ended up in her enclosed patio. Her favorite room. The myriad stars danced around her, visible through the glass, glowing like his silver eyes in the moonlight.

How curious that his eyes could be so blue in the daytime and so silver, almost colorless, in the dark of night.

She walked to the round table at the center of the room, blew out the candle, and stared out the glass walls. All was darkness, but light still reflected from the next room. She would have to make sure all the candles were out before she went to bed. She'd already dismissed the servants for the night, telling them the rest of the cleaning could be done tomorrow. It was just her, and the darkness, and—she startled when she looked up and saw his reflection in the glass.

Her highwayman was in the doorway, studying her as she pondered the night.

"How did you get in?" She didn't even turn to face him. Her heart raced as if he were a stranger still, though she knew full well who it was. Marlow.

"I didn't mean to startle you." He walked into the room. "The door was open. I needed to see you."

"Why?" She laughed, trying to sound jaded as she turned to face him. "What could you possibly need from me that you haven't already taken?"

"This." He placed her hands on the sides of the mask. "I need to give you control."

"Control?" Just the feel of his hands on hers made her pulse pound. She struggled to breathe. He was so close. Her hands stroked at the edge of his mask, a fine soft leather.

"Control of me, of the situation." His voice was

husky, as she remembered the highwayman's to be. Her nerves pricked under her skin. She knew it was Marlow, and yet—he excited her beyond measure with the mask on. "You never got the chance to unmask me, as it happened. There is so much I want to tell you, but first, take off the mask."

"I—" She looked in his eyes, twin silver-blue pools, and she trembled all over. She hadn't quite got used to the fact that he and Dylan Marlow were one and the same. "I don't want to yet."

He cocked his head to the side, seemingly surprised by the turn of events. He smiled crookedly, the highwayman's mischievous grin.

His hands slid along her arms to her shoulders, and he pulled her close. She could hardly contain herself, couldn't ignore the heat spreading from her stomach down between her thighs. She couldn't help moaning from deep in her throat as he pulled her sharply into his embrace.

"Oh, yes," she said, rolling her head back in a gesture of surrender. She'd never known such need.

He kissed her throat, traced the tip of his searing-hot tongue down her neck and across her collarbone.

And then, suddenly, he stopped. "Perhaps we should talk first. I have much to explain."

"No." Her head shot up. Earlier she'd wanted him to talk. Now she'd changed her mind. "I don't want to talk now. I don't want to think. I want—" How could she tell him what she wanted without seeming utterly depraved? She wanted him to make love to her with his mask on, as if she never knew the man who waited beneath. . . .

"I know what you want." His voice was barely a whisper, coarse as gravel. The mere sound of it made her skin prickle and her breath come in shallow gasps. He laid her down on the table and kissed her all over—her neck, her shoulders. He tugged at her gown, revealing the bare skin of her shoulders and the tops of her breasts. "Let's get you out of this heavy gown. I have my fantasies too."

Right then, hearing his voice thick with lust, she almost thought she'd reached the height of ecstasy, but the anticipation dancing in her belly told her she had so much more to look forward to. She couldn't wait.

"What—what are you going to do?" Her voice was weak. She gnawed on the edge of her lip as he tore her gown sliding it down past her hips.

"I'm going to ravish you, princess. Just like you've always dreamed."

She moaned aloud. Never had she known such desire. Her entire chest was enflamed with wanting, needing. She didn't know what to do next, she just knew that she had to feel his hands on her.

Her nipples, erect, showed through the shift. He rubbed his hands across them, and it sent an electrifying jolt of pleasure straight through her. How much better would it feel without the barrier of even the thin cloth between her breast and his hand. That would come, perhaps, in time. He stood at the edge of the table and pulled her body against his. She sat, wedged so tightly against him that she would have to open her legs if she wanted to get any closer.

And she did.

He groaned as if barely able to contain himself. And *she* was so ready for *him*. She writhed against him, her body commanding her to act on her wildest impulses. He was so hard. She wanted to free him from his breeches to look at him. And his chest—she remembered his steely, rippled abdomen. She couldn't help herself. She ripped through his shirt, pulling the buttons off in one sharp tug.

"Easy, princess." He laughed a little. "We have plenty of time."

"All night." She nodded, burying her head against his nape and glancing out into the hall. One last look to make sure all was quiet, that everyone else in the house was asleep and out of the way. They were. "All night."

He trailed his hands lightly across her breasts again. Her nipples strained achingly against the lace, swollen and dying for release.

"I've wanted you for so long." He studied her face.

She stared at his eyes through the mask. "And I've wanted you." She spoke to the highwayman, but when she looked at the scarf she kept imagining his hair underneath. Marlow's hair. A dark mass of silken strands. He seemed surprised when she reached behind his head to tug at the ends of the scarf, untying it.

She smiled, liking that he didn't know what to

make of her, that he had no idea what to expect. She took the scarf off his head. "Oh, yes, that's better. I was dying to see your hair." She ruffled her fingers through the soft strands.

His jaw was taut. A vein pulsed fast at the base of his neck. Did she make *him* nervous too? She kissed him right at the center of his throat, tracing her tongue in circles and following up with a flutter of tiny nips up and down his neck.

He groaned. "God, what you do to me." Tangling his hands in her hair, he removed the intertwined strands of pearls and coral beads that still remained. "There," he said, when the last strand was free. "You looked lovely tonight. Exquisite. But I like you best just like this."

He ran his hands through her hair, again and again. And then, as if he couldn't stand it any longer, he held her to him and kissed her more deeply than ever before.

"My angel," he whispered, his lips brushing her earlobe. He undid her stays, tugged at the laces of her petticoats. He'd done this before, clearly. And the knowledge thrilled her no less. She stood up, her body flattening against the length of him. He stepped back and gave her space to let her clothes fall the rest of the way to a pool of fabric on the floor.

Now she was naked. The cool air kissed her skin, provoking a tingling all through her. She cast her eyes down as he studied her but made no move to cover herself from his gaze.

He smiled approvingly. "You're exquisite." There could be no barriers between them. He untied the cloak that he still wore, though he'd flipped it back off his shoulders, and spread it over the ground next to the table like a blanket.

"There." He took her hand and gestured for her to sit. She did, trying to maintain a ladylike posture by curling her legs under her bottom. She watched him undress, slowly, assuredly. His shirt took just a second to discard since she'd already seen to the buttons. The muscles of his arms rippled as he lowered the dark fabric from them and dropped it to the ground. His hands paused at his belt, as if awaiting her permission. She said nothing, but she smiled to show her approval.

He unbuckled his belt and slid his trousers down his narrow hips. The first thing to catch her attention was the dramatic change in color of his skin, from a healthy bronze to a paler gold. He must have spent some time outdoors without a shirt. Doing what? Her curiosity would wait for later. The dark thatch of hair that began running down just under his navel in a narrow thread captured her interest. It widened out just over his—oh, my!

"Oh, my," she repeated aloud, her breath catching in her throat. She longed for him, wanted to feel him, and yet . . .

Perhaps she had gone too far. Suddenly, she was so nervous. Would there be pain? He was rather large. . . .

He stepped forward, naked now except for the

mask, and she looked up. He stooped to join her on the cloak.

"Relax, angel. I won't hurt you. We can stop any time you like." He pushed her hair back from her shoulders and stroked her skin gently.

"No," she said quietly once, and then louder again as if to affirm herself. "No. You must ravish me."

"Then ravish you I will."

He kissed her full on the lips, softly at first and then harder. And harder. She kissed him back frantically, caught up in her growing need. She drew on his tongue, eager to pull him entirely inside her if only she could. He ran his hand down the length of her, encouraging her to recline, and rested his body atop her. The weight of him was so reassuring, so comforting. And his skin felt so good, warm and bare against hers.

She hadn't even realized that she'd reached out for his discarded scarf. She twisted the silk between her hands, wrapping it tighter and tighter as his mouth engulfed her breast, urging her longing to new heights.

His hand reached between her thighs and he stroked her to near madness. The feeling was incredible, almost completely overwhelming, but she fought against it.

"Stop." She pushed his hand away and sat up, breathless. "You said I was in control."

"Yes?" The sly smile. He mocked her.

"But I—I don't feel in control at all."

"That's good." He perched on his side, supporting his head with one arm, his body still stretched out comfortably. He was erect to the point that it looked almost painful for him. "You're supposed to lose control."

"No." She smiled. "First, *you* will." She reached for his chest first, wanting the courage to work her way down. What would he feel like there? His chest was both rough and soft. Hard planes, soft hair, smooth skin. His nipples were hard little nubs, and she traced each one with her fingertips, caught up in the wonder of him and how he made her feel.

"Mmm." He leaned his head back, allowing her exploration, seeming pleased by her desire to touch him.

She trailed her hand over him, down his stomach, around his navel, and then she picked up the scarf and wrapped it around her hand.

He looked up to see what gave her pause. "You plan to kill me with such exquisite torture?"

"No. Only to make *you* beg for a change."

"Lord!" When he groaned and rolled his head back, she felt a thrill of triumph at her core. Now she was the seductress, and she found it was a role she thoroughly enjoyed.

She touched him with the silk over her hand at first, and she was surprised at his solidity. She really had never imagined that a man could turn so hard. She stroked him all over, amazed.

"That's—very nice," he said. "But I want to feel your hand."

"My hand?" She dropped the scarf. She supposed she was ready.

"Yes." He sat up and took her gently by the wrist to guide her. "Like this."

He closed her hand around his shaft and ran it up and down. His skin felt like the silk to the touch. So soft, and yet so solid all at once.

"Oh," he groaned again, allowing himself to relax. A second later his head shot up. "I'm begging now." He gripped her by the wrist and pulled her hand away. "*Begging*. Let me. Let me ravish you."

When he urged her onto her back, her legs wrapped around him. He felt so right. Before progressing further he leaned in to kiss her. A gentle kiss, so loving.

It wasn't the highwayman's kiss. It was Dylan Marlow's. And she preferred it.

"Wait." She reached up and pushed away his mask. He looked at her, his blue eyes wide and glittering with emotion. "That's better." A deep warmth engulfed her.

"Are you sure?"

"Yes. I am. I want to make love with you, Dylan Marlow. It's you that I want." She wanted this man more than anything she had ever wanted in her life.

It's you that I want. The realization penetrated him, touching each of his nerves in sequence like a wildfire spreading underneath his skin, not stopping until it burned him through. She wanted *him*. Not the highwayman. Marlow. By God, there was hope!

He entered her gently and didn't press her until

he felt her initial discomfort vanish clean away. She urged him deeper, deeper. When he was certain there was no pain, that she needed to feel all of him inside her, he let go and gave her all of him. Every ounce that he had to give. And when he found his release, and she looked up at him with sheer happiness shining in her whisky-tinted eyes, it was the most magical, most perfect moment of Dylan Marlow's entire life.

Chapter
20

For hours she'd been watching him sleep.

The stars were still out. She looked at them for a while as her mind raced. The last thing she saw before he'd driven her so out of control that she could no longer open her eyes had been the stars in the night sky. And with her eyes closed she could see those stars still, again and again. He'd given her the stars, she laughed. She wouldn't have thought it possible, but Dylan Marlow had found a way. He was a rogue and a gentleman all in one.

And she loved him just the way he was.

If he needed money once, he didn't now. He could have anything he wanted. What was hers would be his. She would discuss it with him as soon as he stirred. Her uncle would be so surprised! He'd been so right last night about the wedding. How he would laugh! But she had to get Marlow out of here before the servants woke, of course. It must be nearly dawn.

"Wake, my love."

Wake? Her voice, rousing a lover, was the first sound Chadworth heard as he crept through the halls at Briarwood, and it astounded him. *Wake, my love?*

She had a lover? She was sleeping with him? And not even in the confines of her bedchamber! He crept quietly, following the sounds of the voices.

"I'm awake, angel."

Marlow! Damn him! He was too late. She was already *his*. . . .

They were in the enclosed porch. Hm. A romantic setting at night, no doubt. There was no one about, no one nearby to hear them. It was why he had chosen this time of morning to return. Well, it was why Elizabeth had suggested it, anyway. After he'd made love to her in her husband's bed at Melbourne House, she had sent him out to secure Amelia's hand in marriage before word of Lady Melbourne's frequent companionship with the bachelor Lord Chadworth could reach Lord Melbourne at his country estate. Melbourne knew his wife had lovers, of course. But he didn't give a damn who was in his bed while he was away as long as her affairs were not exposed to public scrutiny.

Chad felt a pang of jealousy when he spied the

lovers from around the corner. He could see only their feet, but he knew they'd made love on the floor. On the floor? He'd never guessed that Amelia was a creative type. Elizabeth was tiringly unorginal in bed—she didn't need sexual skills to lend her more authority. If anything, Lady Melbourne required him to work all the harder to please her. And she was worth the effort, if she could get him the position he was after.

She'd told him he would be a prime minister one day, if she had her way of things. It was a lofty goal, and one that would please him to no end. But he wouldn't get it without taking a suitable wife, and Elizabeth had chosen Miss Benedict for him. At first he'd protested that she wasn't suitable. She wasn't even accepted at Almack's. Wouldn't she hold him back?

But Elizabeth had promised that she would use her power to override Amelia's lack of influence. Amelia held a certain charm, she'd argued. While Amelia had her few detractors, she had managed to win over most of their haughty crowd. In the end Elizabeth's arguments had swayed him. He knew she would feel more secure if he had a bride who couldn't do much for him politically, and now that he realized what a sexual prize Amelia may be prove to be, he was more than willing to oblige his mistress.

But if Amelia had settled on Marlow . . .

Well, they weren't married yet. There had to be a way to separate them. Her virtue was gone, clearly.

That was something he could work with to force a wedding, perhaps. Blackmail. How much did Amelia Benedict care about her reputation?

Obviously, not enough. He needed something more. His plan had been to wait for her to wake and to surprise her with his renewed declarations of love. Lady Melbourne had practically written his dialogue for him. He was to be mad with love, up all night, unable to sleep with thinking of her. He needed to see her very first thing in order to beg her hand in marriage. Ladies of Miss Benedict's ilk could seldom deny a man who begged at their feet, Elizabeth had said. So he was to beg, to plead, to nearly die of need for her, and then to entice her with a jewel. An emerald, and a rather large one at that. It was too big for its setting, but Elizabeth was certain it was just the thing for Amelia.

Just the thing, indeed. He needed a new plan. An emerald was nice, but it was a little harder to convince a woman to marriage when she was still ripe with the smell of another man's seed. Lord, he'd botched it in leaving her last night. He told Elizabeth he should have stayed, but she was so certain Amelia needed only a little more time.

Apparently, what she needed was a good roll, and Marlow had been there, willing.

"I don't want you robbing again. It's too dangerous. I insist." Her voice held a note of desperation.

Robbing? What was this?

"I'm not planning on it, Amelia. But I will keep the mask. It does come in handy, don't you think?"

"You no longer need it." Her voice was full of love. Chad's stomach turned. "What happens now?"

"What happens? I love you. I want to marry you, of course, but—"

But. Chadworth paused at the *but*. It gave him hope. If Marlow turned out to be a cad—

"Right away! My uncle will officiate. We can have—"

"You don't understand, Amelia. I can't marry you yet."

"Why not?"

"I have nothing to offer you."

"I don't need anything but you." She stood. Chadworth peeped around the corner and got an eyeful of her beautiful body. By God, she was stunning! Her tiny waist, her perfect round breasts. How he longed to cradle them in his hands. Firm, *youthful* breasts.

"I need to earn a living, to gain respectability." He stood and blocked Chad's vision of Amelia. Chad leaned back against the wall. Marlow's body wasn't anything he needed to see and wasn't worth the risk of his discovery.

"You won't need anything. I have enough for both of us. Look around you! You must know I've plenty of money."

"I don't want your money." Marlow's voice was hard and cold. Chad was in delights. Perhaps he didn't need to do a thing to win her over—Marlow was making a good mess of things with Amelia Benedict on his own.

"Sit down. Please," Marlow pleaded. "We need to talk. There are things you must know."

"I don't need to know anything but that I—"

"No. You do need to know. Please. I must admit that, at first, I was after your money. Completely."

"That's why you robbed me in the first place?"

Back to the subject of robbery, now? This was getting interesting.

"No. When I robbed you I was honestly trying to make a living at highway robbery. You were my first. It was after that that I'd set my cap at wooing you for your fortune."

She sighed heavily. Chad could hear the rustle of fabric to indicate that she was covering herself more adequately. A sure sign of a woman's distress.

"Go on," she said at last.

Likely, Marlow was dressing too, for he paused a moment before speaking again. "While it is true that I am the nephew of the Earl of Stoke, he disinherited me and broke off the connection long ago. I stay in his house now out of the generosity and lingering fondness of his housekeeper and nothing more. I took up residence there only to impress you."

"And your more regular home is—"

"The warehouse near the Thames. The one I took you to when—"

"The dockyard. Yes, I know the one. Go on."

"It's all I have to my name, honestly. The warehouse and one ship left of a fleet, a ship in such disrepair that it barely stays afloat. I inherited that from my father, as well as a heap of debts. The debts I paid off by selling the rest of the ships and some baubles that remained from the time I was in my uncle's favor. The money left over after the debts had been paid kept me going for some time. Only recently have things been . . . getting tight."

"And you began to rob."

"I thought that if I could steal enough to get the ship in order, I would be well on my way."

So Marlow was a bloody highwayman. She'd never have him now! Could life get any more perfect?

"And since I have plenty of money, why not? I can help you." Chad thought he detected sarcasm in her tone, but he couldn't be certain. As much as there was a hint of bitterness, there was also apparent hope. Clearly, she wanted things to work out with Marlow. For a second he truly felt for her.

"It had nothing to do with you at first. I didn't even know who you were. By the look of your coach, I did assume you had plenty to give and wouldn't miss an extra few hundred pounds. But then, afterward, I felt awful. I thought of you all night. I just sat in a tavern and looked at your ring and thought of you. It's why I kept it."

"As a souvenir? To remind you of me?" She sounded skeptical. Chadworth knew for certain she was being sarcastic now.

"Truly. I told myself I would keep it as a token of my first bold attempt at being a highwayman. I felt bad, true, but I can't deny that it felt right in some ways as well. Until I realized that you weren't one of *them*."

"One of them?"

"The *ton*. As long as I knew I was robbing from a spoiled set of hypocrites, too rich for their own good, I felt justified in my actions. I was wrong. I know I was. You have taught me—"

"Don't flatter me now. Just finish your tale." Good. She grew impatient.

"Very well. I saw you at a party not long afterward."

"Lady Melbourne's tea," she said, still sarcastic.

"And I knew that you were worth pursuing. You intrigued me from the start. That you were the same one I'd robbed added interest, but still what I wanted was your money."

"I knew it! I *knew* that you were like the rest!" She seemed as gratified as she was disappointed. And Chadworth smiled as Marlow continued to dig his own grave.

"I was, at first. The second robbery, I had no idea you would be in the coach."

Chadworth grinned. Marlow robbed the same woman twice? It was too rich. . . .

"And yet I managed to happen on you again. The coincidence was too much to deny. Fate kept throwing you at me. I was only robbing the second time to get enough money to court you properly."

"Why didn't you hold me for ransom?" she said

at once, growing animated. "You had me. You could have taken my fortune then, but you didn't."

After a moment he said, "It was too risky."

She seemed all the more delighted.

"Risky? You could have taken something else if not my money, and you didn't. Mr. Marlow, I think you are far more noble than you want to admit."

"Far from noble, Amelia. My intentions were still to get your money, and I kept after you."

"That you did. And you had another chance to . . . to take advantage."

"Yes. It was then that I knew I could not. I couldn't hurt you. You were so willing, Amelia. So beautiful. You don't know how hard it was to leave you that day. The way you looked, half-naked, the wind and grass in your hair . . ."

Chadworth now had a vivid picture of Amelia naked, and he felt himself growing hard at just the thought. God, he could use a beautiful young woman in his bed.

"But you did leave me. I was . . . I was upset. Only later would I be grateful."

"You were *grateful*?"

"Yes. Because I started to become attracted to you—you yourself, not the man in the mask. My heart was torn. I felt as if I was in love with the highwayman, but yet he wasn't real. You were real, and as much as I wanted to hate you at first—"

"*Hate* me?"

"Well, you were annoying, always interfering with my plans." Her voice was light. She teased him, apparently. "But I started to look forward to seeing you, and I was able to let go of my fantasy of the highwayman. I began to fall in love with you."

Chadworth cringed. She was in love with him?

"Then I'm the happiest man alive."

"But I'm so afraid of something happening to you. You can't continue with robbery. If you marry me you'll have plenty of—"

"I can't marry you now, Amelia. I want to. God knows, I want to marry you more than anything."

"Then, do."

"No. I need to be worthy of you. I need to be able to support myself, to know that I could support you if need be."

"But there *is* no need. I have so much." Her voice was quiet now. She was upset. Chadworth was delighted.

"My pride demands it now. If I married you I would still feel as if I were somehow just latching on to your fortune. I love you too much for that."

"Women have been doing it for years, Dylan. Marrying for fortune is nothing new. If love is in the mix, so much the better."

"Please try to understand. I love you. I will marry you. I just need to get my business in order first."

"How long?"

"What?"

"How long will it take you?"

"I don't know. I need to raise capital, to make repairs . . . a few years."

"Years. And in that time you want me to wait? To be your mistress?"

"I hadn't thought that far ahead. We can make it work."

"We? That's the first time I've heard you speak of this as a combined effort. All I've heard from you is *you*. You're thinking of who you are, what you need. What about me? What about what I need? We can make a go of your business together."

She was angry now, well and truly. She wasn't getting what she wanted and couldn't figure out how to sway things to her advantage.

"I need to do it on my own." He sounded hurt too, desperate for her to understand.

But she wouldn't, and Chad knew it, and how he wanted to laugh out loud! She was a woman. A woman who'd always had plenty of everything. A woman who was used to getting her way. She could never understand a man's insufferable pride. She was hurt, and she was angry—she was right where Chadworth needed her to be.

"Go, then. Go take care of yourself. Get your business going. Good luck to you. And maybe, just maybe, I'll still be here when you're ready."

"Amelia, please. I love you. I need to know you'll wait for me."

"I can't make any promises, Dylan. And now you must leave. It's nearly sunrise and my staff will be waking."

Chadworth would wait to hear no more. He crept to the door and prepared to wait in the fringe of trees near the drive so that he could follow Mr. Marlow and see just what sort of double life the man led.

Marlow may have taken her last night, but he'd left the aisle wide open for Chadworth to take her to the altar.

She'd never said she loved him.

He realized it as he rode away from the house. She'd said she wanted him, she needed him. But love? The words never passed her lips. He thought back over the conversation, trying to be sure.

She'd said that she had begun to fall in love with him. Was that enough? It was as close as she had come to telling him she loved him.

What if she didn't? What if she wanted to be in love, was in love with the idea of a wild romance, but was not in love with *him*?

It was possible. She'd only just realized that Dylan Marlow and her highwayman were one and the same. What she'd had with the highwayman was sheer lust. There was no mistaking that. She was far more ready to give in to lust with the highwayman than she was to explore love with Marlow. And yet she did take off the mask. It touched him deeply and gave him the courage to hold on. He knew he had a chance.

But what kind of man was he if he couldn't provide for his wife?

He didn't need to provide for her, though. She

had plenty without him. But his pride—damnable pride! He'd been after her money from the start. To marry her now and still need her money made him feel as if he were cheating her somehow, even if it was no longer true. Did she not understand that? No, clearly she didn't.

He needed to make a go of his business, but did he truly expect her to wait years to marry him? He'd already made love to her. What if they had created a child? If they had, well, then damn his pride, they would marry anyway. He would do right by her. It was all he wanted to do.

If only he could figure out a course of action. There had to be a way he could repair his ship and marry her by summer's end.

He leaned down and harrumphed into his horse's ear. Good old Fergus, he was always willing to listen.

"Women, Ferg. What's a man to do?"

Amelia had thought she would feel much better once she washed and dressed and had some time to think.

She'd thought wrong. She felt worse. Far worse than she had imagined. Far worse than she ever had.

Why had she let him leave?

She was angry, and she was hurt. How could he not marry her after what they had done? But his reasons made sense. They'd rushed into things. All spontaneity, no plans. He'd asked to talk before he made love to her, and she wouldn't allow it. She'd wanted him so badly.

He'd thought about stealing her money. He ended up stealing her heart. But he never imagined, she would wager, that he could have the whole package. Her love and her money. He didn't have to choose between them. Somehow he thought that loving her meant not needing her. She would have to show him otherwise. They would talk again. There was time to work it all out.

She needed to find a way to convince him to allow her to be an investor. An investor, that was all. Perhaps he would accept her financial assistance if it came through Uncle Patrick instead of through her. No. That would be dishonest. Dishonesty was no way at all to start a marriage. He would just have to put away his silly masculine pride and realize that they could be a team.

She could provide the money. He would provide the know-how. And when he had his business going, he would make enough to pay back her investment if he wished. She'd rather simply take a share of the profits, but they would work it out in a way that he could feel right about it. It was simply a matter of speaking with him again.

Unless his financial reservations were all just a ploy to get out of marrying her. He did say that he loved her, but she'd heard that men say lots of things in the heat of passion that they might not mean later. When he said he loved her, did he mean it?

How she was dying to talk to him again, to put her fears to rest. At least he seemed ready to give up highway robbery. She was worried enough about keeping his love—she didn't care to worry about the possibility of his losing his life.

Chapter
21

The *Marie-Therese.*

Marlow stood—he didn't know for how long—pondering the hull. It was the one ship he had left. A twenty-eight-gun frigate, built in France and redesigned to haul freight. The other two had sold for twelve hundred pounds, a tidy sum that had helped to pay off any number of debts. But it still hadn't been enough. The *Marie-Therese* was in disrepair. She stood in dry dock, waiting for him to gather the funds.

Waiting for how much longer?

Perhaps he was being foolish. Amelia knew he didn't want her money. He'd told her how much he loved her. But what if it wasn't enough? What if his love could never be enough? What if she tired of footing his endless bills and wondered if he had truly married her for wealth in the end? He couldn't stand the thought of her doubting him. It could tear them apart. Their love deserved a better chance. *She* deserved better than he could give right now.

He should have thought about that before making love to her.

He hadn't meant to let it go so far. Last night he'd returned to her for the sole purpose of explaining himself, of letting her know of his past to see if she would be willing to wait for him for the present, until he could make a better future for them together. But she looked so beautiful standing there, looking out at the stars. He had to give her one kiss. And once he kissed her . . .

Never could he have imagined that the mask would excite her so much. He knew that she was prone to flights of fancy. In the past, when he appeared to her in costume, he'd noticed that the anonymity had an inspiring effect on her. But he'd never guessed how far she would be willing to go. And he wanted her so much. Denying her had proved impossible at last, and he'd made love to her with unrestrained passion. She'd left him weak by the morning hours.

When she took the mask off and said she wanted *him*, his heart was lost forever. He would love her until his dying day, of that he had no doubt. But did she love him?

He'd thought back over their conversation and their lovemaking a thousand times since last night— it was all he could think about—and each time he came up with nothing. No declaration of love. It could well be that she'd wanted him but she truly didn't love him. She'd been so angry in the end.

But he didn't blame her. He was a penniless rogue, after all. A thieving, dishonest cur. And he had just taken her virginity. It was no wonder she'd expected him to marry her as soon as possible. And he'd said no. How could he? She was perfectly reasonable to assume he would, to be angry when he didn't. He had no right to expect her to understand. And yet he hoped she would. He had to explain again. Perhaps they could work something out between them that would make each of them feel better.

Hell, he would marry her right away. He couldn't well live without her, and he *had* compromised her virtue. In the end their financial situation didn't matter. What mattered was that he loved her.

"I thought I would find you here."

He turned. "Thomas. I missed you at the ball last night."

"I wasn't there." He motioned to the ship. "A beauty, isn't she?"

"She's stunning. Such news I have—"

"I meant the boat, Marlow. But I can tell from your eyes that you have a different beauty in mind."

"She's mine, Tom. She's going to be mine, that is."

"You've made so much progress in so short a time?"

"It's incredible, I know. But it's true. I love her so."

"You've told me. And she loves you?"

"She hasn't said it in so many words, but yes. She'll have me. I can't tell you how I know." Dylan blushed. For the first time he would keep a conquest to himself. He had no desire to share the slightest detail with Thomas Selkirk. With anyone. "I just know. I must go to her."

"Can it wait? I, myself, have intriguing news."

"Depends on the news, I suppose."

Thomas sighed, smiling so wide that his dimple was apparent. "You lovers are a selfish lot. Aren't you even going to ask why I wasn't at the ball last night?"

"I'm sorry, Thomas. You're right. I've been most impolite. So why weren't you at the ball?"

"Because I was entertaining a lover of my own. Lady Sarah Billings. You may remember her. . . ."

"She was at the Abercorns' weekend, was she not?" Marlow inquired.

"She was. That's where we became . . . special favorites of each other, you might say."

"And you and your lady love were too wrapped up in each other to attend the ball?"

"Actually, no. Her parents invited me for a dinner. Lord Billings wouldn't attend Miss Benedict's affair because your lady is not admitted to Almack's."

Marlow rolled his eyes.

"Instead, Lord Billings hosted a dinner for his friend, the Italian ambassador, Conte Pergamo."

"Conte Pergamo?"

"An interesting fellow, who happened to mention that he can't get enough Venetian lace in England. It seems they can't find anyone to import it."

"You had dinner with a foppish Italian, and this is news?"

"You must be affected, Marlow. Love has gone to your head. Think."

Marlow stared blankly.

"He's looking for an *importer*. . . ."

"Oh!" It dawned on Dylan at last. "If the *Marie-Therese* was back in commission—"

"Exactly. I got him to commit to a contract with you, Marlow. Eight hundred pounds in advance for transport! He wants to meet with you a week from Wednesday to discuss the terms."

"Are you mad? It's too soon! I can't commit to anything yet. What if the *Marie-Therese* can't be fixed in time—*eight hundred pounds*?"

It was more than he'd made on the sale of one entire ship! He'd be turning a profit immediately. A profit large enough to allow him to buy a second ship before long. It was a start. A solid start. And he wouldn't even need Amelia's assistance.

"Indeed. The count's a decent man. You'll like him. Apparently, the demand for this lace is high in Britain and France. You know ladies and their need for the latest fashions. But at this point he merely wants to discuss a contract. I imagine you'd have time to get the ship in order."

"Yes," Dylan replied absently. His mind was working at top speed, going over details. He needed money. But not her money. He wanted this to be a surprise. He would ask for her hand and then explain to her how he had everything he needed to be self-sufficient. But first he had to see to the *Marie-Therese*'s repairs.

There was only one thing to do.

"So? Do you think you can fix her up in time?"

"I know a coach that will be traveling down old Dracott Road tomorrow night." Lady Melbourne. At Amelia's ball he'd overheard that Lady Jersey was hosting an Almack's event. Lady Melbourne, resplendent in all her finest jewels, was sure to attend.

"Highway robbery! Oh, Marlow. Not again. I thought you'd given it up."

"I had. But I don't consider this one a robbery. I'd call it more a loan. Not to worry, Selkirk. This will be my last romp, and I have a perfect plan. . . ."

Lord Chadworth, hiding around the corner of the warehouse, heard Dylan's every word. He was grateful he had listened to his own instincts to follow Dylan from Briarwood all the way to the docks. A few times he'd almost lost him. But at last he'd managed to keep up. And now he knew his rival's plan down to the last detail. Dylan Marlow wouldn't be in

Amelia Benedict's good graces for long. Chadworth smiled, his victory nearly assured. Amelia would be his for the taking, and Lady Melbourne would be so pleased with him.

As much as she wanted to go looking for Dylan Marlow, to tell him how she felt, she knew it would have to wait. Her last words had been harsh, and perhaps they would both benefit from some time apart. She wanted to be certain he truly loved her. Chasing after him would never do. She had to give him time to think and the chance to return to her . . . or not. If he truly wanted her he would be back to see her again soon. If he did not, her fit of temper and avoidance afterward gave him an easy excuse to steer clear of her now for life.

She prayed he would not stay away!

To ease her mind she went with her uncle to Holcomb House. Seeing the boys' reactions to the news of her success with the ball would delight her. A new roof! No more leaks! They would be so pleased.

When her uncle told them, though, with Amelia looking on excitedly, there was a rousing sigh of disappointment.

"No more interrupted classes?"

"No more sleeping in the common rooms?"

It seemed she couldn't please anyone today.

"Not to worry, muffin." Her uncle tried to comfort her. "They're only boys. The roof being repaired means a return to routine. The leaks meant changes, and change is an adventure. We're all better off for your help, and I do appreciate it. They do too. You'll see."

"I know, Uncle."

Sister Hortense interrupted their private discussion in the confines of Patrick's private study to announce a visitor.

"A certain Lord Chadworth to see Miss Benedict." Hortense seemed surprised. She punctuated her announcement with light, girlish laughter, though the sister was all of forty-three years in age. Amelia supposed Hortense took Chad to be a suitor, and she guessed he was.

Last night, when she found him with Lady Melbourne after he'd nearly proposed, she'd written him off entirely. But he was persistent, after all. Would he demand an answer to his suit, or had he come for some other reason?

He had never sought an audience with her uncle. That much she had learned from Patrick this morning on the journey into London. Would he still profess to be a "little bit in love," she wondered.

"A gentleman caller." Her uncle bowed. "I will leave you be. Hortense, you may show Lord Chadworth in."

Sister Hortense exited, still giggling. Her uncle left to check on the lads, and Lord Chadworth's entrance followed directly afterward.

"I was hoping you would receive me." He bowed slightly in greeting.

She turned to the window, looking out to compose herself before she glanced back at him. "And why wouldn't I? Avoidance is never a wise course, Lord Chadworth."

"Too true, Miss Benedict. Too true. With that in mind, on to the business at hand . . ."

She jumped. So he did mean to renew his proposal.

"I have something for you. Something I rather meant to give you last night," he said, reaching into his coat pocket.

Her heart raced. She had to stop him again! But, no, this time she would hear him out.

"It's a donation for your lads, for this house." He gestured around him and held out an envelope to her. It was stuffed with pound notes.

"How very generous, Lord Chadworth. I do appreciate it. We did make enough last night to manage a new roof, though, so if you'd rather—"

"No. Please." He took her hands in his and held on. "I want to give it. And I have so much more to give. So much more."

She pulled back, nervous. What was he implying?

"Well, then," she pulled her hand away to place the envelope on her uncle's desk behind her, "I thank you. Perhaps we can manage some more of the repairs now as well. It is a great help."

"Marry me, Amelia." He dropped down on his knee right at her feet. "Please. I've been thinking of you all night. I'm overcome with love."

From a little bit to overcome in one night? Amazing, she thought wryly. "Lord Chadworth, I—"

"Do not answer too hastily. Take time to think. I have much to give and a strong position in society."

A strong position with Lady Melbourne. She walked away to the other side of the desk, needing a barrier between them.

He rose. "I love you. I need you. Think what we could accomplish together."

"I don't need time to think, Lord Chadworth. I don't love you, and I will not marry you."

He slammed his hands down on the desk, his eyes wild with anger. Then he seemed to take a breath and rethink his display of temper. "Is it because there is someone else?"

She hesitated. On one hand she felt like keeping her new love a preciously guarded secret. On the other she wanted to shout it to the world. But caution was best until she could speak to Dylan again. "I'm not at liberty to discuss it."

"Because there is someone. I knew it! Mr. Marlow?"

"My personal matters are no affair of yours."

"Aren't they? You will marry me. You'll have to wed to save your reputation, after all, and I'm kind enough to have you even though I know you're already . . . damaged goods."

How could he know? Her face betrayed her distress, clearly, as he went on.

"Oh, I know about your tawdry rendezvous. I heard it from Marlow himself."

"You're lying." She strode to the window. He was lying. He had to be. Dylan would never boast about her as a conquest, least of all to Lord Chadworth—unless that's all she truly was to him. Perhaps he had lied to her when he said he loved her.

"Am I? You didn't even have the decency to do it in the bedroom, did you?" In two strides he was at her side, leaning into her. "You did it right there on the porch. You little wanton. I never would have guessed. Perhaps when we're married?" He reached out to grip her by the wrist, trailing his fingers over her bare forearms.

She jerked her hand away. Good God, Dylan *had* told. It was the only way Chad could know such intimate details. "Get out," she hissed.

"I don't think so. There is still much you need to know. To Marlow's credit he didn't confide in me directly. I was eavesdropping. He happened to be telling his friend, Thomas Selkirk. And he told Selkirk something else too."

She didn't even ask. The shock still consumed her. That he didn't tell Chadworth was no less distressing than that he had told Selkirk. Her reputation could be ruined just as easily by friend as by foe. How could he?

"He told Selkirk that he plans to commit highway robbery. Robbery, can you imagine? How stunning!" He took her by the waist and guided her to the chair. "There, there, darling. Have a seat. You look pale."

"Leave me alone." She shrugged him off as soon as she made it to the chair.

"It's true. He plans to rob a coach traveling by the old Dracott Road this very evening. I imagine he could get the noose for this."

Her head shot up. As shocked and upset as she was with Dylan, she was still in love with him. She couldn't help her feelings. And she couldn't allow him to be caught.

"And where would you be then?" Chad hovered over her chair, a leer of satisfaction on his face. "Your lover dead, your reputation in ruins. Well, who would take care of the orphaned lads? They're sure to want for more in the future. And who could provide it if you were left with no friends to contribute at your balls? Marry me, sweet." He lifted her hand and pressed it between his. "It's the only way."

She looked up at him and smiled her sweetest smile. "How kind of you to be so concerned for me, Lord Chadworth. I'm quite distressed by the news. To think I've given my heart to a common criminal. But"—she pulled her hand back from his—"you've underestimated how much I love him. And how much I loathe you." She stood and looked right into his eyes. "I'd rather *die* than be your bride. When I die, in fact, Holcomb House stands to collect a rather large fortune. That takes care of everything. You needn't fret about me or the lads anymore. Now," she walked to the door and opened it, "kindly leave me."

He met her at the door and slammed it shut, pressing his body against hers as he pinned her to the wall. "Oh, no, Miss Benedict. You listen to me. You've just made a powerful enemy."

His face hovered inches from hers. She trembled, though she tried to remain calm. His body was hard against her, the evidence of his desire pressing into her. That rage piqued him to passion disgusted her. She was ill with thinking that she'd ever considered marrying such a man. "Better to make you my enemy than my husband."

"You're lucky I have principles that prevent me from hurting women, because I would love to throttle you right now. Instead, I'll take my vengeance out on your beloved. And when you have nowhere left to turn, I'll be waiting for you."

"You'll wait in hell." She pushed at his chest to extricate herself from his grasp. "Now leave me."

He smiled a lecherous smile and looked her over, up and down. When he was done with his perusal, he opened the door to leave, but he kept his eyes on her. "You'll be worth the wait. Good day, Miss Benedict."

She'd been all over town trying to find him, to warn him.

To Oakley Place, where the housekeeper, Mrs. Fredericks, had been so kind as to ask her in and to chat with her a bit while she'd waited to no avail.

To the dockyard. There was no sign of him in the warehouse or around the docks.

To Boltwood's Tavern. It wasn't a place she could stay in very long, but she'd been able to ask about him at least. No one had seen him since the wee morning hours.

In frustration she returned to her home, only to find he'd been there looking for her.

Lettie sat her down with a cup of tea and explained everything. "He was in an awful hurry. Seemed put out not to find you."

"Lord, Lettie! Such a mess I've made of things. If only I could tell you. Perhaps later I will. He left no word where he'd be going or when he would come back?"

"He did say he would try back tomorrow."

"Tomorrow? Not till then? And he left no other word?"

"No message. But he did seem desperate to speak with you." Lettie blushed. "He had the air of a man in love. At least tell me that much. Are you in love?"

"I am, Lettie. I am, for whatever good it will do me. There's no time." She pushed her teacup away. "No time for rest, rejuvenation, no time for anything. I must find him. It grows dark."

"So important is it, then? It must be love."

"It's a matter of life and death." She donned her cloak. "If he comes back, please, Lettie, do whatever it takes to keep him here. I'll be back when I'm sure he's safe."

She didn't even wait for the team of horses that pulled her carriage to be rested. She took one of the stallions that the groom has just saddled for exercise, and she lit off like a crack of wild lightning down the road.

She had to find him before it was too late.

Chapter
22

Ready at last, he sat at the edge of the Dracott Road. Fergus whickered impatiently. Something had set his horse on edge tonight. Maybe it was his own case of nerves that the aged stallion was sensing. At any rate, he wished the carriage would come so this unsavory part of the job would be done.

It would be his last robbery, he reminded himself. He would be able to repair the *Marie-Therese*, and then he would be a man of some means and he would return the money he was about to steal, every last penny. Not that Lady Melbourne needed it or deserved half of what she had.

He thought he heard a rustling in the distance. It wasn't very late and had just barely grown dark, but it wasn't unusual for Lady Melbourne to make an early start to Almack's, he supposed. She had a reputation for arriving promptly. The carriage could come at any time. It was why he'd stayed on Fergus's back, ready to charge.

The rustling died down. It must have been merely the wind. He would have to wait a little while longer.

His fingers flexed and tensed, gripping the leather reins in his hands. He could hardly keep from fidgeting; no wonder his horse did the same. He wasn't sure which exerted the more positive influence, the pot of coffee he had gone through alone or the shot and a half of whisky.

Just once more.

He wished he'd been able to see Amelia. The sudden urge to tell her he loved her was strong, almost overwhelming. Perhaps he should give it up and just go to her.

But as soon as he'd thought it, he could hear the rumbling of a team of horses coming down the road. He knew it was his chance, his one chance, to get the money to fix his own problems so that he would never have to rely on her for anything more than love.

Shouting a hearty command to his horse, he charged through the fringe of trees and on to the approaching carriage.

As he rode forward, he reached into his waistcoat and pulled out his pistol. Though he wasn't about to actually hurt anyone, it was imperative to give the impression that he meant business. This robbery mattered so much more than the others. It wasn't simply his own interests at stake anymore. He was thinking of Amelia.

Mechanically, he waved his pistol in the air. He thought only of her now. Of how she had asked him not to rob anymore. Fortunately, the driver made it easy on him, pulling over immediately and putting his hands on his head so that Marlow wouldn't shoot him. He had no intention of doing so, of course. He didn't even want to hit him.

"Good man," he spoke, remembering to make his voice gravelly cold. But as he drew closer he realized that he recognized the driver. Dylan had a sinking feeling in the pit of his stomach. Was there any way this could possibly turn out well?

"Marlow," Chadworth addressed him, removing his hat and leaning forward out of the shadowy recess of the driver's box. He pointed a gun. "I've been expecting you."

Dylan's options were few. He could shoot Chad, but where would that leave him? He could try to run, but he wouldn't get far, and running away was as low on appeal as shooting Chadworth.

"Surprised? Lady Melbourne would send her apologies if she knew. I convinced her to stay at home tonight. She thinks I'm proposing to Amelia right now, in fact. Perhaps I'll stop in and do it on the way home. Sweet Amelia. She'll be sad to hear of your demise, of course, but she'll be in need of protection. Her reputation, you know . . ."

Dylan, enraged, stepped forward, suddenly unconcerned with the gun. "You have no right to even speak her name!"

"Tut, now. Stay back!" Chad pointed the weapon, waving Dylan over to the side of the road as he stepped down from the coach. "I am prepared to shoot."

Dylan's last thought was for Amelia. His sweet angel! If only he had done as she'd asked. He prayed he would live to see her again. And if he didn't, he prayed she would forgive him.

"Stop!" She screamed out before they could hear her. All she could see was darkness up ahead and one lantern illuminating a carriage.

She had no idea what went on, who was there. She just knew, in her gut, that it was Dylan, and she prayed she had beaten Lord Chadworth to the scene. Before she'd made it quite all the way there, she slowed her horse, jumped down, and ran.

Then she saw them by the side of the road. Marlow and Chadworth, face-to-face.

"There you are. Please, Chad, if you ever loved me, even just a little bit, please—" Her voice broke when she saw the guns. They each held a pistol pointed at the other. "Dear Lord, no!"

"Amelia." Marlow sounded overjoyed to see

her, and yet his voice was filled with concern all at once. His grave tones were no longer affected, she knew. He was honestly anticipating the worst. "Go back to your horse. Walk away."

She stepped closer. There was no way she would leave him.

"I said go!" His voice was hard now, filled with rage.

"Touching." Chadworth made as if to yawn and cover his mouth. "Are you quite done? Or shall I allow you one last farewell?"

Amelia stepped closer still.

"I said to get away!" Marlow shouted.

"It's all right, my love." She walked confidently forward. She held the trump card. If only she hadn't been so distraught that she'd forgotten about it earlier. "Chad won't shoot you. I know all about his—"

"You said *my love*?" Dylan turned to face her, quite forgetting the man with the gun, forgetting everything but Amelia's words.

And in that second, a gunshot echoed into the night.

In the same instant she reacted. She jumped forward, trying to block Dylan's body with her own. Too late. He fell backward into her arms, his side already spilling blood from the wound. The impact jolted them both to the ground.

"What have you done!" she shrieked at Chad. "You fool!"

She cradled Dylan's head in her lap. He looked

at her, silver eyes dazed before closing tight. His body shivered lightly, letting her know he was still alive, but she kept close watch on his chest, rising, falling, rising . . . just in case.

"I did what I had to do," Chad said smugly. "Now, to wait for the constable. I told him to meet me here at half past nine." He withdrew a watch from his pocket, looked at it, and replaced it. "Ah, ten minutes to go. You'll never get him home in time."

"You bastard!" She would have flown at him had she not been looking after Dylan.

"Now you'll have to marry me, hm? What with your lover dead and all."

"He won't die!" Amelia shouted. "He won't die, because you'll help me get him home and get the attention he needs."

"So he can live to testify against me? I think not. Perhaps I'll shoot you as well, and then neither of you will live to tell the tale."

"I don't need to be alive to tell it, Lord Chadworth. I left instructions with my maid. If anything happens to me, all of London will know of your affair with Lady Melbourne, and her husband's wrath will come down on both of you."

Chad stood still, stunned. She had him there. He hadn't thought anybody knew. "What? I—"

"I'm prepared to use the information against you if anything happens to Dylan. Nobody doubts my integrity. And—" she paused, "it will be enough to touch off a scandal. You know how Lord Melbourne detests a scandal. You'll be ruined."

He seemed to mull it over, still keeping the pistol trained on her. "I should shoot you anyway, just for the satisfaction. It felt so good the first time. If only I had aimed the arrow higher."

"You *did* do it deliberately!"

"I was furious to see you were fool enough to follow Marlow into the woods. What would people think? By God, you were probably sleeping with him then. Whore!"

Of course, she had not been, but she felt no need to defend her position.

"I saw you making love to him too. He never told a soul. I saw you." Chad threw back his head and laughed wildly. "I saw you."

She was glad Dylan's pistol had fallen beyond her reach, because if she had it handy she would have shot Chad now herself. Right through his heart, if he had one.

"Well, which is it, Chadworth? Shoot me or salvage your hope for political glory?"

"Oh, all right." He tucked his pistol into his waistcoat and came to help Amelia. "I can always find another wife to please Elizabeth. Exposure might bring about an investigation. I can't afford to be tied to a double murder. Or a scandal."

"Hold on, Dylan. You're going to be fine." She stroked his hair and kissed him gently on the forehead before helping Chad lift him into the carriage.

"You come around and take his feet. I'll carry his torso," Chad instructed.

She obeyed willingly, as his feet weren't as heavy. The last thing she wanted to do was drop him and make his injury worse. And Chad was sufficiently cowed to be trustworthy now, she felt. A scandal would ruin Chad. It was the last thing he would want.

They got Dylan into the carriage in time, just before another carriage started rumbling up the road. "I'll stay inside with him. You drive us to Briarwood. And hurry! If anything happens to him, I won't hesitate to expose you anyway."

"But the horses?" Chad asked. Dylan had his horse there and Amelia had left her mount at the side of the road.

"No matter. I'll send a man out for them later. There's no time. Get going!"

Chad dashed to take his seat in the driver's box. Seconds later, they were off.

The constable and his men never happened by them. Amelia could only assume that Chadworth had bluffed about that part of the deal, just as she had bluffed about Lettie having instructions to spread news of his affair with Lady Melbourne.

Chad could have easily shot them both, and no one would have ever known a thing. Amelia couldn't think now about what might have occurred. The worst *had* happened, as far as she could imagine. Two days ago, she wasn't sure if she truly loved Dylan Marlow at all. And now, the thought of a world without him made her ache with a force of pain greater than she had ever known.

He had to be all right! He simply *had* to!

At Briarwood, Chadworth helped her carry Dylan into the front parlor. She didn't dare try to move him all the way upstairs. Her sofa in the parlor was large and rather comfortable. It would do for now.

She said a silent prayer—the hundredth of the night, perhaps—and was both grateful and distraught that her uncle was at Holcomb House and not present at Briarwood. On the one hand, it would be so hard to explain everything that had happened. On the other, she could use his support.

A sob rose up in her throat, and she let it out at last, a wail so loud and filled with pain she felt as if she had been torn apart. He was so pale!

She'd torn her petticoats to use as bandages and wrapped him with her coat, but it wasn't enough. Blood still seeped through. She was tucking the coat around him tighter when she felt a hand on her shoulder.

"I'm so sorry." Chad's voice, low and concerned. "I never meant to hurt him. Or you."

She bit her lip and contained the bile that rose up. "Never meant to—" she began to shout and stopped herself. Chadworth was a wretched man, and she hated him, but her anger would settle nothing now. She had to think of Dylan. He needed peace, not chaos.

"I lied when I said I shot you with the arrow on purpose. I shot *at* you on purpose, yes. But I never meant to hit you. It was an accident."

"No need to explain," she said quietly, not turning her attention from Dylan. At least, Chad hadn't hurt *her* on purpose. It was something, but not nearly enough.

"I must. Please. I lost my temper. I never meant to shoot him either—I mean, I did. I was so angry. But seeing him now, seeing you . . . you're so in love with him. I'm so ashamed. Lady Melbourne and I . . . we didn't think of your feelings at all."

"Lady Melbourne." Amelia had been wondering what the woman had against her. Why had she become the lady's target? Amelia needed to hear Chad's confession.

"Yes. Elizabeth, Lady Melbourne, caught me looking at you once. Shortly afterward, she decided you would make a fine wife for me. Her explanation was that my marriage would keep people from guessing at my affair with her. At first, I was reluctant. To test Elizabeth's determination to carry out the plan, I began to flirt with you to make her jealous."

"When you destroyed her pansies, for instance?" It all made sense now. Chadworth hadn't been thinking of her, but of Lady Melbourne.

"Yes. But it didn't work to dissuade her. Despite her jealousy, Elizabeth remained insistent that I marry you. Lord Melbourne started to write letters to Elizabeth. Angry letters. He'd heard of us—Lady

Melbourne and myself—being seen together frequently, and he mentioned that it didn't look proper. She insisted you were the perfect choice for me. She knows how I want to succeed and that you couldn't help me with my political ambitions. And, I began to enjoy the thought of having two women to myself."

"Why me? I'm clearly no threat to Lady Melbourne if political success is all you want," Amelia said aloud.

"But you were, in a way. My physical attraction to you was, anyway. She felt that by marrying you, my attraction would fade and—"

"And she could still maintain control over you." Amelia would have been hearing what Chad was willing to endure for the sake of his ambitions, was she not so worried about Dylan's health. Dylan was her only concern now. Chad could go to the devil for all she cared, and with Lady Melbourne as a lover, perhaps he had.

"I don't like to look at it that way, but yes. I suppose that's her hope. It's turned out badly and I'm so sorry. I will leave you alone now. I promise."

"Because I've ceased to serve your purpose. You'll find some other poor girl to marry, no doubt." She was disgusted. "Not to worry. I'll keep my counsel. Your secret is safe as long as Mr. Marlow is."

"No one will know of his robbery and—" Chadworth's voice broke off in a whimper. "I'm so sorry."

She didn't have the patience to ease Chad's guilty conscience, nor did Dylan have the time.

"Very well, Lord Chadworth. I forgive you. Now go. Go and fetch the surgeon!"

"The stableboy has already sent for—"

"Well, go yourself, anyhow!" she shouted, unable to control herself any longer. "Get out of my house and never come back. Understand me!"

"I—I understand." It was the last she heard of Chadworth as he quietly went out the door.

She sat beside Dylan Marlow while she waited for the surgeon, whispering his name over and over, telling him she loved him, and that everything would be all right.

As if through a fog he heard her voice.

"I love you. Don't leave me, Dylan. Don't leave me."

He didn't want to leave her. Ever. But the pain was so great, nearly unbearable. He tried to breathe—in, out. In, out. It was as if he had to talk himself through every step. He felt as if he was lying on the edge of forever. Deep, peaceful sleep awaited him on one side. Harsh, restless pain was on the other. But the pain wouldn't last, he told himself. And her love felt better than any heaven he could know.

He had to fight.

And fight he did. It was no easy struggle. In, out. In, out. His sleep was fitful, brief. He tried to open his eyes. He could feel her hands on him—light, gentle, like the feathers of an angel's wings. And then he heard another voice. A loud, masculine voice. The surgeon?

He heard Amelia and the man talking. He felt hands on him, roving over his flesh, a fierce sudden pain, and then—he wasn't certain if he'd been dreaming. He flitted in and out of awareness, but he couldn't manage to open his eyes. He was determined to see her again, to tell her that he loved her.

He would tell her how foolish he had been, how wrong.

It wasn't up to him to succeed alone or up to her to provide for him. It was up to both of them together. Her fortune was his. His misfortune was hers. Their joy, their pain—it belonged to both of them. He could feel her tears as she cried for him, like drops of healing ointment on his open wounds. She was hurting for him emotionally as much as he was feeling the physical pain.

And that was love. *Love.* He was blessed with the brightest of angels. Amelia—his angel, his love. He would make her his partner, in marriage and in business, in sickness, in health . . . as long as they both should live.

And he planned to live a very long time—if only he could open his eyes to tell her.

Chapter 23

He'd rather rob than be her partner.

After two days of thinking about his actions, trying to understand his motivations, it was the only conclusion she had been able to reach. And it roiled inside her like a sickness.

She couldn't marry him. There was no way she could allow herself to be with a man who thought so little of her.

Dr. Clark had been in several times throughout the past two days. While Dylan was in danger she'd stayed by his side, had slept on the floor next to him, had tended to his every need. But now that Dr. Clark had said he would be all right, she was struggling to maintain her distance. When his life had been in danger, all she could think of was how much she loved him. And she still loved him so much that it caused her physical pain to think of being without him. But she would do it. She had to.

As soon as he woke and recovered, she would tell him that she never wanted to see him again.

Her parents had had a real partnership. She'd been thinking of them so much lately. They had done everything together. Her mother had been able to tell her father anything. He'd respected her advice on business and politics as well as in trifling domestic matters. Would Dylan be that kind of husband to her? He'd already shown her how much he respected her opinion by disregarding her request to stop robbing. He'd gone out and nearly gotten himself killed!

And could she imagine the man who absolutely refused her financial involvement in his business matters coming to her for advice? Hardly. No, he didn't know what it meant to be a partner.

He was not the man for her. No matter how much she loved him.

A successful marriage, to Amelia, meant mutual love and respect, helping each other through difficult times and enjoying the good times that much more by sharing in the process of achievement.

It made her heart heavy, her whole being sluggish and weak, to think that he could not be the man she needed him to be because of his ridiculous pride.

Women married men of wealth and property all the time, even if they didn't have the resources to match. It wasn't fair for society to frown on the reverse. It was unusual, yes, but why should it matter? What hurt most was that she didn't expect Dylan Marlow to turn out to be a man to bow to society's dictates. She had thought he was different. But from his actions she could only deduce that she'd thought wrong.

"He's awake and asking for you," Lettie ducked her head in to inform her. Amelia had been sitting at her escritoire in the informal drawing room. She'd been unable to return to the porch this week, for all the memories it brought back.

"Thank you, Lettie." She rose and walked out to the front parlor, where Marlow still lay on her sofa.

He was sitting up a little, and the color had returned to his cheeks. He would require a longer convalescence, for which she had hoped to be able to move him upstairs to one of the vacant bedchambers, but for now he was awake. Though she tried to keep an emotional distance, she couldn't keep her heart from beating faster with relief that he was awake and aware.

She said nothing but pulled up a chair and sat beside him.

"There you are." His voice was a soft whisper, as if it hurt him even to speak. "I thought I would wake up and find myself in the constable's holding cell. But what a surprise. This is far nicer."

"You are welcome to stay here while you regain your strength, of course." She hadn't meant to look at him, but her instincts required her to meet his gaze as she spoke. His blue eyes were clearer and more dazzling than ever. She tried to look away quickly, before she was overcome with the temptation to pull him into her arms and thank God that he was alive.

"I see." He apparently made note of the coldness. "I thank you. It is most gracious of you, considering that you are angry with me."

"Angry?" His accusation put her on the defensive. To defend her position gave his words credence, and she didn't want to discuss it now. Later would be a better time. She forced herself to smile. "No. I've been so worried."

"I'm sorry, Amelia. You should be angry, after what I put you through. I thought I could steal the money from Lady Melbourne and return it later. But I had no taste for the deed, and . . . well, Chadworth called my bluff, didn't he?"

"You needn't worry about Chad. I've ensured his silence." With blackmail, she added silently. It was something that she wasn't entirely proud of. But sometimes, she realized, there is no black and white, and right and wrong must meet in the middle. She did it for him, and she wasn't sorry. "He won't be troubling either one of us again."

"Good. I need you. I can't have him keeping us apart any longer."

Her head shot up. "Yes?"

"Amelia, I—I need a very large favor. Please, just listen. It's hard to talk and I must get it out."

"All right." If talking pained him, she would do her best not to interrupt. For now. There would come a time when she would have her say. It could wait for him to be better.

"I have a business deal pending with Conte Pergamo of Italy, to ship Venetian lace to England for a tidy sum. I imagine it will involve exporting something from England as well"—he winced, then continued—"but there's no way I can do it without making repairs to my remaining ship, the *Marie-Therese.* I'd thought about stealing the money, but that was a ridiculous plan, clearly. Why would I do that when I have a willing investor ready to help?"

"An investor?" He couldn't possibly mean *her.*

"I'd thought about asking this investor for a sum of money that I would return at a later time, but I think I've come up with a better solution. I want to sell her half my business."

Her? Was she hearing him properly? "What makes you think she'll buy?"

"It is a risky venture, I admit. But if she buys half the business, she'll be entitled to half the profit, and I think we could make a go of it. Pergamo's willing to pay more than the cost of the repairs, but we need an able ship before we can accept the contract."

"What exactly do you want from me?"

"I want you to be my business partner. A fair split, down the middle. With the money you invest we'll be able to make the *Marie-Therese* seaworthy."

"We?" She could hardly believe it. He was willing to allow her to help him, to make her his partner—his equal. It was everything she'd hoped for.

"Yes. As I said, it is a risky venture. And, as I'm out of commission, you would have to see to negotiating the terms of the contract and getting the necessary repairs under way."

"You think I can do all that? It sounds like an awful lot to—to entrust to me."

"I trust you with my life, Amelia. Why not my business as well? Our business. What do you say?"

"I love you." Her eyes were filling with tears so fast that she couldn't blink them all back. It was all she could say. "I love you."

"Then, can I assume you will invest?" He smiled weakly.

"Yes. I—I would love to. I don't care if we make a profit or lose everything, as long as we'll be doing it together."

"That's one more thing I want to talk to you about." He reached for her and she went to him, kneeling at his side and gripping his hand in hers. "I love you more than life itself. When I was shot, all I could think of was you, of telling you how much I love you, how sorry I was—" His voice broke off.

"I understand. Hush, now. We can talk more later."

"No." He struggled on. "Now. I need to say it now. I want to marry you. As soon as possible. Please say you will still have me."

"Of course I'll have you. I love you."

He smiled, his eyes twinkling, showing all the life and happiness his weakened body wouldn't allow. "I haven't a thing to my name, you know. Just the business. What will the *ton* think?"

"Who cares? We needn't bother with them." She beamed, holding his hand to her cheek and cuddling as close to him as the narrow sofa and his injuries would allow. "I don't give a hang what anyone thinks. I'll be a trader's bride—a trader myself, come to think of it, since half of the business is now mine. The *ton* may well shun us both for good. And that's very well. We'll turn enough of a profit to keep the lads of Holcomb House in style. Who knows—maybe our orphaned lads will be society's future elite."

"What a lovely thought . . . I can picture little Andrew's future wife crossing the Lady Jersey off Almack's guest list. Oh, but it hurts to laugh."

"Then don't laugh." She leaned her face in closer to his. "Let me kiss you, instead, unless . . . will that hurt too? Are you capable of—"

"Let me show you how capable." With his good arm he tugged her closer to him.

His lips met hers, at first as gentle as a caress. Then his kiss deepened, becoming more erotic, less controlled. She almost forgot his injury as his tongue darted between her lips and swirled around her own. A moan escaped her as she pulled away, and she fought the urge to climb atop him to celebrate his recovery, right there in her parlor, in the middle of the day.

"Well?" He wore his wicked grin as he awaited her approval.

"You are most definitely capable, my love. Any more capable and we'll have to worry about offending the servants, let alone the *ton*."

"We're together now." His mischievous grin was replaced with a genuine smile. "We don't have to worry about anything ever again."

Epilogue

The bride wore a veil of sheer Venetian lace, a gift from the Conte Pergamo.

Dylan wasn't supposed to see her before the ceremony, but he'd come aboard the *Marie-Therese* early to make sure things were in order for their journey. It was then that he'd caught a glimpse of her through the porthole of the captain's cabin. She looked more angelic than ever. He was the luckiest man alive.

She'd stayed aboard the ship last night with her maid and her uncle. This morning she prepared for their wedding on board. He was supposed to have spent the night at Briarwood, but he ended up staying late at the restored warehouse, going over the books. After the ceremony they would sail to Italy for the maiden voyage of the *Marie-Therese*. In the future they would run the business from England and not make the trip personally, but this time was special. This time was their honeymoon.

The man they'd hired to captain the ship would take care of most of the business. Dylan and Amelia would simply be along for the ride, for their pleasure and some sightseeing in Italy. Captain Jackson had graciously volunteered to bunk in with the first mate and give up his cabin for the journey, to allow the newlyweds to stay in the more luxurious captain's quarters. Thomas Selkirk and Uncle Patrick would be looking after things in England while they were away—Briarwood, the business, and Andrew, Dylan and Amelia's son.

The adoption wouldn't be official until after they returned from the honeymoon in Italy, but they'd already made the decision. Andrew was overjoyed. Dylan had never seen Amelia look more pleased. And he was so eager to become a father. A father! He had so much planned for them. Kite-flying in Hyde Park. Riding lessons. Maybe they'd even climb trees together. That ought to get the boy over his fear of heights.

Andrew stood at his side, fussing with the cuffs of the velvet short pants they'd dressed him in.

Dylan wanted to laugh. "Easy, son. You can change clothes almost as soon as the ceremony is over. One day you'll get used to the finery."

Dylan straightened his own ascot; the boy's fidgeting was contagious.

"Yes, Father." He straightened up and glanced down the makeshift aisle, avoiding the gazes of his friends—the other orphans scattered among the gathered crowd—who occasionally pointed up and teased him.

"Like father, like son?" Patrick smiled. He may have been adorned in his official robes as he waited to perform the ceremony, but he was the same old Uncle Patrick. Dylan steeled himself for the jest that he'd learned would follow that twinkle in the older man's eye. "I wonder what will get *him* thrown out of Oxford?"

"He won't do anything foolish, as I did," Dylan answered. And even if he did, Dylan would not desert Andrew or cast him cruelly away. He would love the boy as he deserved to be loved, without condition.

"She's late." Patrick rocked on his heels, impatient. "It's a habit she has had since she was a little girl, to be unconscionably late."

"It's all right, Patrick. For Amelia, we'll make allowances." Dylan smiled, watching for her appearance. "She's worth the wait."

At last she was ready.

Lettie had helped her dress. She had slept in the captain's cabin with her maid so that she would be there when people started to arrive and she wouldn't have to climb up the plank in her wedding dress. It was a little inconvenient for their guests, she supposed, having to board the ship—but it was the only place Dylan and Amelia could imagine getting married after all of the work they put into the *Marie-Therese* together.

Together.

Her things were all packed for the trip. Everything was in order. It was the sentimental last touches that kept her lingering in the cabin. They would sleep here tonight, and she wanted everything to be perfect. Her sheer lace shift was laid out on the bed. There was wine. New silk sheets. A light snack already packed in a picnic hamper.

Amelia looked it over one last time.

"Come. You have to marry him first," Lettie said, urging Amelia to hurry up. Her guests were waiting. Her family was waiting. . . .

Her family! It made her so happy to say it. Dylan, Andrew—they were everything she could ever want in life. And she suspected they would add a second child to their family before long. But she would keep the news to herself until she was sure.

She adjusted her veil one more time in front of the looking glass, then allowed Lettie to pull it down over her face. She admired the workmanship, the intricate needlework. Conte Pergamo was right: Venetians did make the best lace, and the veil was perfect to go with her gown of ivory silk and tulle dotted with tiny pearls.

In a short time she would be Dylan Marlow's

bride! When next he loved her, he would appear not as a highwayman or a gentleman, but as her husband. It was his most appealing guise of all.

"You look lovely." Lettie reached out to take her hand and give it a gentle squeeze. "Absolutely beautiful. Here."

She handed Amelia an ivory lace handkerchief. Amelia didn't anticipate tears—but she had ordered the deck of the ship to be filled with flowers to overshadow the offensive odor of the Thames for her guests. She might very well start sneezing the moment she walked out on deck, but she felt better knowing that her guests were happy and not resigned to spending the whole ceremony holding their noses.

Fortunately, a fair, light wind blew today, blowing the murky scent of the Thames off in another direction. All that remained was a faint tinge of roses and brine on the air. The sun was shining, and it seemed everything was perfect for her wedding day.

Selkirk rapped lightly at the door. It was the third time he'd come, but every other time she'd sent him away, saying she wasn't ready. Thomas would walk her down the aisle in place of her uncle, who was to perform the ceremony.

"Are you ready now?" He offered his arm. She took it and stepped out onto the smooth, polished wood.

"I'm ready."

A collective sigh rose up as they started down the makeshift aisle. Their dearest friends were here, and all of the boys from Holcomb House. Some of the younger lads giggled and squirmed in their seats; she knew how they felt about romance. And what was more romantic than a wedding?

Not so long ago, she recalled, she'd thought her life dull compared with the stories she used to concoct for the lads. How silly it seemed now. Life with Dylan Marlow was one grand adventure.

She peered through the lace to the end of the aisle. Patrick smiled approvingly. Andrew stood tall, his chest puffed out proudly even though she knew he was embarrassed to wear what he'd called "sissy breeches." The darling boy.

And there he was. Dylan Marlow. Today he looked like a prince. Even through the veil she could see the twinkle in his blue eyes.

He was everything to her. Highwayman and husband, pirate and prince. All the things she used to dream about, make up stories about, and more. So much more. He was her fantasy come to life.

Her partner.

Before she knew it, she'd made it to the end of the aisle. Thomas handed her off and gave a little bow before stepping back and leaving her to Dylan Marlow, who stepped forward and lifted her veil.

She looked into his bright blue eyes, and he looked at her, his happiness well apparent and matched by her own. He took her hands, and they turned their attention to Patrick as he started to recite the vows.

With Dylan at her side, she knew she would live as her tales to the boys of Holcomb House had always ended . . .

Happily ever after.

SHERRI BROWNING is a graduate of Mount Holyoke College in South Hadley, Massachusetts, where she currently resides. *The Scoundrel's Vow* was her first novel. Readers may write to her at P.O. Box 115, South Hadley, MA 01075 or visit her on the Web at www.sherribrowning.com.